CITY OF
WORDS

BOOKS BY STEVEN J. CARROLL

The City of Words Series
City of Words

The Histories of Earth Series
In the Window Room
A Prince of Earth
All the Worlds of Men
Worlds Unending

&

The Road to Jericho

CITY OF WORDS

WORDS

A Novel by Steven J. Carroll

-Globe Light Press-

City of Words
Globe Light Press :

All rights reserved.
Copyright © Steven J Carroll 2015

Globe Light Press
Printed in the United States of America

ISBN-13: 978-1514282595
ISBN-10: 1514282593
BISAC: Juvenile Fiction / Dystopian

For questions regarding large or bulk orders of this book please address: Globe Light Press, Globelightpress@gmail.com

my email [handwritten annotation]

Connect with other City of Words fans:
facebook.com/stevenjcarrollauthor
www.stevenjcarroll.com

That we may see with our eyes,
and hear with our ears.

Joclyr,
Congratulations!.
You won. Thanks for taking
the time to find my book on Goodreads.
I hope it doesn't disappoint. If you have
any questions, as you're reading, or if you have
a suggestion, please send me an email. This book
is not technically released yet, so it
can still be improved.
Thanks for reading,

Thanks to my editor, Christine Hysell, and to my proof-readers (Natasha & Bridget), and to my many Beta Readers — your help was extremely appreciated. Also, thanks to Chad Lewis for taking my very basic cover design ideas, and making them so much better. And a special thanks to my wife for her perpetual support, and encouragement.

1

The pain is immediate. My eyes shoot open, but they are blocked. It's happening again, and all my ears can hear is the shrill metallic grinding.

I've heard a schoolmate say once, before he was reprimanded and retracted, that he'd thought these sounds served no goodly mechanical purpose, that they were only used as a means to torture and intimidate; and now that I hear it again I am tending to agree. Not that I would say this out loud (even as piercingly awful as this noise is now, it is far better than retractment).

My heart races. My eyes are open but they see black. Though, at last, the painful sounds centered in my brain begin to wear away; and from out of the darkness covering my vision, their symbol slowly seeps into my optic nerve.

"*Who could it be this time?*" I wonder, and I find that I am beginning not to care so much if it is an old laborer, or an instructor, or a militant, or any of the other various designations, as long as they are old, for they tend to know precisely the words to say. But when it is a younger schoolmate, they tend not to know the proper words. They don't know any better, and those are always the bloodiest, and the worst to watch.

And it is no good looking away, or even closing my eyes. This is not natural sight. My eyes are closed tightly already: for I have always thought it to be far too unsettling to have my eyes opened and to know that I'm being controlled. It is better to trick the mind into thinking it is all a dream. And so, within my dream that is not a dream, I can still see the video image of the stage and the confessional podium, and their symbol—the red circle—projected onto the curtain behind the platform.

The tension in my chest begins to settle.

"*Good, a laborer,*" I think, seeing his standard blue uniform, like all laborers will wear.

Yet, instantly I know there is something unusual about this man. And there is something else, something strange and bizarrely familiar in his face, as if I had known him my whole life; though, I've never seen him before. How could I have? My concentration is fixed, raking through my internal memories to think of any reason why I should know his face, or his eyes, which do not seem half as blank as a normal laborer's eyes.

His crimes are read by the orator:

"Treasonous speech and incitement." Which is such a standard accusation that I wonder why he should be treated so cautiously.

"What have you to say for yourself?" the orator asks.

But the laborer remains silent. "Sir, I will ask it of you again."

But still nothing, just his piercing eyes staring straight ahead into the camera.

"Do you not wish to retract?"

And I can see it: there is a purposeful intensity in his non-speech. His jawline tightens, as if to keep his words even more firmly held.

There is a murmuring among the audience of spectators. Perhaps this is as unexpected for them as it is for myself. A woman, a Leader by her dress, goes to speak into the orator's ear. There is some hushed interchange, and the woman is helped back to her seat.

They won't let him stand before the podium, as they always do, but instead they hold a microphone in front of him, possibly so that it can be pulled back at any time. And as the orator steps to the confessional podium to give the judgement of the Leaders, it is obvious what it will be. It is clearly said on his face before a word is ever spoke.

"The Common has found him unrepentant," the orator says. "His citizenship shall be taken," he continues, as his puffy white hair and stern face are wafted slightly by a wind that must have blown into the stadium.

"All together now," the orator says, beginning the Ritual. "My heart feels the shame of his deceit..." he says.

If I don't say it, the grinding will begin in my ears again, and there might even be consequences tomorrow morning, and so I repeat every word. "My heart feels the shame of his deceit... My voice speaks a condemnation... I consent to his termination."

I hate that—I always hate the Ritual, if and when it comes to that. I wish, instead, that I could only watch, and would not have to speak, and could pretend it was all a dream. And from my place, lying in my sleeping quarters, with the images from the retractment pouring into my vision, I can see the wind that had begun before continue to rise, fluttering the corners of even the thick fabric of the orator's collarless shirt.

And it is during this unanticipated wind that another unexpected thing happens. The laborer shoves away from the middle of the stage, pushing back the militants who were charged with watching him. He knocks into the orator, toppling him to the ground, so that the puffy-haired old man slides across the stage.

And the laborer, who is now standing before the confessional podium, he lowers his mouth to the microphone, and says—does not shout, but says—with a force of words I have never heard before, only a single word, with a deep voice, and a nod of his head as he speaks.

"Revolution."

Blast!

There is a single shot taken from the front of the stage. A spark burst comes from the muzzle of a firearm, and drops of red land against the all-white rear curtain, on which the symbol of the Common's red circle is projected. An audible gasping shock of terror comes from the audience.

Instantly, the images from the retractment go black.

2

"Awake, awake, awake..." says the prerecorded message of a woman's voice, transmitted into my inner ear.

My eyelids are shut, but I haven't been sleeping well. I open them as a reflex, so that her voice will be cut off. Theta says that she has always liked the woman's voice—she imagines her to be a kind, familiar young woman waking her up from her dreams—though that seems like far too much for me, and I have always despised that voice, although I would never tell Theta that.

My feet slip from my bed onto the cool grey slab floor. This is the world as it should be, and even though my personal quarters are cramped and uncomfortable, they are mine. And I am always grateful to see them with my natural eyes after each retractment, or after every instance in which my vision is controlled.

"Who was that man?" I wonder, as I dress in my stark white uniform as always, fastening the straight silver buttons, and reaching down to tighten my shoes.

He was not a laborer at the School, for my internal memory is by necessity always very keen, and I would remember that. I press my hand flatly against the metal door plate; it flashes blue, and opens, leading out to the covered walkway, which overlooks the lawn and beyond that the perimeter fence.

Beside my quarters, in a long line beneath the awning, other doors begin to slide open. And the walkway starts to fill with schoolmates, several of them in their same white uniforms as myself, all marching on their ways to morning lectures. I do not walk so quickly. How could they hurry like that, as if they had not seen anything the night before?

There is a rustling in the bushes near by: a red-chested bird is gathering sticks for a nest. Perhaps the whole world will not stop for one man's death, and so my steps are taken more quickly, or else I will be demerited for tardiness.

The main building of the School is crowded with schoolmates darting in all directions, rushing to make it to their allotted lecture halls. And there, very far ahead, mixed with the surging crowd is Theta. She is walking away from me, so that I cannot see her face. Though I can see her hair, and that is enough, the color of fire and cut straight across her shoulders, yet it won't lay flat like the other girls' hair, but does what it wishes, so that I can always tell that it's her.

I run ahead to catch her pace.

She must recognize my footsteps, so that she begins to speak even before I have reached her.

"Did you have trouble sleeping, again?" she asks.

"Like always," I say. "Too many bad dreams." Though this is untrue: I did not dream at all last night. However, I was not referring to real dreams. "Bad dreams" is our code for a nighttime retractment, and Theta of course knows this.

"Same for me," she says. She stops unexpectedly in the center of the pressing line of schoolmates that flows on all sides of us. This will take up precious amounts of our time, but I don't care.

"We should talk after lectures," she says. "Will you wait for me?"

"Yes, of course," I answer.

We part ways at the top of a set of stairs, and I rush, pushing through the crowd. Though I should not have been so slow this morning: my location sensor indicating that I am fifteen seconds late as I enter the lecture hall doors. A message flashes in the lower righthand portion of my vision, until I slide it away with my hand.

"Demerited," it reads. "Credits: 5," it continues to flash, as I take my seat within the bowl-shaped lecture hall, and until I swipe my hand again.

"*Only five more credits to last me till graduation... One for every year,*" I say to myself. I must be more cautious, or I will never keep my rank as an instructor.

3

The instructor stands on a circular platform at the low center point of our lecture hall, that is easily filled with nearly a thousand of my male schoolmates, who still hold instructor rank, as I do, the highest rank available. And he addresses us, turning as he speaks. Though for the purposes of sound this is not necessary, since his voice is automatically amplified within our audial sensors.

"I'm sure you are all aware of what transpired last night," he says. "Are you?"

"Yes," we all say in agreement.

"Very well," he says. "Then I will tell you that I have received instructions from the Leaders that you will all be forbidden from speaking of it. You will not allude to it, or use words like 'that thing that happened'. Even any passing remarks will get you demerited."

He steps to the center of the platform and presses the metal plate on the podium, bringing up the lesson cube for the whole class to see. But he speaks up again quickly, as if he's forgotten to mention some important part.

"Oh, yes... and this will be retroactive. So, in the unlucky instance that you had said something about this on your way to class, your memory logs will all be scanned, and you will be demerited."

At this, many of the boys in the hall let out open groans of frustration. And a second later, several of those same boys' desks begin to glow red, showing that they have just been demerited, and that that has demoted them to militant rank. I count ten boys in all, who begin to stand up from their red desks, all walking out of the hall, some shaking their heads in disbelief; including one schoolmate, who was on his last year, Delta 647-40-1, a favorite of the instructor's, and whom had been a certain pick for instructor rank, since he'd only had seven days left till his eighteenth year.

"It's not fair," he says aloud to the class, as he rises to leave, surely knowing that this will demerit him further, but with all of us knowing that he can easily keep militant rank, with only seven days left until his graduation, and so he doesn't seem to care.

"Those are the rules, Delta 647-40-1," the instructor says, visibly sorry to see him go. And as the door slides behind them, shutting them out, our lecture hall feels slightly more empty.

The lesson cube slowly spins in the air above the instructor, awaiting him to begin the class time.

"Now that this is understood," he says, standing with his hands griping at either side of the podium. "Are you all aware of what transpired last night?" he asks again.

"No," we all say.

"Good. Let's begin."

After daily meal, and second lecture, at the end of our classes for the day, I find Theta seated on a stone bench out in the lawn, not far from my personal quarters. I am not surprised by this, since it is a favorite meeting place of ours, peacefully secluded behind a hedge of bushes, and it gives an unhindered view of the setting sun.

I sit down beside her.

"I was demerited today," I say.

"Oh, I'm sorry," she says. "It was my fault, wasn't it?... for stopping you in the hall."

"No, it's not. It's my fault. I should have hurried," I answer. However, the blame could be easily split between the two of us, since she was the one to stop on the way to lectures, and without that I might have been on time. Though I won't say anything about that, and so we sit in silence for several more minutes, as I try with all my ability to think of a way to mention last night's retractment, and my thoughts about it, without seeming too obvious, or getting us both in trouble with the scanners.

The School is quieting, as schoolmates begin to settle into their personal quarters for the evening, well ahead of curfew. Nearby us in the lawn, that same bird from this morning is still gathering twigs for its nest. That's my chance.

"So I had a bad dream, last night," I say.

She gives me a fearful glance, obviously knowing that we

should not speak so openly like this, and risk giving away our codes, that we'd worked so hard to keep secret. But I have to speak to someone about it, since it has been piling up in my brain all day.

"I had a dream about a red-chested bird, last night," I continue. "And he looked so familiar, like I had seen him somewhere before."

Her eyes are still concerned. This is such a poorly coded message, and it's blatantly obvious that we both know this.

"But when I left my quarters this morning, I saw him out in the lawn, and realized that I must have seen him somewhere before, and hadn't remembered it."

The bird flutters nearer to us, gathering another set of twigs from the ground.

"Doesn't he look familiar to you?" I ask.

It's clearly seen in her eyes now, that she knows that this is a dangerous line to tread, but still she answers, "Yes, he does..." She tightens her lips, as if she knows she should not speak another word, though strangely she does not stop. "It's his eyes," she says.

The bird flies away to his nest, and returns for another twig, hopping still nearer to us.

My brain is overwhelmed. "His eyes?" I ask, shocked that she had seen that strange familiarity, the same as I had. How could that be?

Then she continues, "They're your eyes, Alpha." She stares deeply at me. "That's where I've seen them before."

And deep in my heart I know she must be right. Something flashes across my vision.

Oh, no! I close my eyes trying not to show my anger, and hoping not to say anything else aloud, now, that would get us into even more trouble.

"What is it?" she asks, likely seeing my face change in an instant.

I swipe the air with my hand, shoving away a newly appeared message from the bottom righthand corner of my optical display, it reads, "Report to the Schoolmaster. Immediately."

I shake my head, angry at myself for being so careless.

"I'm in trouble," I say. And as I stand up from our bench, I add, "Maybe two demerits today."

4

I was given fair warning. Why did I have to press it? My instructor was inexcusably clear. Do not speak of it, he warned. And even seeing my fellow schoolmates demerited, and de-ranked, that didn't sway me. Why had it mattered? And what could Theta mean by saying that "he had my eyes"? Of all the things that she might have said: that our eyes are similar, perhaps, or that they both have comparable colors of blue in them, but this is not what she said. She said very plainly, that they were my eyes, as in the very same, an identical pairing.

Echoing footsteps on the hardened walkway, the sun is setting behind me, and mine are the only footsteps heading back toward the main school, where the Schoolmaster keeps his personal quarters.

To keep four credits for the next five years seems almost unattainable. I can almost feel the loss of my instructor's rank, even before it happens. This is hopeless now.

The empty school halls are silent as a bone, and as alone as I now feel. My feet traipse a steeply inclined flight of stairs to a higher level. The School, which seems to have no end in size when it is full, seems even more massive now that it is vacant. The stair rail is cold in my hand, and after many steps I come to the higher level, and to the School-master's private quarters. His door is not squeezed on either side with other doors, like my quarters' is, but it stands alone, and is likewise more intimidating.

Epsilon 581-38-5 is shown above the doorplate, the Schoolmaster's designation. The entry scanners sense my presence and announce my arrival.

"Alpha 7-40-3," they transmit into my audial sensors, and as I assume, into the audial sensors of the Schoolmaster's ears, who must be there in his quarters, since his designation is shown above the doorplate.

His voice is the oldest voice, of which I am aware. "Enter, please," he says, his voice being amplified from the speaker above the doorplate. The door slides open, and I enter.

He is seated at a work desk. But for myself there is nothing to be sat upon, though his personal quarters are much more spacious than my own, and so I stand. This is my first time ever being allowed into the Schoolmaster's quarters. And likewise, I am the only of my fellow schoolmates whom I know of to be asked.

Most of the hair on the top of his head has been lost, though there is still some. He begins almost as soon as my feet enter through the doorway.

"Is this what you would call 'immediate', Alpha 7-40-3?" he says.

What to say?... something to save myself. "Should I not have thought of it as such, Schoolmaster?" I ask.

"No, you should not have," he says, like his voice were the oldest thing imaginable. And he examines my face intensely, perhaps to see whether I was being openly defiant, or just unaware that my slowness would not be welcomed. Though I am not punished.

"You should learn to come when called," he says.

"Yes, Schoolmaster," I answer.

He breathes in a heavy breath that sounds like it's scratching in his throat.

"Do you know *why* you are here?" he asks, with a slow voice that seems skeptical of me.

"No," I answer, purposefully lying in order to save my few remaining credits, if that is possible.

He licks his dried lips before beginning again. There is no way he believes me.

"I have been reviewing your memory log today," he says. "It appears, you have had some *bad dreams*," he continues, overemphasizing our code words for a retractment.

My skin jumps, the veins in my neck flinching.

"Yes, Schoolmaster," I reply.

He takes another extended breath, in through his nose this time.

"But a dream about birds does not seem upsetting to me... Can you explain yourself?" he asks.

My hands wring nervously behind my back.

"I do not like birds, Schoolmaster," I say, desperately lying to save myself from these spiraling turn of events. Perhaps, I will lose all my credits today.

He leans across his desk.

"This is not something that has been shown in your log," he says.

"It is a new feeling," I say. I could be docked one credit for every lie. I may not even stay at militant rank, after today.

He takes several more breaths while his straining chest rises and falls, as if it is being pressed upon.

"Then it is something you should have made mention of," he says, with his frail and raspy voice. Then he continues, before I have a chance to comply with his request.

"You know, there are many watchers who might have misinterpreted you words, today," he says, inhaling quickly to regain his breath. "You should be *careful*," he says, vastly overemphasizing his words, and rising up from his work desk that sits at the center of the room, at the central point between his door and his bed, coming to stand near the door to lead me out.

"Yes, Schoolmaster," I say.

He stands very close to me now, staring deep into my eyes, which he can do since his posture is slightly slouched. He grabs my hand with quite a lot of force, opening my fingers so that my palm is flat. This is so bizarre that I begin to glance down, until he seizes my chin with his other wrinkled hand, and proceeds to speak again.

"But I will make a clear note that I have addressed your words today, personally."

He is drawing something into my palm. I desperately want to look down as a reflex, but he still holds my chin tightly with his other hand.

Letters—it takes me till the end of his second letter before I can tell what it is: a message in capital script.

"That way, the watchers will know full well that you have already been dealt with, [now numbers, and dashes, a designation] ...regarding this misunderstanding, and you will not face any further scrutiny. But again, please make mention of any fears you might have, ahead of time, so that this will not be an issue, in the future."

My pupils widen as he finishes the final drawn number on my palm. He wrote slowly, so that I did not miss any number, and only the first letter of the designation, since I was unprepared to begin with.

"LPHA 7-39-1" is what was written, or as I would very logically assume, ALPHA 7-39-1. This is not just any designation. It is the designation of my progenitor. My own breaths are hard to take in.

"Yes, Schoolmaster," I say. "I *understand*," I continue, over enunciating my own words. Since this is obviously a new code, that we now have amongst ourselves.

"Good," he says, with an almost imperceptible grin coming upon his old face, that hides itself in the lines of his wrinkles, and I'm sure is only something that I would notice.

■ ▧ ▨

I close my eyes, and see a red-chested bird, that same one from the lawn. He is gathering twigs for what I think might be a nest, but when I look into the trees, there is not a nest at all, but a word built from twigs. A single word, which he weaves his twigs into, completing his work. A word that I have never heard spoken before, except for one time: One terrible, bloody time.

"Revolution."

And I do not even have a clear knowledge as to what it might mean. Perhaps it means something like evolution, I think. Perhaps, to re-evolve. But I don't have time to dream of this, for the bird begins to speak, and his voice is a woman's voice, an awful mechanical woman's voice.

"Awake," it tweets. "Awake, awake."

I hate that voice. I always have.

5

This time I am waiting for her, beneath the covered walkway where her personal quarters are kept, along her normal path to morning lectures. She quickens her already brisk pace; she must have seen me.

"What did the Schoolmaster say to you?" Theta asks, when she reaches me. "Were you demerited?" she says, and her mouth cringes.

"No," I say, still shocked by it myself. We make sure to keep moving so that we will not be docked for tardiness.

I need to speak with someone about this: it's exploding in my brain, and has been all night.

"He only said, 'I should be careful,' and that my words might be misunderstood by any watchers who may review my memories."

She glances at me with a peculiar look stuck upon her face. "How... fortunate," she says, stretching out the word *how*.

But it is not enough—she needs to know. So we must result to code again, and hopefully it will not be ruined like yesterday's code for "bad dreams."

So, I flash the number three across my chest quickly, then reach up to scratch behind my neck, so that ideally our most secretive code is not found out. Of course she will know this is serious, since we do not use the number code often, only when we have something of upmost importance to say.

Three. She will ask three questions from the initial one, and then I will give the real answer to her question. At first, this code was a challenge for us, but now it is as easy as plain conversation.

"Did you hear about Delta 647-40-1?" she asks. Question one.

"How could I have?" I answer. "I was with the Schoolmaster until just before curfew. I barely made it to my personal quarters in time."

"Would you like to hear about it?" she asks. Question two.

"Sure," I say, "as long as it's open knowledge."

"Well, I heard he was so furious after being demerited, and de-ranked to militant, yesterday morning, that he volunteered for a staged battle, and put three schoolmates in the infirmary. He's being considered for a lead militant position now."

My jaw drops.

"After only a day?" I ask, as we come into the main school hall.

"I know," she says. "I could hardly believe it myself."

This would be the final question. We hurry up the steps to where we usually part ways.

"Have you thought of anything interesting, today?" she asks. Question three, time to tell her what I'd really learned from the Schoolmaster, last evening.

"Designations," I say. "I've always found it intriguing to learn new ones. It's like a brief lesson into someone's past."

Hopefully this would be clear enough for her. Her eyebrows lift instantly. She must understand, by the way that she looks at me.

"Really?" she says, her eyes locked onto mine.

"Really," I answer.

I'd not kept up with the time. We part ways, and I sprint to lectures again, pounding my feet on the stone floor, and once again I am demerited. More than a full minute late this time. I will never be an instructor, at this rate, swiping away the de-crediting notification in the lower right portion of my vision as I find my seat. Four credits. Four credits for five years. This is impossible.

6

During daily meal, I sit alone, slurping my nutri-mix from my bowl. I don't feel like speaking with anyone, and so I found a place at the far end of a long table.

Crammed into my head are all the images of things that have happened beyond my control. It is too much to fit into meaningless conversations, in which I cannot even use my own words, for fear of retractment; and, if it came to that, would they shoot me, the same as they did to my progenitor? These thoughts boil inside my head, so that I don't even notice an old laborer, who is sweeping too near to me. His broom scrapes the ground and prickles against my shoes.

"Can I help you?" I ask, in no mood to be bothered, especially of all, today.

He turns his head toward my direction, and holds up a three, while still griping onto his broomstick handle. He then returns to his sweeping. I almost spit the nutri-mix from my mouth. It was an obvious three. He knows the numbers code. But how? Was he watching us in the hall this morning?

"What's your designation?" I ask the laborer. Question one.

"Chi 333-38-3," he says. His voice is slow and drawn out, in lazy deep syllables.

"Do I know you?" I ask, hoping he might reveal something about how he knows our code. Question two.

"Do we ever really know anyone?" he says.

"Maybe not..." I answer.

The last question, but what to ask?

"Would you like me to do something?" I ask. Question three.

"Yes," Chi says, lifting up his face to speak to me. "You should leave. Things get awfully dirty around here, and I'd hate for you to get any of this dust on your feet," he says, moving the broom closer to me.

"You want me to leave?" I ask.

"As soon as you can," he says. "Here, *let me help you*," he adds as he pulls my chair back, and overemphasizing the words "let me help you."

▩　▩　▩

The lawn is perfect, and green, every inch manicured as it always is, with square cut hedges. We sit on the bench, our bench, and for this little piece of time there are no "bad dreams," no secret codes, no lectures to endure, no demerits, and the Common can't harm us as long as we are silent. It is my favorite portion of everyday.

But I cannot hold it in any longer, so I speak. "Look at the sunset, Theta. Just look at it," I say. "I can't take my eyes off of it," I continue, hoping she will get my hint, as I open up her hand, and draw my fingers across her palm, writing the same designation that the Schoolmaster had drawn into my hand last night.

"Wow..." she says, after I finish. "What an amazing sunset. I knew it would be these colors tonight—somehow I just knew."

"So did I," I say, thinking that perhaps she was referring to my message, and my progenitor, instead of the sunset. So this is added to our growing list of codes.

We watch in silence, as I write the details of my conversation with Chi, the old laborer. I wish that I could tell it to her with my own words, but that is impossible, and so palm-writing will have to do. Why we had never thought of this before is peculiar to me. After all, touch cannot be monitored like vision or hearing can be, and it cannot be controlled either: except for sensations of pain.

Long ago, the Common wished to implant a sensor into that portion of the nervous system, but it failed, and the sensors had caused too many delays in their hosts. Too many citizens were either burned or cut without their knowing, until it was too late. So they gave up on touch, in favor of those senses that could be easily controlled.

I tell her through writing that I am almost sure that he was offering to take me away from the School.

"And go where?" she writes.

A voice behind us, sharply brings us back to reality.

"Alpha 7-40-3?" this voice says.

I turn, pulling my hand away from Theta, and standing up from our bench in a singular motion. There are twenty or more schoolmates, militant ranks, with Delta 647-40-1 as their obvious leader.

"What do you want?" I say to him.

"You have to come with us," he replies.

Theta stands up as well. "Go away. Why don't you just de-rank already? No one wants you to be a lead militant anyways," she yells at him.

Slap! Without warning he strikes her with the back of his hand.

"Neither do I," he says.

I rush at him, but my schoolmates surround me, seizing my arms. Theta is on the ground, holding the side of her cheek, and someone kicks her in the side, for what I can tell is no good reason.

"Theta!" I yell.

Instant pain—I'm struck in the face by Delta's fist, and there is wet blood now on my lips. I am not going to win. Two last-year schoolmates grab my arms so tightly that I feel like they could break; I am kicking, biting, but nothing helps. These are skilled militant ranks, and I am still only an instructor rank. Being dragged across the walkway, I place my feet down, trying to stop them. Something hard beats against my back—I will not win this—and so I let my body go completely limp. If they want to carry me, they will have to do it themselves.

The main school is as empty as it was the night before, except for the horde of militants surrounding me. I am carried through the first level of the School, below the tall stairs that I'd climbed when I was called to see the Schoolmaster. All their hardened boots pound the polished ground. Why so many of them? Am I really such a challenge? Maybe they think I'm stronger than I really am, or this is Delta trying to prove himself.

We stop in front of the door to a personal quarters that I've never wanted to enter. And every time I've heard stories of schoolmates who've entered here, it always ends in a retractment, or in bruises and a loss of credits, but anything less than that, and the Disciplinarian would not be doing his job.

Gamma 616-38-2 shows above the doorplate. The two bulky militants, who were carrying me, toss me to the floor. The entry scanners shine over my entire body, and I am announced, both within my own head, and through the speaker above the doorplate. "Alpha 7-40-3," it says.

Though there is no answer from inside to welcome me. Instead, the door opens at once, and a stark, blinding light shines out at me from an otherwise totally black room. I will have bruises, for sure.

7

I am kneeling on the floor in front of the Disciplinarian's door.

"Come in, Alpha," he says, although I cannot see his face. Oh, no! He must have reviewed my memory log. He knows what Theta calls me.

I stand, desperately hoping not to show any concern or fear in my expression, and walk into the darkness of his personal quarters, taking my seat in the lone wooden chair; though I still cannot see the Disciplinarian's face. And the door slides shut behind me.

"Why does she call you Alpha?" he asks, in an innocent way that also sounds like it's tinged with violence.

I do not answer immediately, and am struck across my face, reopening the wound that I'd had in my mouth from when Delta hit me earlier. I try my best not to glare at him, but it happens anyway.

"Because that is what I like to be called," I say.

The noise of his footsteps solidly reflects off the black walls as he walks behind me, though I keep my eyes straight ahead.

"But that is not your designation... Are you ashamed of what the Common has given you?"

"No, sir," I say immediately.

The clacking of steps follows around my chair, until he is again standing in front of me, though I still cannot see his face. He makes a subtle, "hmm..." as if he is thinking.

"Then why not use your full designation? And why only with her?" he asks.

Again, I take too long to answer; there is nothing permissible that could be said that would not bring her trouble. His hand stings against my face.

"Because with her it is not required," I answer.

He leans in. The outline of his sharply pointed nose is now visible within the silhouette of harsh light that blurs in my eyes, but obscures all else in blanketed darkness. "And who has told you it is not required? Your instructor? A schoolmate perhaps?" he says.

"No one has said that..."

He places a hand on my face, and I flinch expecting to be slapped, but I am not. Though his soft touch makes me sick inside, and I would rather be slapped.

"Alpha..." he says, using tender tones that bite like ants upon my skin. "Then how have you had the idea, if no one said it?"

I gulp and shiver, because his hand still rests upon my face.

"I just knew," I answer. " ...that with her, Alpha would be enough."

"Why?" he says, running his fingers through the strands of my hair.

"Because she knows me," I say. "She knows who I am, without a full designation, and I her."

"Then can I call you Alpha?" he asks, holding my hair between his fingers.

"I'd rather you not," I say, for some reason, knowing it to be dangerously foolish.

"And why not?" he asks, griping slightly onto my hair.

"Because I don't know you," I say. "We've never met." Why am I doing this? I should be compliant, but I am not.

"Alpha," he says louder, pulling forcefully on my hair, tightening his grip so that every piece feels pain. This is what comes from saying things I shouldn't—nothing but pain.

"But I do know you," he says. With his other hand he pulls open my eyelids. "I can see, everything that you see." Then pulling at my earlobe, he says, "And I can hear, everything that you hear."

He pulls at my hair harder, so that it feels like a fire on my scalp, but he speaks softly again. "I know you, as well as you know yourself."

Slap!

I want to scream and fight back, but that would send me down to militant rank for sure. He lets go, and begins to pace around me again.

"Tell me, Alpha... Can I call you Alpha?" he says rhetorically, and I know it's just so he can taunt me. "Have you heard any words lately, that you have not recognized?" he asks.

"No," I lie.

"Really?... And what about the other night, during the retractment?" he says, quickening his pacing steps.

It's a trap. I know it is. So again I lie. "What retractment?" I say.

Slap, to the side of my head, causing a ringing, reminiscent of the night before. That was obviously not the right answer. Perhaps a simple "no" to his question would suffice, and so I try that, but I am struck on the other side of my head, now with two ringing ears.

"Yes," I answer a third time, clenching my jaw at him.

"One demerit," he says, abruptly. "You should be careful, Alpha," he says, while never altering his pace. "And this new word, have you ever thought of it before?"

"How can I have thought of it, if I've never heard it?"

"Oh, you may have thought of the idea of the word, without knowing it," he says. "Tell me, Alpha... Can I call you Alpha?" And he looks for an answer this time.

Though, I do not answer. I will not be his game.

Slap!

"This new word, what do you think it means?" he asks.

I run my finger below my nose, and find a trickle of new blood. "I'm not sure... to re-evolve?" I say.

"Two demerits, only two remaining. I would hate for you to lose your ranking. After you'd worked so hard to keep it. Be *careful*, Alpha," he says, straining the word "careful." It's possible he'd also done this the first time and I hadn't noticed it. My eyes open wide in shock. This is a new code, between myself and the Disciplinarian, a threat: not only for me, but for the Schoolmaster as well. He must have seen that part of my memory log too, and figured us out.

He smirks. "Perhaps..."

And then he begins again quickly, addressing his audial scanner, "Assign *three* demerits to Alpha 7-40-3, for good measure," he says, patting on the top of my head, which is still brutally sore. "Open door."

At his command, the door slides open and I am dragged away into the night, with bruises all over, lots of bruises.

■ ■ ■

Though the beatings do not end with the Disciplinarian, as I wish they would. I am pulled into the courtyard, and Delta wants to have his fun as well. He slams his fist into my gut.

"You better not be trouble, Alpha 7-40-3," he says, looking like he might actually enjoy it if I were.

My stomach churns, and I cannot help but fall to my knees, coughing as I speak, "You don't have to do this," I say.

Why am I saying this? Do I really want to be hit again?

He reels back, and I half-heartedly attempt to block. There are too many of them, and Delta is a militant now; he would never risk his new ranking, by allowing me to win anything. I shut my eyes; maybe then this could be just a dream, just a terrible, painful dream.

"Stop!"

The Schoolmaster is running out of the archway, and panting as he hurries. He snatches Delta's fist out of the air.

"What are you doing?" says the Schoolmaster, using all the remaining air in his lungs to say the words.

All the other schoolmates take a step away from their militant leader, not wanting to be implicated. Delta's face is stern, and unfeeling, yet still unresponsive.

"Answer!" the Schoolmaster says, as gruffly and as forcefully as he is able.

"We had orders to escort him to the Disciplinarian," Delta admits.

My nose bleeds as a thin line down my face, and my saliva is tainted with the taste of blood, and my stomach is still reeling from the punch.

"And I'm sure you were not all ordered to beat him, as well. I'll take this from here," he says, and shoves Delta away as he continues, "Now run off to your quarters, or I'll de-rank all of you for being out after curfew."

And with that, every spectating militant scatters almost instantly. Though Delta 647-40-1 glares distrustfully at me, and at the Schoolmaster as well, while taking a few slow steps away from us, until he turns and runs away like all the rest.

The Schoolmaster's hand grabs onto mine, and I am lifted up. The old man is slouched and winded from rushing out to save me, and suddenly I remember I must return the favor.

"Be *careful*, Schoolmaster," I say. His eyes twitch back and forth; he must understand my meaning, and surely his reaction is one that only I would notice. But still I continue, just to be certain that my words would not seem out of place to any watchers. "I mean, I would hate for you to be injured, while trying to protect me," I say.

The seriousness of his stare I can almost feel. What if that was not a clever enough code? Could I have caused even more trouble, not intending to?

"We should be going. Allow me to see you to your quarters," he says.

And I agree, not wanting to be left alone any more tonight. Our steps are painstakingly slow, but all the better; with the Schoolmaster holding me up by the arm, it is the perfect opportunity for inconspicuous palm-writing.

"Who?" he writes, while we hobble beneath the walkway awning, well after curfew.

"Disciplin—" I begin to write, until he brushes me off, presumably knowing what I would write ahead of time.

I am the next with a question. "Chi?" I ask, in writing.

"He will help you," he replies.

"I leave?" I quickly scribble into his palm, as we approach my quarters.

"Yes," he answers.

"When?" I ask, slowing our steps, but not so much that it would be noticeable. And we halt in front of my door. The Schoolmaster releases my hand.

"*Tomorrow*, I should hope, you will be ready for your classes," he says. "And I trust you have not mistaken my kindness for familiarity. I have only been interested in your good study," he adds.

"Yes, Schoolmaster," I reply, placing my hand against

the doorplate, so that it slides open immediately. "I understand," I add.

"Good," he says, gazing intently at me, stroking the side of his wrinkled face.

The door shuts behind me, and I am once again alone, in the lightlessness of my personal quarters. I place my clothing in the bin for cleaning. Hopefully the blood that had dripped upon my white uniform shirt will be washed by morning, and hopefully there will be no more "bad dreams" tonight. I think I have had enough nightmares for one day.

8

The lawn is dreamlike again, and I am standing beneath the tree where the red-chested bird has left his message. Behind me, there are shouts, and lights shining out from the main school; a mob is forming, led by Delta, and the Disciplinarian, whose face is still obscured in darkness.

They rush at me. They must think that I was the one to write the message in the tree. Their shouts come closer and I turn away, sprinting with all my strength, but it is not enough. And so I shout in reply as they draw nearer, "It's not me. It was the bird," I yell, but my words seem to gargle in my throat. Until I scream out with all my might, "It was the bird!"

And I am finally awake, and dripping with sweat. Ironically, there might be a decent chance, that after all of this, I will actually develop a real fear of birds. A nervous, exhausted quiet laugh leaves my mouth, and though none would see it in the darkness, I am grinning.

"It was the bird," I repeat, and I cannot help but chuckle at this silly phobia I am creating for myself. And unable to fall back to sleep, I dress in the darkness, and wait for my door to be unlocked for the morning.

Devastatingly early, I stand in the archway to the main school, waiting for Theta until I can almost afford to wait no more. I will leave today—whatever that means—but if I've the chance not to lose my last credit on my final day, I will try for that.

The time is moving on. The rush of schoolmates pouring into the archway is becoming a more manageable trickle. Though turning to leave, her voice calls out to me. How could I not have noticed her? She is hobbling toward me, and her hand is against her side as she walks.

"Alpha..." her voice says frailly.

Running back down the walkway to help her, I let her lean her weight on my arm as we attempt to hurry along. Her face squeezes around her eyebrows with each step.

What do you feel?—I ask her. And she says she'd had a pain in her ribs since the night before, since she was kicked. My face heats with anger. If I ever get a chance at Delta I will take it, no matter how many credits would be lost. He deserves to be kicked, himself, for what his militant squad has done to her.

"You should really be in the infirmary," I tell her.

With what strength she can give, she smiles. "Where do you think I'm going?" she says.

Making our way through the flow of foot traffic, we come to the open infirmary door, with a handful of our other schoolmates spread around on beds or on couches, some of them red-shirts from militant training. It is clear to see that Theta is not even the most badly hurt of them all. Could these be some of the schoolmates whom Delta had beaten on his first day of training? Likely they are.

"If you're released after courses, I should like to speak with you tonight," I say, delivering her over to the less comforting care of a medical rank.

"I should like that too," she says.

The time has come down to the end. Sprinting away from her, I fight the surge of schoolmates. I will not lose my last credit. And with only seconds to spare, bolting past the door scanners, it is kept safe, for now.

The spots that were made vacant have already been filled by first year schoolmates: barely six years of age, and visibly overwhelmed, with their tiny hands and miniature faces. And with their addition, our bowl-shaped lecture hall is brimming to its maximum capacity, once again. Yet, something about their eagerness to prove themselves seems strangely pointless to me now. Was this what I was like when I was shipped in from the infantarium? And now, seven years later, fighting to keep my instructor's rank, clawing to keep every last credit, which now for the first time seems like an imaginary number that only appears in my vision every so often, though now more frequently. And what is leaving worth, then, if I will exit in the same way that I came in? After all, leaving would likely mean an automatic de-ranking to laborer, either way.

And so, for perhaps the first time, I have a different thought about credits, and the grasping onto them in my mind begins to weaken. I will never be an instructor now. That was all that I'd wanted for years, but that seems now, in light of my leaving, pointless as well. And what use is it to hold onto something that is imaginary, like a credit, if I can only keep it till the end of the day?

■　■　■

The lesson cube spins methodically above our instructor. He is sliding his hands across the podium, guiding the cube through a lecture on past events of the Common, namely its beginnings. This is probably meant to be beneficial for the great number of introductory first year schoolmates, who have filled into the newly vacated seats. Most of them will not make it as instructors, though they are at least required to know this. And as such, it is a lecture I have heard repeated till my ears feel numb.

Yet, perhaps I should give it my attention, since this shall be my final day, whatever that will mean.

Images of happy citizens shine out of the lecture cube in shades of tinted green. "In the forty generations, since our creation, the Common has been always improving, always striving to fashion a better existence for our citizens," our instructor says.

From out of the cube flashes scenes of smiling laborers, in their perfectly pressed blue shirts, and technology ranks, and medicals, and militants in exact formations. And so on, and so on, through all the various rankings.

"Thus, in order to maintain a more perfect cooperation, during the first generation, the Leaders enacted our system of ranks and credits, and implemented the process of sensor implantation into the nervous system to guard against rogue elements," our instructor is blank faced as he says this, having repeated these points many times over. "And for all these forty generations, we have lived in complete peace and harmony."

Something triggers in my brain. How does this make sense? How have I sat here for so many years and never once questioned this? I will. Today I will.

My feet stand, as if I cannot control them. I slide my hand across my desk to show that I would ask a question. It blinks green to alert my instructor. And my designation, I know from experience, transmits into his audial sensors.

He begins to speak, even as he is still finding my blinking desk, "Yes, Alpha 7-40-3. Was something not explained to your liking?" he asks.

All eyes are fastened onto me. No one stands when they ask their questions, and so I don't know why I have done it. "Well... no, sir. You have been very thorough, but I would like a clarification," I say. None of my schoolmates could be expecting this. Every question rests finely on the edge of a demerit, but what does it matter anymore.

"From our previous lessons, sir, you've said that before the Common, there were only mindless bands of half-men..."

"Yes, and what is your question?"

"Well, if there were only ever half-men here, then where did our first Leaders come from? Were they half-men themselves?" I ask.

At once, all the air is sucked from the room with a gasp. Our instructor has a questioning look in his eyes. And he pauses the lesson cube, so that it freezes in the air, showing images of the Central City, locked in a green haze upon the cube.

Lifting up his hands to shush the growing murmuring, he says, "I should warn you, Alpha 7-40-3. You are venturing into dangerous territory. Would you care to rephrase your question, so that it will not be so disrespectful to our Leaders?"

Glancing around at all the eyes upon me, and at these new first year schoolmates, whom I am being a terrible example for, I say, "But if I should want an answer, sir, then I have no idea how else to phrase it."

I will be demerited. I know I will.

"Then, let me help you"—using a very deliberate voice. "You might say, 'Since it is impossible that our illustrious Leaders might have ever been half-men themselves, from where, O good instructor, could they have come?'" he says.

"Yes, could I say that?" I ask.

He nods his head in agreement, but I am forced to repeat his words exactly, before he will answer. And the first time, leaving out the phrase, "O good instructor," I am forced to say that as well. He smiles at me, once I have asked the question in the manner he would like, and he continues, "Very well, since you have been *so* respectful, I will tell you what you would have learned in an upcoming lesson, that your older schoolmates already know, that our Leaders were not half-men themselves... but were evolved from half-men to become fully human, as we are today."

"And what has happened to the half-men?"

"They have all died," he answers, abruptly.

"And how have they died?"

"They have gone extinct," he answers.

"Yes, but—" I begin to say, before he stops me.

"Please, you have taken up far too much time. You should leave space for your schoolmates to ask their questions."

I scan the room. There are looks of terror in all their eyes. "Would anyone else like to ask a question?" I say. They stare at me with their blank and frightened faces. No one says a word. Though I do not take my seat.

"Just one more question, sir, please," I say.

He glances even more intently at me, though I am begrudgingly allowed to continue.

"What comes after human?" I ask.

"I'm not sure that I understand your question."

Trying to make myself more clear, I say, "Our Leaders, as you say, have evolved from half-men... then is there something more than human?"

Some of my schoolmates are snickering at my line of questioning, but some are still too nervous to make any sounds at all, but short gasps.

Our instructor takes a steady breath in through his nose. "Let me see if I have this straight, and I will hope, for your sake, I am mistaken. Are you saying that you are dissatisfied with our Leaders, and with your place as a human citizen?"

I protest, vehemently saying that that was not my intent. "It just seems to be logical, sir, that if it has happened once before, that it might happen again. That we could be re-evolved," I say. Not one eye is directed away from me in the whole room.

"And who would begin this new evolution? Would it be you, Alpha 7-40-3?" he says, as if angry with me.

Don't say another word. There are frightened eyes all around me that are telling me not to speak. But today I am leaving, and so for once in my life I will say what I want to.

"Well... it could be any of us, I suppose. And so yes, it could be me," I say.

Our instructor snidely grins at me. "Then I will help you learn your place... Assign one demerit to Alpha 7-40-3," the instructor says.

"Credits: 0," shows in the lower righthand corner of my field of vision. And suddenly, in bold red script in the center of my view is the word "De-ranked." This has never happened before, and it is frightening to see text so big, and all encompassing. I swipe my hand to remove the notification. My desk glows red.

I glance around the lecture hall, seeing all of my schoolmates' scared faces. I have been like them, for so long, griping onto my high ranking, hoping to keep it until my final year. But now that it's gone, I realize now that it's never meant anything at all.

"It doesn't matter," I say. And my credits, that had been reset to ten, are now ticked down to nine.

"It doesn't matter." Eight.

I am walking from my desk, and headed to the door. "It doesn't matter." Seven. And I leave, without looking back. I am a militant now.

■ ▦ ▥

The chime for daily meal sounds almost as soon as I step outside of the instructor ranks' hall. And in my short walk to the dining area, it seems rumor of my outburst this morning has already spread so quickly.

I step into the meal hall, and the air loses its conversation, as if everyone had been waiting for me, so that they could unsuccessfully pretend that they hadn't seen me, and then continue to whisper to one another. And now no one will sit near me, or even in the several open seats surrounding me. My bowl of nutri-mix tastes bland and tepid. Far away at the other end of the room Chi is sweeping aimlessly.

Does he know? Does even he want to stay as far from me as possible?

Several minutes later, the Schoolmaster steps into the room and stands beside Chi as he continues to sweep. The Schoolmaster is gazing out over his gathering of male students for daily meal. And although he does not turn toward Chi's direction, his mouth might be moving. Are they speaking about me? Have I ruined my only chance to leave? Have I squandered my instructor's ranking for false promises?

I must have. There's no way they would try to help me now. The watchers will surely be intently tracking my every move through my location sensor: Uninterruptedly viewing my whole life through my visual sensors. There will be no way to leave this place. Perhaps, there has never been. How could I have been so foolish to waste all of my credits on an impossible hope? The Common controls what I hear and what I see, and so they control me. And they have controlled the forty generations before me. How could I have been such a dreamer?

I'm a militant now, and militants cannot afford these sorts of dreams, or hopeful emotions that might make them weak. And after all, would I really want to leave the School if Theta could not come with me? Of course I wouldn't, and I know that almost instantly, without much thought, as if I had always known that.

9

The militants have their own battle training facility, just past the main school. Arriving several minutes early, there are already groups dressed and ready in their blood-red uniform suits. They are running through the high obstacle course, as if they could never miss a step, or they are practicing their sparring, or defenses, with the greatest agility.

And then here I am, still in my white instructor's uniform, and several years behind in training: since I had held out for so long in my previous ranking.

And at the very far right end of the gymnasium is Delta. His knuckles are wrapped in padding, and he is pounding the life out of a punching doll, that is held in place by his training partner. And without warning Delta spins and kicks the doll, flinging his partner to the ground as well, with such ease, and as if this were the ranking that he was always meant for.

His mouth is curling up in a smirked grin; he must have seen me. There is a terrible high-sounding ringing in my ears. This must be the notification for militants that class has begun, since they all take their seats on the floor, as if this were expected.

This is a mixed class, and from what I've heard, it is the

first and only time this will ever happen. And it seems fairly logical, as we've all assumed, that the reason for this is that the Leaders wish to thoroughly break any habits of gentleness we might have toward our female schoolmates, and vice versa. And looking around it must have worked; all of their faces are so brutal and bloodthirsty, just like Delta's, though he is the worst of them.

Our class begins and we are seated on the floor in a half-circle, awaiting our militant instructor to give us our directives. She is the most vicious woman I've ever seen, with dead expressions and flat white skin.

"This afternoon, we will continue with our target practice, and hand-to-hand combat training, but first, a matter of importance. As you should have noticed, we have some newcomers," she says, with her grotesque eyes staring into me. "Though, if these new militants would like to stay, they should prove themselves." I glance over my shoulder, but can see no other white-shirts besides myself. "And therefore, since there are only two of them, we shall have a battle to the death... or as near to it as we are allowed," she says, as if the concept of restraint is a disappointment to her. "And so, the *winner* will be allowed to stay, and the *loser* will be de-ranked."

There are subtle cheers from my militant schoolmates. To see them so without feeling is dreadfully appalling. It sits uneasily in my stomach, and makes them seem more animal-like than human, to me: As if militant rank for them is a devolution, degrading them back to half-men status, and they are reveling in that loss of humanity.

46

My designation is being called.

"Alpha 7-40-3," she says.

Some familiar faces are cheering me on as I stand, or cheering for my demise; it is hard to tell which.

A militant, older than myself, who at one time long ago shared a row with me in instructors' hall, he is wrapping my knuckles in white padding.

"Tough first day..." he says to me, but I am not giving him much attention, and instead I'm scanning the facility for my opponent's face, though there is no one else that I can see. "Good luck," he says, as he is finishing my last hand. His genuine demeanor catches me off guard, being so unexpected in a place like this.

"I've never fought with anyone before," I say.

"Shouldn't matter," he answers. "Your opponent probably hasn't either... but if you fall to the ground, just try to block your head."

"I'll try," I say. "Thank you."

He finishes the last wrap, and gently slaps at my head as if to motivate me. "You'll do alright," he says, and then takes his seat back in the crowd.

I close my eyes, trying to forcibly remember his designation, the only person in my new ranking who might ever be nice to me, at least for now. Tau... Tau, something. Maybe in the hundreds... 116. No, 114, I'm sure of it. And he is obviously a 40, like myself, though I cannot remember his birth order number, but Tau 114-40 is probably enough.

Though I am interrupted, as our instructor begins to call my opponent's designation. My eyelids shoot open in a terrible shock. It's Theta.

"Theta 87-40-2," our militant instructor says.

How? How could this happen? She was perfect. She never lost a credit in all her seven years since we were both transported from the infantarium—and I remember the moment, the exact moment I first saw her, seated across from me in the transport hull, and I knew it then that she was perfect—and now she's a militant in a day? That's impossible. It has to be my fault, somehow. Maybe the Disciplinarian is punishing her now, to get at me.

She stands at the far end of the gymnasium and limps toward me. She is still visibly hobbling. She's injured! She's still injured and they're making her fight. Of all the people whom I might have to fight, she is the only one that would mean anything, the only one I could never fight.

Now, she is standing in the open space in front of me; a militant girl is wrapping her knuckles as well. Wet marks around her eyes show that she's been recently crying. And her face behind her fiery hair is the most hopeless that I've ever seen it.

We are brought to the center of a circled floor mat. For the briefest part of a second we have the chance to talk.

"I won't hit you," I say, but that seems to disappoint her even more.

"No, you have to. I want to be de-ranked. I can't stay here, not like this, and I wouldn't want to," she answers quickly.

The militant instructor orders for us to touch gloves, and to begin our battle. Which the first part we do, except I cannot bring myself to punch at her, neither of us have any will to fight. She is standing there, an open target: The only person who's ever known me, and how can I hit her?

"We request a de-ranking," I say, turning to our new heartless instructor. She glares at me, and with one hand she is rubbing her thumb against the tips of her fingers, as if that helps her to think.

"No," she answers, plainly.

There must be someway to stop this. "Alpha, please," Theta says, in a whisper, but I have to try, for both our good.

"But if we will not fight, then we are useless to you," I reply, taking a soft step toward our instructor.

Her jawline juts out like a pointed knife.

"If you will not fight... I will make you fight," she says, giving the most violent smile I've ever seen.

I've made a terrible mistake, a gross miscalculation.

"Who will fight in his place?" she asks, addressing my schoolmates. An overwhelming show of hands raises instantly, as nearly all of them wish to prove themselves, thus improving their militant status. How can they be like this? Can't they see they're becoming exactly what she wants them to be?

She picks a raised hand from the seated crowd, and whom would it be, but none other than Delta 647-40-1. He steps condescendingly onto the mat, his knuckles already wrapped from having stayed through daily meal to work on his training, taking advantage of what little time he has left until his graduation.

My mouth hangs open. I cannot form the words in my shocked state. "You're next," he says, pushing past me. And then, he shoves me to the ground, so that it's easily seen how much stronger than me he is.

"Stop! I'll do it. I'll hit her," I call out.

"You've had your chance," our instructor states, as unfeelingly as hardened stone.

I am yelling desperately, as I jump to my feet. "Let me do it!" I plead. But this terrible woman is no longer responding to my cries. If there is something that can be done to stop this, it has to be done now.

Something almost physically snaps inside my brain, and I am running, sprinting. Delta rears back to give his hardest punch. And now, I slam my shoulder into his side, sending both of us sprawling to the ground, even though he is easily one and a half times my own size.

The rage is uncontrollable. I am screaming as I beat my padded fists into his jaw and eye sockets. However, my arms are weakening. I'm unprepared for this. I've never fought anyone before. Air escapes my mouth in panted quick breaths, and in my tiredness I give him an opening. He grips my right forearm, then the other, and shoves me off of him with his natural brute strength. And using his knees to pin my arms, he has free range to do as he pleases; and I cannot do as Tau suggested, I cannot block my face. Grabbing me by the collar, he pounds his fists at me—my white uniform shirt is spattered again with red. Then his fingers are wrapped around my neck. I am not able to breathe; it's been several seconds since I've taken a breath.

And then Theta's voice breaks through the cheers and excitement of my schoolmates.

"You creep!" she shouts, as she pounds at his back and head. He turns and shoves her away, pushing into her side. An excruciating cry leaves her mouth—that was the same still tender place she'd been kicked in last night.

My arms are inescapably pinned. My heart seems to be beating more slowly, though my anger is overflowing. These could be my last images of the world. The last face I might see is Theta's pain-ridden face; and Delta's uncompassionate contentment.

"Enough," our instructor orders. Delta doesn't stop. "Enough, Delta 647-40-1," she says again.

A snide grin eases onto his face as he releases my neck. He bends low to whisper into my ear, "Next time..." he says, threatening.

And as he leaves, Theta crawls to me, laying on her "good side" staring into my eyes.

"Are you ok?" she says.

"As long as you are..." I answer.

Our instructor interrupts. "Theta 87-40-2, you are deranked. Please, vacate my facilities at once," she says, without any visible emotion.

And the only visible emotion in this white-walled building is shining out from our faces, twinkling out of our eyes.

"Thank you," she says. "Thank you," she repeats, and then coughs devastatingly. And the grossness of this cough, it breaks all of our fleeting happiness. After several more spasmed coughs, she pulls her cupped hand away from her mouth, and there is a drop of blood spattered in the center of her palm.

10

She is shuffled out of the gymnasium by some unsympathetic brutes, and the part of me that was relieved to see her de-ranked to a much needed medical ranking, that same part is also sad to know that this single half-day of classes was our last time we would ever have together in our courses. And especially today, this feeling is expounded, since who can say whether or not I might still have a chance at leaving.

But seeing her being shoved out of the door, I watch and our eyes meet before the final moment. I can't leave without her. And if anyone deserves to escape this place, it's her, above anyone else, even myself. Maybe if I ask Chi, he would take her instead, if it's not possible for both of us to go. And so that's what I'll do—my mind is made up—if Chi can not take her, then I won't go. It's either her, or both of us, or none of us: that's what it'll be. But first I need to get through the rest of my first and hopefully last day as a militant, with raw puffy eyes that can barely see straight.

Tau 114-40 is hurrying my way. He drops an automatic rifle into my hands. "Here, take this," he says.

The gun's metal is cold in my hands.

"What's this for?" I ask.

"Would you rather run the high obstacle course?" he answers.

The harshness and the weight of the gun is something I'd never felt before. It's distractingly brutal.

"Well?..." he asks.

"No," I say, though without much confidence.

Not speaking another word, I follow him briskly out of the main room and through a dimly lit hallway to the range. The blasts of automatic gunfire are already greeting us, before we even enter the room. But as soon as we cross the threshold, the sound is instantly muffled, to levels that are breathtakingly loud, but still manageable.

"You can thank the Common for that," Tau shouts, close to my ear. "Your audial sensors are programed to instantly dampen the explosions... if they didn't, you'd be deaf right now," he shouts.

My eyes, still feeling the effects of Delta's fists, are growing more swollen and red than they were, even a few minutes ago. But I can still see fellow militants hurling fire blast grenades and firing with insane speed at bulletproof target dummies. Now, finally, all the stories I've heard about young militants being accidentally maimed or killed, they all seem to make sense. This place is maddening. Any misthrown grenade, or ill-fired rocket, and we'd all be dead.

We set up behind a barricade, aiming at a human-shaped target that is so far down the hall that you would barely notice it. Tau arranges my grip, placing the back of the rifle firmly into the curve of my shoulder, and he kicks my feet to adjust my stance.

He half smiles. "You're a natural," he says in his loudest voice, to get above the blasts, and obviously exaggerating. Then, tilting my head down to look through the sight of the gun, he continues, "Hold your breath when you fire. You'll need one hundred thousand points to graduate as a marksman, and you're already behind schedule." He readjusts my arms, which are already beginning to slouch from the weight of the gun, then continues, shouting into my ear, "Each hit is at least one point; each kill shot is at most ten. It'll take you years to get to that marksmen level, so you'd better get started now."

Glancing up at him, through my squinted and now watering eyes, I ask, just as a matter of curiosity, "How many points do you have?"

He pushes the end of my rifle up again, because it has swayed from its mark.

"About a million," he answers.

I can't believe it. "Then why are you here?" I say, since he obviously doesn't need the practice.

"I'm not here for me... I'm here for you. Now shoot," he orders, pushing my face back toward the gun sight.

Magnified in the sight, my visual sensor produces a target analysis and distance readout.

"Subject: Human," it reads. Then drawing circled markers in my vision to outline the kill zones, it shows, "Distance: 684.35 feet."

I swipe my hand in front of my eyes to clear these notifications, but all my gestures do nothing.

Seeing me struggle, Tau speaks up. "That doesn't work in here," he says. "You see what they want you to see," he adds, pointing around as if the Common were all around us. And perhaps I've never realized how true such a statement was until right now.

He lowers my head back toward the sight. One hundred thousand points, and I don't have any, yet. My finger eases to pull the trigger, but then with my magnified eyesight I notice the target dummy's face; I see his eyes, and my mind flashes back to the previous night, to my "bad dreams", and the retractment, to my progenitor and to his determined glare as he says that word, "Revolution," repeating it over and over in my brain.

I shake my head and pull back from the rifle. "I can't."

"You have to."

"I can't."

"Do it." He tries to shove my head toward the gun sight.

"I'm not a militant," I say, for some reason. Not entirely sure what I even mean, since obviously my ranking is militant now, and so therefore I am, by definition, 'a militant.'

He stares at me with his mouth twisted to the side, and with a look of disappointment, and he sighs at me before speaking.

"Do you think they're just going to de-rank you? That they'll let you walk out of here like nothing ever happened?" he asks.

For a moment, I'm slightly embarrassed. I hadn't known what would happen, but perhaps, without giving it much thought, I had imagined it would be something like what would happen regularly in instructors' training: a schoolmate would lose his last credit, and his desk would turn red, and there was nothing more to it. But here, there are no desks to turn colors, and so I don't know why I was so silly to think it would be that easy. And all these realizations go shooting through my brain in an instant, as Tau continues, "You're beaten into militant ranking, and you're beaten out of it... And they'll put you up against Delta 647-40-1 again, and you're not ready for that. He'll kill you just for fun. At least wait a few days until he graduates."

I nod in agreement that I'll keep trying, but he doesn't seem convinced, so he continues, "What do you think happened to those schoolmates who went up against him, on his first day?"

"They lost..." I answer, "and they went to the infirmary, I think."

"Yeah, and one of them was paralyzed, after that," he says. "And they revoked his citizenship, yesterday morning."

I can see his jaw clench as he says this, and I don't know if I've ever seen someone so visibly angry as Tau is at this moment, yet without speaking, or saying a word against the Common: like his anger is a boiling rage inside of him, and his jaw is a lid to keep it in.

"I never heard about that," I say, in response to our schoolmate's loss of citizenship.

"Yah, well they don't tell you everything, do they?" he replies.

And twisting my head back toward the gun sight, he directs me to shoot; and helps me to pull back on the trigger, since it is surprisingly difficult to manage. Yet, in all this, I somehow spectacularly get a kill shot, and even with my swollen and still watering eyes.

11

The clouds burn in regular embers of orange. I am at our bench again, waiting for her as the sun dips toward the treeline, toward the forest that stands just outside of the perimeter fence that surrounds our school. Where is she? She should have been here, nearly a half-hour ago.

Maybe the medical ranks in the infirmary have kept her over for the night. I should leave; there might be a chance I could still find her along the way.

Though as I stand and turn, she is there standing behind me, looking as pale and as feverishly weak as I have ever seen her.

"I tried to hurry," she says, and continues to take stuttered painful steps toward our meeting place, and these are the most awkwardly slow steps I could ever imagine. She must still be in excruciating pain from her bruised or broken ribs, and maybe it's grown worse, and her tiny steps are a way to compensate for that.

"They let you leave like this?" I ask, completely astounded that anyone in their right mind would let her leave an infirmary.

"Yes," she answers, as she finally reaches our bench, though then she touches her nose, which is our code we use when a "yes" would really mean a "no."

"They left the door open for me," she adds, and then in what I assume is a statement for the watchers, she continues, having her seat on the hard stone bench, "I thought that meant they wanted me to leave, since they left the door open... but with all my pain medication, it's hard to know what to think." Her face wincing as she speaks, and I don't know if I've ever seen anyone look both as strong and as weak as she now looks.

Her fingers stretch out for my hand.

"Look at the sunset, Alpha," she says. "There's no way I would have wanted to miss this." Though as she is speaking these words, her fingertips begin to make the words, "Are you leaving?"

"No," I write back, once she finishes, being sure to keep my eyes fixed onto the sunset. "Not without you," I add.

She bats my hand away in what might be a reflex of anger, before reaching for it again and staring into my eyes with a determined glare.

"I won't let you kill yourself for me," she spells, being sure to keep her eyes locked onto mine, and with both of us keeping our hands away from our peripheral views.

We turn back toward the sinking sun, as a way to avoid suspicion in case we have watchers monitoring our visual feeds.

"Kill myself?" I write, as the usual oranges of the sunset turn to their standard deep red.

It will be curfew soon, and so she writes quickly, and I struggle to keep the letters straight.

"Why do you think the Schoolmaster is helping you? Why is Chi risking his life for you?"

She has always been smarter than me, and now she's proving it.

"Because they know something you don't."

I stare into her eyes again, knowing that she's right. "Come with us," I scribble onto her palm.

The corners of her eyes twinge, with a sad look in them, as if I'm being naive. "I can't even walk," she writes.

The sun is a sliver of frail light now. We rise to leave, knowing we have so little time before curfew. Though, a grouping of medical ranks are already coming to take her away. She makes her case about the unlocked door, but they very obviously don't believe her. Yet there is little they can do to punish her in this instance, as was her plan, though regardless they still tear her away from me, for what might be our final time, which is the worst punishment they could give.

She is being led away, at a more rapid pace than she would be comfortable with, given her condition. And I have to say something, since this will be the last time I might ever see her. I quickly try to think of something that might not raise suspicion. "Good evening, Theta," I call out, below the covered walkway as they direct her away.

She turns her head, and I can see and tell in her voice that she is crying. "Good evening, Alpha," she answers, in a way that I can tell that what she really means is "good-bye," the same as I do.

I will lose a credit for being out after curfew, but I don't care. I watch her until she is pulled through the archway of the main school, until she disappears from view. And there is nothing more that I can do, so I place my palm on my own doorplate, nearby, as the last sun rays are pulled from view. My new tally shows in my view, "Credits: 6," and a swipe of my hand removes it.

Entering the stark darkness of my quarters, I lay upon the bed. Maybe Chi won't come tonight; maybe we won't leave. Though still I stay in full uniform with my shoes on, on the off chance that I haven't ruined everything by my outbursts in instructors' course this morning, or with my defiance in militant training. My eyes sag and still there is no sign of him. My wandering consciousness searches through any way I can think of to bring Theta with us, but there is none. This is an impossible thing to wish for. And my eyes close, creating a darkened seal within the deeper blank darkness of my quarters.

12

I wake with an instant fright; hands have reached out from the shadows beneath my bed, calloused and wrinkled hands. They are covering over my mouth, so that I will not scream and are pulling down on my eyelids, so that I could not force them open, without pain.

Heart racing, I strain to breathe in stuttered breaths through my nose. How could someone be in my quarters? The entry door is sealed until morning, as it always is, but here he is all the same. The heavy hand that clasps onto my mouth places its index finger over my lips to shush me.

Slowly my nerves begin to settle. He does not want to murder me—he only wants me to be quiet. And my brain begins to wake from its drowsiness, so that it is obvious now: these old and calloused hands must be Chi's. He, or the Schoolmaster, or both of them working together are the only ones I can think of who could get through my door without triggering the computer scanners, or alerting the watchers. And the thought that it might be him begins to calm my fears.

He reaches down, opening the palm of my hand, and he begins to write.

"Do not speak," he writes, forcibly pushing his finger into my hand to emphasize the word "not." "Do not open your eyes," he continues. "Never open your eyes."

I would naturally, here, ask why, but he has already begun to palm-write an explanation. "As long as your eyes are shut, their scanners will assume you are asleep, and that will give us extra time."

"Location sens—" I grab his hand in return, and start to palm-write a question, but he does not let me finish.

"I have to remove it. Your location sensor will stay in your quarters until they come to check on you," he writes.

"Remov—" I begin to write, but again he does not let me finish. Apparently, there is no time for full questions on my part.

"It has to be cut out," he writes, and he points his finger at the place near the base of my skull where it will have to be removed.

"But I will die." He lets me write the full message. Since everyone knows that our sensors are grafted into our nervous systems as infants, and that any attempt to remove them will instantly kill us.

There is a deep silence in my quarters as I wait for his response. "That is not the full truth. You might die," he scribbles into my hand. "But if you stay here past tonight you will die. They will force you into a retractment, and they will <u>kill</u> you." And after he writes the final word, he pulls my hand up so I can feel the bandages at the base of his own skull.

"It will <u>hurt</u>, but it is possible," he writes. And then adds, "Never trust the Common to tell you the full truth."

If this is what it will take to leave the School, maybe I don't want it. "What are the chances—" I begin to write, meaning to ask, "What are the chances this will kill me?" But he doesn't let me finish, as if we have no more time for questions. He grabs my hand forcefully. "Yes or no?" he writes.

Which I assume is his way to ask if I would like him to cut around my brain stem to get at the location sensor.

"T—" I want to write, "Theta?" but he slaps my hand away, and won't let me finish.

"Now! Yes or no?" he asks.

What an impossible question... deep inside I want to say no, but my mind flashes back to our bench, and to Theta writing, "I won't let you kill yourself for me." I take a few readying breaths to prepare for the pain, and I realize what I have to decide—there is no choice for me. At least this way I might only die in my quarters, alone, with Chi, instead of what would certainly happen if I stayed, having my retractment transmitted into Theta's visual sensors, so that there's no way she could close her eyes.

I reach for Chi's hand.

"Yes," I write.

And without waiting a moment, he shoves a wad of cloth into my mouth to quiet me, or to give me something to bite down on. And he locks my arms between his knees, since he's now seated behind me. Maybe this is so I won't out of instinct reach behind to bat him away when he starts to cut into me. That's not comforting, when I think about it like that.

The cloth wadded into my mouth dries out my saliva. Then I feel the prick of a blade so sharp that I almost don't sense the pain of it, but I still feel the pressure, and the line of blood that flows down the back of my neck.

The cutting stops. I breathe through my nose, and realize that it's been so long since I've even allowed myself to breathe. Each quickly inhaled bit of air is trembling in my lungs.

The blood is still substantial. My whole neck is dripping, like it does when I have my daily sanitation, letting the water fall over my head and down to my feet. This is that same feeling, except now I am the pouring liquid, and it comes from my own body, and not a spout in the corner of my quarters.

I want to vomit from the thought of it, but somehow I hold it in. A fiery pain singes in my neck and runs down the length of my spine like needles, or like a column of biting ants. He reaches the fingers of his unused hand—the one that is not being used to cover over my eyes—he takes those fat fingers and he shoves them into the opening that is obviously too small an incision. The size of them tears at the edges of the cut. And the tip of his finger grazes against something that should never be touched, not by anything, and especially not by his rough (and probably dirty) hands.

Uncontrollably, I scream out in moans that are muffled by the wad of cloth in my mouth. And yet the computer scanners might only think that I am having a bad dream, since my eyes are still clenched shut.

His fingers poke under my skin searching for something, and I can feel his fingertip drift over a bump at the base of my skull. More tightly, he holds his hand over my eyes, and he pinches my arms firmly, struggling to keep my head still. Then he pulls at the device, and there is nothing more excruciating. My mind is a fog, and a haze. And the acids in my stomach heave up into my nose and mouth, soaking the already moistened rag from the inside out.

Bandages on my neck, and something that pulls at either side of the wound to keep it closed. Everything is weak.

And after the bandage is on, another strip of cloth is tied around my head. When he told me to never open my eyes, he must have meant it, and this blindfold will make sure of that. Some little bits of hard and tiny ovals are being forced into my mouth. They are pills. I can tell by the slick coating, but swallowing anything while blindfolded is so unnatural. Though I finally get them down.

All my muscles have never been so weak. And after several feeble attempts, he finally gets me to stand, and he leads me hobbling out of my quarters, through my door which is not locked as it should be, and out into the night, after curfew, for the first time in my life. And the door scanners do not announce my exit, since they do not register that I've left. My location sensor is gone. And for the first time ever, I can be where I want, and the Common can not control that, because they don't even know I've gone. And this is terrifying in a way, and yet the greatest sense of "good" uneasiness I've ever had.

13

The ground is not especially bumpy, but with blind-folded eyes every unexpected dip is a drastic valley, and each minor stone is a great mountain. We step across the lawn. The cut grass subtly pokes the soles of my shoes. My fingers clasp onto Chi's still bloody hand. My limbs are weak, and nothing seems to make sense without eyesight, and my mind has gone cloudy. And I am lighter and hollower inside—I guess this is what it feels like to lose so much blood. It is a disheartening, empty feeling.

We shuffle across the evenly cut lawn. There is a metal rattling. That must be the surrounding fence that closes the School in. Chi drops my hand. The fence tinks and snaps with a high-sounded snipping. Then those noises stop, and something falls, or is thrown toward the open grass beside me.

And there is Chi again, grabbing my hand and guiding me, bent over as we walk, through a place where the perimeter fence should have still been. That was that sound of something thrown on the grass. It was Chi, throwing a section of fence that he'd cut, and those snipping noises must have been him using some tool to break through the metal.

This blindfolded world is confusing, but my other senses are starting to adjust to this new way of living. Beyond the fence is the breaking noise of something that we walk over, and its shattered pieces poke into my shoes, and beyond that is hard packed sand, and small stones, and random patches of bristly grass that hit against my uniform pants, but most of it feels like what I imagine the covered walkway to the main school would feel like, only if it had been broken up and destroyed.

Is this what a forest feels like? Not that I have ever been in a forest, having come straight from the infantarium to the School, and never anywhere in between, but this is not the sort of ground I would have pictured.

Surrounding the perimeter fence, there has always been a forest. Where is the soft grass, like we have in the lawn? Where is the crunch of leaves under my feet? Not that I have stepped foot in a forest, but still, I have seen trees up close in the lawn. And I would think that a forest would be something like a single tree, except that it would be multiplied over a hundred, or a thousand times, if forests even get that big.

In the night, beneath the blackness of my blindfold, I reach out a hand to feel the trees, but after a few minutes, without the slightest bit of tree bark against my fingertips, I palm-write to Chi, "Trees?"

"There are none," he answers as we walk ahead through the night, which is slightly colder than I had expected.

But how is this possible?

"Forest?" I write, while nearly tripping on what might be a stone, since I am not giving as much close attention to my steps as I was before.

"There was no forest," he writes.

"But I saw it."

"You've been seeing imaginary things your whole life, and now it bothers you?" he answers.

"What?"

"The retractments, your credits tally in your vision, your lesson cube in your classes—all of it imaginary."

My already tired and cloudy mind is reeling.

The retractments, of course, and my credits—all that was obviously transmitted in—but our lesson cube in the instructors' classes? It does make sense. I'm so silly for not realizing it before.

"If you think about it, you'll realize those trees were the exact same height they always were, since you first came to the School. You grew, the grass grew, the trees in the lawn grew, but those forest trees were always the same," he writes.

It's true, of course it is. Am I that oblivious? What else could have been made up, if the trees weren't even real?

Oh, no. Perhaps the one thing I wanted to be real most of all.

"The sunset? Real?" I ask. He waits a long while to answer.

"Sunsets are real," he writes, which is not an exact answer to my question, and is, therefore, my answer.

Sunsets exist, somewhere, but ours didn't. Ours were imaginary, just like the forest. Seems like the only thing real in that whole place was Theta.

"Never trust them to tell you the full truth," he writes, repeating what he'd said earlier, probably to make his point. And now I'm beginning to understand what he means by "never." It means, that if they can lie about the sun and trees, then nothing is safe from being lied about. Even my most certain truths could be a lie. My stomach feels sick.

14

After several more hours of walking and stumbling, with little palm-writing, we finally reach a space of uninterrupted grass, and then a forest, a real forest, with leaves spread all over the ground, and softer dirt below my feet, and the smell of trees that wafts in the air with a sticky, natural-smelling aroma.

My limbs are empty and lifeless, and my neck is stiff and raw. And the pain pills that Chi gave me at the start of our trip are wearing away. So he reaches into a dangling pouch he carries across his shoulders, and he feeds me another set of pills, without me having to ask for them, and a few dry nutrition squares that he must have stolen this morning.

Once the pain medication starts to take effect, I want to ask him whether he has enough medicine for himself also. My hands stretch out to get his attention. What is this? My fingers brush the edges of a ripped strip of cloth that is wrapped around his own head, covering over his own eyes.

Frantic, I pull at his hand and palm-write, "What are you doing? A blindfold?" I ask.

"Did you think I was somehow so much different from you?" he asks. And then explains, before letting me respond, "If we had our eyes open, then there would still be a low-level signal cycling through us that could still be detected at close range."

"But one of us needs to see," I write.

"If I don't know where I'm going, then neither do they," he answers. That seems like wishful thinking, but I don't try to correct him. I'm too tired for that.

And so we continue on, until I can not keep my head from hanging down as we walk, and until my feet feel like they have weights connected to them. And Chi lets me rest my arm around his shoulder. We can not stop. My consciousness is growing hazy from my weariness. I can not stop. I should pretend to fall, just to have a few seconds of rest, with the forest leaves as my bed, before Chi could come to retrieve me. Though before I can attempt this, there are chirps of birds that deter me from those thoughts, and there is the warmth of a real, unaltered sun on my right cheek and forehead.

Quickly, this true sun is hotter than I ever remember it being at the School. And so much so that I almost wish for the false one again. But going back toward the School now would mean an instant retractment for me, and so we continue on, even though the bones in my feet ache, even though my muscles are burning with pain. I've never walked this far before. And my body is fighting each step, but still we stumble through this "real" world, with no obvious end, and no direction.

My mind drifts somewhere between sleep and consciousness. Suddenly, there is a tree with leaves that poke at my skin, like small bendable needles. This tree seems to be bent over, or either has fallen to the forest floor. We crawl on our hands and knees below the branches. I am dirtier than I can ever remember, yet also happy for the cool shade, and a place to rest my head and sleep.

■ ■ ■

Something small, with legs, something crawling—I swipe at my face in a gut heaving hurry. There was an insect on my face when I awoke. I'm never going to sleep in the forest again. But there is something good in this also... This is the first time I have woken on my own, without that fake woman's voice to pull me from my sleep.

I've always despised that mechanical human-like voice, but even so, it is hard to feel truly awake without her "voice" ringing in my audial sensors, and especially with my blindfold still tied tightly and with my eyes still shut. It's as if I have been dreaming since Chi covered my eyes last night, and except for the fact that I can reach behind my head to feel the bandages, or for the fact that I am still in need of pain pills fairly regularly, except for those things I would imagine that I was still in my bed, dreaming of this all, but what a bizarre nightmare this would be.

We leave our covered tree bed. Gradually the flat forest starts to steepen. More than once my foot slips on loose dirt and I collapse with a thud onto the ground, and one time scraping my hand in the process, though it's not a substantial injury.

It has to be alright, now. How much more of this could

we possibly do? It's not like we can walk aimlessly like this forever. We will have to find out where we're headed eventually.

"Can we look, yet?" I write.

Without much hesitation—"No," he answers, digging his finger forcefully into my hand as he palm-writes, to emphasize its importance.

Bits of loose gravel drop below my feet; I fall again, bruising the flesh on my hands, as if I had done it on purpose to prove my point. Why not just raise up the corner edge of this scrap of cloth that's tied around my head? Just a few peeks wouldn't hurt. If I were quick about it, maybe the watchers wouldn't even know it had happened.

"Please," I ask with palm-writing.

"Never," he replies. Which I have been thinking all along has only been an exaggeration, meant to make his point... but what if that's entirely true? What if I must keep my eyes shut forever?

More walking, we continue on for hours, until my feet are fully swollen and blistered. And we stumble ahead through this real forest, which is not so clean or as well trimmed as the School's lawn. Every so often a low branch surprises me, scratching at my face, and almost continually I am kicking roots or rocks that crowd our path. And the warmth of the sun creeps over me slowly, until it is falling on the top of my head.

Up ahead there is a deep splashing sound, stronger and fuller than the noise of the water that flows over me during my daily sanitation, and more intimidating than the sound of liquid sloshed around in a bowl. This is a watery noise that seems like it is continually passing by us, while at the same time staying in place, like it will always drift by us, but never truly leave.

I palm-write to Chi, asking what this noise is, and he replies, "a river." Of course, they have these around Primus, the Leaders' central city. I've seen them before in pictures during instructors' course. But those were just lifeless photos, and it is hard to guess at the sound of something without ever hearing it.

"We have to cross it," Chi writes.

Whatever that will mean, I should guess it will be wet and uncomfortable to do in my full clothes.

"Couldn't we wait until it dries?" I ask.

"It will never dry," he writes back.

"And what if it's too deep to cross?" I ask.

But his reply to this is not what I want to hear, saying that I should never let go of his hand, no matter how deep it gets.

I've made the wrong decision to leave the School; I know I have. Who says that they would have called me to a retractment? Or that they would have, after that, revoked my citizenship? And if that did happen, would it really be any worse than having my location sensor ripped out, and after that, worse than us wandering around in this empty wilderness, blindfolded, until we die? At least a retractment seems more civilized, and less painful, or less drawn out.

We stand at the edge of the river, with layers of smooth rocks beneath our feet. Chi picks one off the ground and tosses it forward, a splash of water. He grabs another, throwing it slightly harder—I guess—and there is another splash, beyond where the first was. Though on his third try, throwing with an audible strain, there is no splash, only the sound of clinking rocks on the opposite edge of the river.

He grabs my hand firmly and we enter. The water rushes into my shoes, and my feet are instantly frigid. Rivers are cold, or at least this one is. Within the Central City, I bet they warm their rivers, because this is unbearable.

In the rushing water, the rocks are slick beneath my steps; on one of them I lose my footing and fall with a yelp into the biting flow. Chi lifts me to my feet again, and we move on. Cold water creeping up my ankles, then to my thighs, and torso—the deep water makes it difficult to walk as quickly as I want to. And I press through the water as I struggle against the passing force. The water gets to my neck. It stings against my bandages. I am whimpering from trying to keep in the agony of cold water against my still healing cut. There's nothing worse than this. Water is touching my face, chilled river water running along my cheeks as I try to keep my lips above the surface.

Then my feet give way, and there is nothing else I can do but to hold onto Chi's hand. Desperately out of control, helplessly hoping that he is tall enough to hold me up. And hoping that the water won't take both of us under, but it does not. And after what seems like another minute, my feet can touch again, and a little after that the water begins to diminish, and I am found on the opposite side of the river, freezing liquid dripping off of every part of me.

There is nothing comforting or happy about rivers, except when you reach the other side. The cold water drips from the tips of my fingers. Leaving the School has turned out to be the most difficult, and horrifically painful, decision I've ever made... but what if it was also the best? After all, I don't want to end up like my progenitor, to be discarded by the Leaders, when and how they see fit. And maybe this is what re-evolution feels like; maybe it is not a comfortable feeling.

15

The warmth of the sun is hitting our faces now, though its rays are not as strong as they once were. Which is unfortunate, since my uniform clothes are still damp and they chafe against my legs and underarms as we hike up a seemingly barren hill. It has been nearly an hour, or more, since I've felt the crunch of leaves beneath my feet; and several hours (I would think), since we left the edge of the river, after taking sips of it to "quench our thirst" as Chi wrote. Though I wouldn't have gone back to that deathly water, if Chi hadn't forced me to, and if he hadn't waited until I had promised that I had drank from it. But now, with the sun setting lower, and my uniform still damp in places, water is the last thing I would want.

We are climbing up a hill with dry wiry tall grass.

"Can we stop?" I write.

"After the hill," he answers.

But "after the hill," I can see is a general term, and we walk until we find a wide path, some of it that feels hard and evenly level, like the walkway between my quarters and the main school has always been. But also there are random patches of unevenness, where the hardness is broken up, and where grass or small plants have grown through the cracks.

And almost when we can not feel the sun at all, we find a thinner gravely path that breaks off from the main one. And we follow this much thinner path, until it leads us to a building, or to what I guess is a building, with wooden steps which almost break under our feet.

Crunch.

There are sharp crunches as we near an entry door, and Chi touches or twists something, which allows us to enter. How can he have gotten by this building's door scanners without authorization?

But when I ask, he writes that the door was unlocked. Though nothing is ever unlocked at the School, without reason, so I ask, "A trap?"

The sounds rumbling in his throat might be him chuckling at my question, which I thought was a decent one.

"No, a *gift*," he writes.

"Gift?" I ask.

"It means, something you're given that you haven't earned."

"Like luck?" I write.

We step through the doorway, greeted by the smell of dust and oldness, and the feel of cushy floor beneath us.

"Luck is chance... gifts are purposeful," he writes. And after this explanation it seems to make sense, but I can't focus on words and meanings of words; it takes too much energy to concentrate enough to learn anything new.

It's good to sit, after a full day of endless walking. The soft ground that I lay upon is so peculiar. It's like tiny bits of cut thick string, that has been sewn into the ground. But it is much better than laying on the dirty forest floor.

After a while, when the aches start to slowly seep from my legs and feet, I begin to get a feeling for how old this place is, and how forgotten. There are spiderwebs in any place that will have them. And the whole building even the stringy floor smells like it has not been cleaned for ages.

"Why would the Common abandon this?" I ask. They never let go of anything, and it seems so unlike them to let this place go to ruin.

"It's not theirs," he replies.

The Common controls everything. What is he talking about? And if not the Common, then who could build this place?

But then he answers my questions without my having to ask them.

"These are half-men quarters," he writes.

How is that possible? And buried in the back of my thoughts is the notion that there is so much more I have to learn, and so much I've never been taught in the School. It's almost as if my instructor was there more to protect me from ideas, rather than to teach me anything with truth in it.

Seven years of instructors' training, and they never taught us that half-men built anything.

My cut begins to throb again, and so Chi hands me the last pill and another nutrition square. Two nutrition square meals in less than one day has never happened before, but I think I've earned it, or maybe it would be considered a gift —not sure if that's the proper use of that word.

"Are there more quarters like this?" I palm-write.

The sun must be set now, since the darkness behind my blindfold is more overwhelming.

Chi must be amused by my questions. He laughs with a heartiness and a low rumble to it. This is the first time I've heard him laugh like this. No one laughs at the School, except for Theta sometimes, when we're alone. And there is something hopeful in the sound of Chi's laugh, and pleasant.

And since there is obviously so much I do not know about half-men, Chi palm-writes from the beginning, all that he has ever learned about them, information that was probably very treacherous to gather, over the course of multiple generation cycles, since well before my pregeneration.

Half-men, he writes, built giant cities, with transit systems stretching between, connecting these cities to one another. And almost everything that we have can be traced back to their contributions.

Everything I thought I knew about half-men is turning out to be lie. I lay on this fabric floor, distraught. The Common lies about everything. Chi was right. It seems obvious now. My face fills with anger; apparently the only true thing in the School was Theta, and maybe myself. I've been lied to since I first arrived there. So that in a very real sense, it's not a school at all. Maybe if there is a word for the opposite of a school, it would be that.

"What really happened to the half-men?" I ask.

Our newfound quarters are entirely silent, around us.

"I don't know, not for sure," he writes. "But I would think they were an-i-hilated." I miss the last word.

"Repeat," I write.

"*Annihilated*," he replies. "It means murdered, all of them."

I know this is just a guess on Chi's part, but it sounds true. Maybe when things are true you just know. Though since this is such a new feeling for me, to hear the truth, it's hard to say whether I'm right or not. Maybe the truth sounds different than a lie; maybe you know it when you hear it. And murdering whole masses of men, or half-men in this case, that sounds like something the Common would do. It sounds true.

All my body is weary. And my eyes feel tired from being closed for so long. But I eventually sleep, and late at night I awake for a brief moment. There is some small animal that has made his nest in the corner.

I should wake Chi, to let him know. I should... there is no more strength left to stay awake.

■　　■　　■

Chi is groaning. He seems angry. I hope it's nothing I did.

"Ahh..." I hear. These are the closest things to true words I've heard in more than a day. I reach out for his hand, trying to find out what's wrong.

He's too busy to give a full answer. "No food," he writes.

"Why?" I begin to ask, but he cuts me off at the "*W*".

"Mice," he answers.

That must have been that sound last night, in the corner of the room, that animal I heard. We don't have mice at the School, that I know of, but they must be mean creatures to have taken all our food away while we slept.

Chi throws something, which I guess is his pouch. He throws it, and it breaks a glass item, somewhere in the quarters. Obviously, we've no more food, and I've no more pills left, so that pouch is useless to us now.

Without writing a word, he grabs my hand and we head out of our "gift door," which doesn't seem much like that anymore. Chi is not in a mood for long explanations this morning, and so I don't ask him anything else. All I can tell is that the sun is at the back of our heads, and our stomachs are empty. And we have vicious mice to thank for the second part of that.

16

We leave the half-men quarters, finding our way down the creaking stairs, traveling back over the thin gravely path toward the larger harden path that is broken up in places. And the next few hours are taken up with listening to the tapping sounds of a branch that Chi has found, knocking on the path ahead of us, and with the feeling of the sun as it creeps over our heads.

There is the noise and stirring of birds making their usual sounds, and this follows us for our whole journey, until suddenly there is nothing, as if every bird stops its movements at the same time, and then an explosion of flapping wings all at once. What could make all the birds want to leave at the same time? I lift my head up toward the direction of the sky to have a better listen, but I have little time for this, because now I am being forced to run. My steps stutter and almost stumble. Chi is pulling me faster than my feet can safely go.

And we are off the path again, scratching our hands and faces on spiky low hanging branches, and getting tangled in thick bushes that we push through without thought. Usually we would be better than this. But we're running, down a steep embankment. No footing. We're falling—the ground is not where we suspected it would be. And we fall a short distance off a ledge, of sorts, and onto hard dirt.

Something's rumbling from the path where we came from. That must be what the birds had heard, even before we could. It's getting louder, shaking the dust off my internal memories. Where have I heard this before? It was long ago... It's a... It's a transport vehicle. I heard that same repeating sound for hours and hours as they moved our group from the infantarium.

Chi shoves me to the ground and begins to throw dirt and leaves on my face. You crazy blindfolded man, what are you doing? He's pinning my hands. He's writing almost faster than I can read it.

I want to ask why he's doing this, but I can't move my hands. My whole body has been piled over with dirt, and leaves, and sticks, and anything within his reach.

"Wait 3 hours... Walk away from the sun in the morning, and toward it in the evening. Walk blindfolded, until you feel a wetness in the air, that smells like the taste of tears, and keep walking until you find the golden path over water. If you find this, you'll be safe."

Wet tears? A golden path? Safe? Why is he telling me this? Won't he be here with me?

The rumbling stirs nearer. And with the last bit of dirt, I am completely buried. There is not a speck of me that has been left open. Then I stop feeling the weight of new dirt and leaves being added. His footsteps shuffle away from me as fast as they can, and he is gone.

The rumbling stops. Something heavy squeaks open with a metallic ring.

"Stop!" a voice yells, from the path above us, only barely audible beneath my pile of leaves and dirt.

Another heavy squeak, and another voice speaks, sounding agitated, "What are we stopping for! The sensor drones aren't even out this far yet. There's nothing here."

"That's what everyone else thinks too, and that's why we're going to find them," says the first voice.

There are many more heavy squeaks, in a long ordered line, which must be the sound of transport doors opening, a whole row of them.

The first voice speaks up again, sounding like he's addressing a large group.

"The thermal scanner picked up something in the forest down there," he says.

"Probably, another *deer*," another quieter voice answers, and his jeering encourages a spattering of snide laughs.

Blasts in rapid succession. What's happening? They must be warning shots, because there are no more comments, and no one is firing back.

"That's it!" the first voice calls out, sounding oddly familiar this time. "The next one of you infants, who says anything, I'm going to personally shoot in the face, and leave here. You got it!"

There are no answers, and no more snide remarks.

"Now go find them," he shouts out an order.

This voice is familiar. It's burning inside of me. Then his

face flashes into my mind. It's Delta's voice.

There are rustling footsteps following down the steep slope where we came from. There are boots hitting the ground all around me, but thankfully none on top of me.

"If it wasn't for this useless thermal scanner, we'd have found them by now," Delta's voice says.

The second voice, that had spoken before when they'd first arrived, he comes to stand beside Delta. "Or it's because they're not here," he says. I know this voice also... but whose is it?

The two are standing not far way, though it sounds as if they are facing away from me, staring into the forest beyond.

Something is being hit with a hand. "Come on, work you stupid machine," Delta says.

"I don't think the graduates want us to find them," the other voice says, and suddenly its characteristics match with a face in my mind. It's Tau.

Off in the distance, some younger female voice shouts, "How far do you want us to go?"

The sarcasm is dripping from Delta's tongue as he answers. "Why? Have you found them yet?" he asks.

"No," the female militant replies with a bewildered inflection.

"Then keep walking," Delta orders.

A mixed group? None of the militant groups are mixed after graduation, and since this is obviously a militant search group, it has to mean that these must be undergraduates, led by Delta and Tau, from the sound of it.

"Let me see that scanner... maybe I can get it to work," Tau says.

Gun blasts, only a few seconds after. There are so many of them, and shouts following each shot.

Delta and Tau are running away, toward the blasts.

"He ran that way," a different young voice calls out above the explosions.

The chaos of sporadic gunfire continues.

"I got his leg," another voice shouts.

And above it all, Delta's voice begins to yell, "Don't—"

But a closer single gunshot stops him short. And then there are cheers, disgustingly horrible cheers far away in the forest.

"Tau, you low-rank," Delta yells. "We were only trying to wound him."

"I missed," Tau answers.

"Yeah, right, I'm sure you did," Delta says sarcastically.

"Ok, fine, I didn't... but what does it matter? They were going to torture and kill him anyways. This just saves a few steps," Tau replies.

"The Disciplinarian wanted him for interrogation," Delta answers, loudly.

"Well, I didn't know that," Tau answers back.

"Well now you do," Delta says. And then turning to yell toward his young militants, he calls out, "Grab his body and load it in the transport."

And there are moans in the distance, where there were once cheers. And with heaving sounds that are even audible beneath my buried pile of dirt and leaves, and with a final heavy metallic squeak and a slamming noise, Chi is taken away from the forest.

There are some low words exchanged, but nothing I can hear.

And then, transport doors are opening and shutting. And as the rumbling noises begin again, Delta shouts above the rattling, "Anything else show up on that scanner?" he asks.

"No," Tau answers.

And with that, the line of transports rumbles away back toward where they came from. And when there is no more of their sounds in my ears and audial sensors, the full weight of all that those noises meant—and all that those sounds have destroyed—it hits me, hits me like a stone in my chest. And my whole world that I'd come to rely on is shattered, or maybe the better word for it would be annihilated—killed, all of it.

17

I hate them. It doesn't matter whom, nearly everyone: Delta, the Common, and even Tau—though it's hard to hate him entirely, since he was so helpful to me during militant training, but I'm going to hate him anyway.

This whole time I thought he was against the Common like I was, but now he's fighting for them? Hours, and days, and years spent practicing his kill shot, even after he didn't need to any longer, and for this? Of course for this... why else would he obsess over killing? He's a killer, and I hate him for it.

The decaying leaves and black soil shakes from my uniform as I rise—alone, completely alone. The transports have been gone for a while, but I haven't had the will to move. Why give up this shallow burial place? I'm dead, if I stay or if I leave, so why does it matter? But what would Chi want? He told me to walk, blindfolded until I feel a wetness in the air, to keep going, and so I have to: To do anything else would be lying to him.

Besides, I have to stay alive, if I'm going to punish Delta and Tau for what they've done, and if I'm going to strike back at the Leaders for what they did to my progenitor, during his retractment, and if I'm ever going to find a way to rescue Theta. And really, I might have stayed buried, if not for Theta. She's the only part of this whole world that seems alive, and I have to protect her... protect her by leaving, if that even makes sense.

Heading back toward the hard path, where the transports were, I find a branch, not far away, to use as a tapping branch. The sun is hitting into my face, as I strike the path ahead of me. Just like Chi said, "walk away from the sun in the morning, and toward it in the evening." He's got me this far, and I won't give up and waste him.

The rap of my tapping branch strikes on the hard surface; what if this is Chi's same branch that he'd been using, that he threw to the side as we were running? Maybe it is. The repetitive knock does sound familiar. It has to be the same branch, not for any logical reason, but because it makes me feel better to think that it is.

The sun rays slowly dim, and their heat is gradually less intense. It's going to be night, and I have to find my own way now, not that the night makes finding my way any more difficult than usual. With my eyes closed, behind a thick blindfold, the night is just another shade of darkness.

■   ▨   ▨

The air is more chilling, and, in a way, damp without the sun to warm it. And without that light, there's no way to tell whether or not I'm headed in the right direction. But what's better: to put more distance between myself and the transports full of search parties, and in so doing possibly walk for hours in the wrong direction, or to stop somewhere along the way, and wait until sunrise, until I can be sure of where I'm going?

Fresh thoughts of the gunshots in the forest flash upon my brain. Maybe it's better to be tired and lost, than to be rested, and shot for it, eventually. But after what might be several hours of tapping, with short stuttered steps in the darkness, with no one to lead me now—after this my branch hits against the side of something metal, that has been positioned in the very middle of the path.

I strike against the sides of the object, that is not substantially large. Around the base of it, my branch beats on flat, thin sounding metal. And as I raise my branch up higher, there is a more hollow, smoother sound, that is not exactly like hitting wood, or stone, or metal, but something else.

Placing my hand to the upper surface, it is cool to the touch, and rippled in waves and as delicate feeling as water, but also dusty and filthy against my already dirty skin. Sliding my fingers down the surface, there is a moveable handhold near where the hard rippled portion and the metal meet. I pull at it. And a part of the object opens with a loud grinding noise, as if that object has not been opened for years.

The inside is musty, and damp smelling like the half-men quarters from last night. Though there is a soft area inside, like a padded bench. This must be a seat. Maybe this was a regular resting place for half-men as they walked along the path.

And then it finally occurs to me, this was never meant to

be a walking path, or solely a walking path. I should have known it from the first sound of the transports this morning. This path was made for transports. And with a cushioned bench to sit on, this must have been, at one time, a half-men transport.

Climbing inside, I shut the transport door behind myself; which makes the odor of this place that much more repulsive, but it's probably safer this way. If there were vicious mice last night, then who's to say that there aren't other things, larger and more mischievous than mice, out here in the deep, wild half-men forest, beyond the protection of the Common's gates and walls. And a closed door might be the only thing to protect me.

The padding of the bench is soft, but I lie awake for nearly an hour, until some speeding insect, about twenty times the size of an ant, runs across my hand. And after this, it is another hour or more, before I can fully sleep.

■ ■ ■

My feet are pounding on the grass, though the more I try to run, the further away the fence surrounding the main school seems to stretch. I am running on the lawn, that is growing wider and wider with each step. Behind me a crowd of militants is chasing and gaining ground.

Somehow, also behind me, I know that the red-chested bird has been captured, the bird from before, who wrote its message in the trees with fallen twigs, the bird who wrote "revolution."

I turn my head to see that I was right, that the Disciplinarian is carrying that sad creature in a cage, and he is running at the head of the mob. And the bird is chirping, or yelling in a high-sounding human voice, "Help me, Alpha!"

There is a series of distorted gunshots, and then I awake.

■ ▧ ▥

Heat, from my own sweating face and racing heartbeat, but also from the sun. The transport vehicle must have warmed in the blazing sun, and now it's considerably hot. How long have I been asleep?

I shove the transport door open, and grab my tapping branch from off the ground. The burning sunrays are directly above me. Which way to walk? It's not morning now, so I can't be sure. How many times did I circle around the transport before I entered? And which direction was I coming from when I found it? Any mistake in this, and I could be walking all day toward the Common, instead of away from them.

I begin to walk one way, but then quickly realize that the distorted gunshot noise that had begun in my dreams is only growing louder. It had dulled to almost nothing in the commotion of trying to find my way, but now it is only increasing as I continue forward.

Though it is not a true gunshot: it is too crackling, and too electronic to be a natural explosion. Suddenly, these sounds make sense. My feet turn instantly, and I am almost running in the opposite direction. These are not gun blasts. They do not have the same depth in my ears as normal sound—which means it's distortion, signal distortion, from the search groups. They must be trying to transmit a message into my audial sensors, but I must be just out of range.

But as my pace hurries, and with each new heavily breathed step, the sound is lessening, until it is... gone. I'm sure it is gone. Ha! What they meant to use to their advantage was, instead, the only reason why I didn't just walk right up to them and turn myself in. And maybe, as long as I can stay ahead of the false gunshots, I can stay ahead of the real ones. And my pace hardly slows as the overhead sun begins to shine rays into my face. For sure now, I'm headed in the right direction. But I've wasted hours of daylight, and an additional half-hour of it spent walking in the wrong direction. And the search groups are most certainly gaining ground, with their surge of transports and armed militants, so that it won't be just Delta and Tau, but all of them.

▦ ▦ ▦

There are hours of walking uphill. In this area, the trees are lessening. There are not so many birds, and the sound of rustling branches in the wind has gradually declined until there is nothing. This path cannot keep climbing forever. Sooner or later, I must be approaching the crest of some great hill. And without trees on either side, I must be visible to anyone nearby, or to any rifle with a scope.

Crack. Snap. Static...

The distortion is coming back again. Being out of the forest must be helping the signal to reach my sensors.

I must be at the top part of the hill, because any other steps I take will only lead me down, and there does not seem to be any other place to climb. I would almost continue, but the signal breaks in finally.

Her words are in my ears.

"Stop, Alpha. Please listen." It's Theta's voice. She sounds tired, and frail, as if she still has trouble breathing.

"You might think that Chi is doing right, by taking you away, but he's not. It's dangerous away from the School. Please, come back, and no harm will come to you."

This is not how she speaks, nor would she ever say this, and so it's obviously a prepared message... and it's on a repeat loop, because it begins again. This time with picture, transmitted into my visual sensors. It is the first thing I've "seen" in days, which makes it that much more disconcerting.

She is in the same chair that I was in, in the Disciplinarian's quarters. There is a stark light on her face—on her face, which is washed, and on her red hair that has been combed to make her best impression. But I can tell in her eyes, that she is still uncomfortable and fragile from her injuries. She rubs her nose before beginning, so subtly that maybe only I would notice it.

"Stop, Alpha. Please listen." She takes a deep breath, that somehow doesn't seem to help her.

"You might think that Chi is doing right, by taking you away, but he's not." Her face is expressionless, like she does not believe anything she is saying. "It's dangerous away from the School. Please, come back, and no harm will come to you." Her face freezes still and fades to blackness, but then reappears, saying the exact same thing.

A wind on the hill blows up and wants to push me back the way that I came. But I'm standing firm. Their message has done the opposite of what they intended: For one, now I know she's alright. And they won't hurt her as long as they think they can use her against me. And secondly, they don't know all of our codes, apparently, or else they would have never have allowed this message to go out.

I'm grinning at the top of the hill, with the wind still in my face. She rubbed her nose before she spoke, which is our code for when a "no" would mean a "yes." Or in this case, she's telling me to do the exact opposite of what she's said. So that, what she's really saying is, "Don't stop, Alpha. And don't listen... Chi is doing the right thing in taking you away from the School where you can be safe. And if you came back, they will hurt, or kill you."

I can see it in her eyes that that's what she meant, and so I walk heading into the wind, over the crest of this high hill, toward the sun. And almost instantly the signal begins to break. Her face is flashing in and out of my vision, until I can no longer see her. And the last of her words in my ears are these, before the static, and distortion wipes them away entirely. "Please, come back..."

18

I am well outside the trees. The ground on all sides of me is hard, like the walkway to the main school. My footsteps, and the tapping of my branch makes a sound like there are walls on one side of me, but the echo is not continuous. Every so often, it dissipates for a few steps and then reemerges, as if the walls or buildings are broken up into freestanding sections.

Pressing my hand against a nearby wall, I feel that it is a building made of stacked rectangular sections with rough grooves in between, and in one part of the wall, an entry door. These are more half-men quarters.

Each one of these echoing walls must be a half-man quarters. I would have imagined that there would only be a few half-men quarters, built into small clumps, and placed here or there, but as I walk they seem to stretch on without end. This is like a forest of buildings, where each one is like a single tree. They do not end, and seem to be crowding closer and closer together, until there are almost no breaks in the walls at all.

What brutality and hatred, to kill so many of these half-men. And what sorts of weapons would they even use to overtake so many of them. All along I'd thought, and we'd been told in instructors' training, that the half-men were a minor race, though I can plainly tell that this was yet another lie. I have been walking, since before the sunset began, and even now with its dropping rays, there is still no end. Could this half-men colony be even larger than Primus, the Leader's City? Or could there be more abandoned colonies, like this one?

Blip.

Away in the distance, a set of animals are crying, or yelling, or howling, or whatever it would be called.

Blip. I freeze in my steps.

A noise that even I can only barely hear is hitting my audio sensors, followed by a yelp, or a shout, from the creatures a long way off.

Which clearly means that these animals can hear this blip as well, and that logically this is not merely another silent signal transmitted into my sensors, but instead it has to be an actual sound.

Blip. Ah! There it is.

I'm flailing around, tapping my branch trying to find another half-man entry door. There's no doorplate for me to press my hand against. Though, there is some type of handle to turn, but the door does not open.

Running to find another entry door, I trip, scraping up my leg. There is a tiny dab of blood.

Blip. And the animals howl.

I reach another door, still no doorplate, but the handle turns this time, and I almost fall through the entry door, kicking wooden corners, and an item that shatters on the

100

floor. Slamming the door behind myself, the animals' yelping is drowned away to almost nothing.

blip.

The sound that I cannot even hear, but that the animals can hear, is hitting my sensors in only the most unnoticeable way, but if I stand still, and do not breathe, it is still there in the unperceived corners of my brain.

This sound, it's coming from something, like the rumbling on the path that Chi made me run from, before I knew enough to be afraid of unknown sounds. That rumbling was the announcement that the transports were coming. So this sound has to be the marker for some other mechanism that the Common will try to use to find me, to take me back, to punish me publicly for leaving, in a retractment. And then, they will kill me, whether publicly or privately I can't be sure, but they would never let me keep my citizenship after this. I'm as good as dead if that machine, or person, or thing that "blips" finds me... Was that it again? I wait another half-minute, but this time it seems to be getting stronger.

Blip.

There has to be a place in this giant empty quarters to hide from that sound. And maybe if I can't hear it, it won't be able to find me, or for no other reason than for my own sanity, there has to be a way to escape it.

And so I plod onward into the quarters. Stone squares cover the floors of one large area, then the floors seem to be made of planks of wood. Another door leads to another smaller area with dusty uniforms hung on hooks and lining all the walls. Though these are not uniforms in the true sense, since they are all differing shapes and sizes, and of varying fabrics and softnesses or coarseness.

Could half-men have really had these many uniforms? And how would they know when to wear each of them?

Blip.

This will not hide me from it. And shoving through the rest of the quarters, I knock down some rectangular items that had been fastened to the walls, and they shatter as they fall, making more of a mess for me to walk over, until I feel the handhold of another door. I push forward, but the ground drops away. The air in my chest is seizing with terror, but I catch myself on a railing. These are stairs, and they bend and creak with neglected rottenness. Somehow, they are leading me below ground level. The air in this new place is cool and damp, and uncomfortable in almost every way. And as I step to the flat ground beneath at the base of the stairs, within an uninterrupted stillness, I hold my breath, until my body forces itself to breathe again, but there is not even the slightest sound.

My mouth smirks at the edges, in the overwhelming darkness of this underground location. It's so odd to smile. I must be going insane. Though I'm so excited to be away from that sound in my sensors that I don't even care how strange it is to smile.

And perhaps, if Chi's burying me below the leaves and dirt had protected me once before, then maybe this underground quarters will do the same.

Along the wall, I find a place to lie down, shoving aside mushy container boxes. And I am almost drifting into sleep when the sky in the outside world begins to crash and break, and there is the sound of a thousand tiny tappings on the roof of the quarters. Are these explosions a weapon that the Common is using against me? And I wait to be destroyed but nothing happens, until something minor catches my attention. In the corner, there is a drip, like the sound that the water from my daily sanitation makes against the floor of my quarters. Water? I rush to see what it might be, and feel a splash on the palm of my hand. My tongue laps the drop and it is bitter and stale tasting, but it is water, and I drink from it. I hold open my mouth and let the detestable water quench my desperate thirst with each tiny droplet. It's incredibly bitter, but I cannot help but drink, because it has been days of endless walking with very little water. And even though these tiny dirtied drops should not count for real water, I will not spit them out, nor will I criticize the disgusting state of these quarters, nor of a bed of hard stone, if it will keep me hidden from the sound that made the creatures outside yell and howl, and from the crashing and the breaking of the sky.

■ ■ ■

It must be hours since the sun has set, though I am finding it exhausting to try to sleep even though the blasts outside have subsided. In the far corner, there is another creature sharing this space, but it seems small enough so that it might not bother me.

My mind is restless, unable to keep from imagining Chi's body being loaded into the back of the transport. And the sound of the transport hatch slamming, with all its finality, it continues to shut over and over again in my mind.

And Chi's last words to me were nothing more than aimless babble, that I can tell. Maybe I had misread his palm-written message: "Walk blindfolded, until you smell the taste of tears in the air, and then continue, until you find the golden path over water."

Should that make sense to me, because it doesn't?

And how would a golden-colored path keep me safe from the Common? How could it be better when I get there? Or more precisely, how could there ever be a place where they could not find me? And I finally drift into a weary sleep: in my hunger and still persistent thirst, in my confusion, in the underground of a desolate, abandoned half-man quarters, with no honest chance of ever escaping now, not without Chi to lead me.

■   ▥   ▨

The sound of boots are on the creaking, warped stairs.

" ...I knew him, which is the strangest part of it, I think," says a male militant's voice to the other sets of footsteps that are walking on ahead of him.

"Well, it's shoot to kill now, so don't forget that," another deeper and more serious sounding voice says.

Though, they stop in an instant when an authoritative voice at the lead interrupts them. Their footsteps stammer.

"Quiet. There's something in the corner," the authoritative voice says.

Nothing moves. The blood in my veins and the beat of my heart are still, as well. Then, the tiniest sound, like sand being shaken in a cup.

"What is that?" says the first voice.

"It doesn't even have any legs," the deep-voiced militant adds.

Breath fills into my lungs again, though in the quietest puffs. They're not talking about me, so at least there's that comfort—but it's minimal. And what kind of animal doesn't have any legs, or at least what kind of living creature?

"Not so close," warns the first voice.

A scream shatters in the silence. It is all of them at once. "Ahh!"

"Stupid thing, it tried to bite me!" yells the authoritative voice.

And they are turned and are running out of the underground, fleeing from the no legged creature.

Snap! The wood of an ancient stair breaks in the darkness.

"My foot!" yells the deep voice, obviously in pain.

"Just come on," the first voice shouts, from the top of the steps.

"I can't," the deep voice answers as a retaliation. "I'm stuck, you low-rank."

Gunfire breaks in, skipping off and nicking the hard ground all around.

The authoritative one shouts above the commotion, "And that's why they gave us guns," he says, and then in normal voice, continues, " ...infants."

"Yah, well you wouldn't be talking like that if it had bit you," the first voice replies.

"Well, it's dead now—whatever it was," the authoritative voice answers.

And then, there are more sounds of splintering wood. There are some mumblings about pain, and questions about whether the deep-voiced militant can walk, which he says he can't, in between moans of agony.

"Help me carry him up," the first voice says.

"You do it. I have a job to finish," the authoritative voice replies.

"Oh, you're so important," the first voice mocks. "The building is clear. There's no one who would stay down here with that thing."

And reluctant as he might be, the authoritative voice seems to relent, and they both heave the deep-voiced militant up the remaining stairs, and out of the half-man quarters.

And I am saved by some vicious and biting, legless animal.

19

It's hours of uninterrupted darkness, and my stomach burns with hunger, though it's not like leaving would find me any food, when instead it might get me captured.

Those three voices sounded like graduate militants, which means the search parties have finally overtaken me. And so it might be better to stay in a place that's been "cleared," as they called it, instead of walking out into what could be a crowd of bloodthirsty militants, who will do anything for recognition, and who have the regrettable orders now to shoot to kill, as if that changes anything. They didn't have a kill order with Chi, and that didn't stop them.

So I should stay here; I should stay buried here until they think that I've escaped them, or that I've died. Until they think that there's no way that anyone would have stayed hidden so long, and only after that would it be safe to leave.

And on and on these hours blend together in an endless darkness. I play over in my head the internal memories of what had happened in the underground, and the three militant voices. What could that first voice have meant by, "I knew him"? Knew whom?

107

Those were graduate voices, probably too old to be speaking about me, as if I were the one they knew. Maybe Chi was the one they were talking about. But that doesn't make sense either: no one I've heard of even talks to laborers, so why would any militant ever say he knew one of them?

Gurgling, my stomach grumbles with a hollowed echo. This is useless. This plan of staying hidden is never going to work. I have water, that I collected in a container from that dirty, sour drip in the corner, if anyone would call that water, but without nutrition squares I'll die, maybe in only a few days, though it's hard to say for sure. Before leaving the School, I'd never gone a day without them, and by now it's been at least two days.

My brain flashes back. There is something in my internal memories that might help, but it seems so foolish to consider. The "other meal," which is more like a joke or an infant's story by now, but the way that I heard it is like this: Supposedly, a few years ago there was a slip-up within our female schoolmates' instructors' course, in which their instructor, who was quickly punished and decommissioned from her post, she mentioned something about the food in Primus, and specifically, she was believed to have said, "...the food they eat in Primus," as if it was something else, something other than dried nutrition squares and gelatinous nutri-mix. Of course this was hardly proof, but it didn't matter, and soon we were all whispering about the "other meal" in the School hallways, until the watchers quickly caught on, and would demerit anyone who said the phrase. Which I, and Theta, have always thought has to be proof that it does exist; since they are always content letting us believe any lie they tell, but if a truth ever comes up, they'll squelch it as soon as they can.

And though no one ever mentions it outright anymore, still every so often, a low ranking schoolmate during daily meal, who has nothing really to lose, and who's as good as a laborer anyways, will yell out a single word, like: "hair," or "snot," or "rocks," or "ant legs," or anything else that they could guess, that would be the "other meal" of the Leaders in Primus. And if it's especially clever or funny we might smile with the edges of our mouths, though we never laugh for fear of demerits.

Though the one negative, other than demerits, about making a joke about the "other meal," is that there's an unspoken requirement that whatever you yell, you also have to try to eat, which means that I've sensibly only heard "sticks" and "rocks," one time each.

Yet, the unknown benefit in all this, it appears, is that we now have a growing list of things that won't hurt us. And Theta even thinks, which she told me in code, she thinks that the Leaders are always eating whatever they want, which means that maybe we can too, and since she's smarter than I am, maybe she's right.

So... with no nutrition squares, I just have to find something that might not hurt me, and see what happens. Though still, all in all, I'd rather die from eating something foul, than from militants' bullets, so I take my tapping branch, and strike around the room.

A stack of crumpled container boxes: In one, even more uniforms, as if the half-men did not have enough already. In another, hard hand-sized rectangles that in their centers have been sliced into hundreds of tiny pieces, but nothing here that seems edible. I strike my branch around, and reach a pile of mushed wetness in the far corner. This has to be that no legged creature: Its body like one long muscle that has been broken up with bullet holes.

Something stirs in my gut, and I don't know how or why I might know this, but I think I can eat this. It's not so tough that I couldn't chew it into small bites. I pick it off the floor. And its thick legless body is lifeless, and still wet and dripping blood in my hands.

I open my jaws and bite, tearing into tightly wound slimy flesh that tastes awful, but I have to try to live for Chi's sake; and so I bite and tear and chew, and bite and tear and chew, until my stomach feels like it will burst open from being so full, and until I feel utterly nauseous and cannot continue, not that I would even want to.

■　■　■

The darkness now is an unending cycle. My eyes have been closed for so many days that nothing feels entirely like awake, and when I sleep it is hard to remember that I had.

Though the only way to fully tell that I am not dreaming is by the winding unsettledness in my gut that will not go away, and by the acidic, stale water that I sip from my container, whenever I'm thirsty enough to suffer through drinking it.

110

My feet pound into the lawn. There is gunfire blasting off behind me, hitting every bit of fresh grass, and every tree, and all the leaves from the hedges. Until the School lawn is a broken mess with barren tree branches and hedge bushes, and for some reason the lawn is now filled with dried and desolate grass. Yet, every bullet misses my skin, and I make it to the perimeter fence around the School lawn, where a portion of the fence has been cut open.

I bend through the opening and the metal fencing which seems to melt, warps and molds back into place as it should be, leaving me stranded on the outside of the School. To my right and left, to either side the massive fence stretches out to infinity with no breaks.

And seen through the fence's wire mesh the Disciplinarian, and his mob, slow their pace and stop behind the woven barrier without saying a word.

And then the silence breaks with a heart-shattering high sound. It is the red-chested bird, held within the locked cage that the Disciplinarian holds in his hand.

"Alpha, you left me!" it yells. Then suddenly, the bird's demeanor changes from violent yells, to the softest spoken question. "Why did you leave me?" she says.

And I awake again in the unending cycle, with a nausea in my stomach, and a deep down thirst that cannot be quenched with only these tiny sips.

◼ ◼ ◼

Perhaps it has been a week, or only a few days in the

cool underground darkness, with a dirty bed constructed from piles of dusty half-men uniforms.

Around the third day, or what I would guess would be the third day, a grouping of mice, or what I think might be slightly larger than mice, come to devour the parts of the limbless beast that I could not eat.

And then, when there is no way I could physically stay any longer, I am leaving. My steps depress and bend the ancient wooden stairs, but none of them break under my feet. Though the world above is still too dark for it to be daylight hours, and so I wait in a lighter darkness than I had below ground, but still darkness nevertheless; and I wait until the morning sun dawns, and until I can finally escape out of the half-man's entry door, heading away from the sun as Chi said to do.

In many places the path is broken beneath my feet. But this half-men colony continues on without end. This place must be larger than Primus, the Leader's city, the grandest in the Common, the pinnacle of our perfection as we were taught in courses.

But what if this place were actually larger? Could this have been the half-men's version of Primus—the pinnacle of what they would have called their perfection, before they were evolved into what we are now?

The well-welcomed heat from the sun once again creeps over my head. The wind blows and there is a faint wetness on the breeze, blowing on my face. Tears? Like the combination of chilled tears, and a misting spray. Is this really it? Maybe Chi wasn't crazy after all.

And as I walk, the smell only continues to grow, until it is unmistakeable. This is the smell of tears, or similar to it at least.

"Walk blindfolded until you smell the taste of tears," he said.

And so I reach behind my head. My hands skim over the soiled bandages that Chi wrapped around my neck, until the knot of the blindfold is in between my fingers.

With some trying it is let loose, and my eyes open for the first time. What could this place that I've walked through look like? Or what if there are really militants on all sides of me now, who have just been playing with me to see how far I could come?

Pure white blindness. I never thought that sunlight could be so painful as this. If there is anything here, I still cannot see it. The real sun with its fiery light is impossible for me to see by, after days and days of blackness. My free hand goes up to shadow my eyes from the horrible brightness.

Lungs panting, I drop to my knees on the hard path, burying my head back into my blindfold.

They are laughing at me; if militants are around me now, they are lining up their kill shots, and chuckling to themselves. "This pathetic infant," they must be saying. "He's gotten to the wet air, but he can't see it."

And I drop my tapping branch, using both hands to block my eyes, until the agony of opening my eyes becomes only a general stabbing pain, that then becomes a grinding discomfort; until, after awhile, I can see shapes and colors through teary eyes that cannot seem to stay open for more than a few seconds at a time.

My eyes are beginning to learn how to see again. Maybe the more time they spend in darkness, the more painful the sun feels when it finally arrives. But now I can see again—my blindfold is off—and this city is strange to me.

20

This is nothing like it was at the School: There, all the buildings are built from giant hardened slabs, but here, these half-men structures are made from stacks of a thousand small rectangles, or built from old rotten pieces of cut wood, and in all places these half-men quarters are missing entry doors, or windows, or sections of walls, so that nothing is complete, and everything is a vacant mess, with piles of rubbled debris in the centers of the transit routes between the buildings.

Ahead there is an intersection of two routes, and an odd shaped eight-sided placard displaying a message, a warning for travelers. "Stop," it reads. And so I stop, awaiting further instruction. There is silence and emptiness all around, and no other message is displayed. My feet inch forward. Nothing happens. My pace increases, but still the message remains the same.

The display must have glitched. It must have been stuck forever with this final message. And here I was like a fool, obeying a broken old half-man display. Though there is something strange about this word: the letters don't glow as they normally do. And when I come up close, reaching up to feel this dusty piece of red metal, my fingers rub over letters that have been for some strange reason, permanently fixed to its surface.

The breath in my mouth begins to chuckle.

"How would you even know when to go, if it never changes?" I mumble, the first real words to leave my mouth in over a week.

This feeling of spoken words, after so many days without them rumbles uneasily in my throat.

"How bizarre?" I say out loud, if only to hear the sound of a human voice in my ears, even if it's just my own.

And something else, unlikeable, begins to pierce into my ears—it's that screaming or yelping that I heard the other day, but this time much closer, and not associated with that same steady electric blip. When I was running from that blip before, I'd hardly thought about how unsettling their howls or cries had sounded, but now that it's only those animals' shouts, not so far away, it's easier to be frightened of them, like maybe I should have been all along.

My eyes trace around the decayed buildings. I have to find a place to hide tonight, somewhere secure that's not half-broken apart like all these half-men quarters. And I'm running, away from the sound of the animals' yells. And as I continue, the buildings are growing larger and larger, more like they would be at the School.

The night is covering layers of darkness upon itself. Soon everything will be black and colorless. My chest is beating in a feverish weakness; I haven't eaten in so long that my body must be stealing energy from itself. My legs feel like water. Up ahead, there is a massive building with a half-man word that I don't understand, that has been permanently fastened to the outside wall.

"I-K-E," it reads.

At the front, the glass entry doors are shattered apart, but my feeble legs won't stop running. There has to be some place to hide within a building as large as this. I burst through the broken entry doors and up a set of stairs. Square holes in the ceiling let in only a minimal amount of light, though my eyes can still make out shapes.

What is this place? There are segmented quarters, yet without fourth walls or entry doors, and there are rows and rows of cushioned benches and chairs of all differing shapes and sizes. How many half-men would live in a place like this? I should hope hundreds, to account for the amount of beds and chairs. Or maybe this is a pattern or a trait of half-men, like their obvious obsession with having the proper uniform for every conceivable occasion. What if there was only one half-man who lived here, and he'd just continued to gather up so many beds and chairs that he could never possibly use them all?

Half-men were so weird...

The animals' cries again, but this time echoing. They must be inside. My mind comes back to its senses. I sprint past sections of desks and shelves, and into an eating commons.

An entry door, at the far corner, finally some place I could lock myself into, but the door only swings open, with an awful squeak, as I push through it.

There are no locks, or knobbed handles, like most half-men doors.

Yelp! Yelp!

They must be right behind me!

This must be where the half-men stored their meals, and now I'm about to be a meal for some ravenous creatures—how fitting.

It's so dark that even shapes are difficult to make out. There is a wide table nearby. I fumble to climb on top of it, any way to keep out of reach of the screaming animals. Hurrying, my foot kicks at something that pricks into my uniform shoes.

"Ow!" I say, as a reflex.

What was that? The darkness is almost as black as it was in the underground. My fingers grab for it, tracing around the shape of it, to find out what it was. I can only see shadows.

Slicing, it cuts at my pointing finger, severely. Drips of blood pour out.

Is this a weaponry? Maybe I was wrong, and this isn't a storage for food, but for weapons. With my uninjured hand, I grip the handle of a long knife, and then the door breaks open, with a flow of four-legged furry beasts of various shapes and sizes, but all of them with flashing teeth and ugly growls.

They howl and yell, standing up onto their hind legs around the table, snapping their jaws and trying to bite at my legs, but some of them are so small that they could not possibly reach me.

There is a tall one with a pointed nose and ears. He snaps, trying to bite the fingers of my already cut and bleeding hand, but I kick him in the nose before he can. He's yelping and I've made him angrier, it seems, and his yelping is causing all of them to yell all the more.

And then a hulking one with puffy hair covering his whole body, he pulls himself onto the table, and clamps his teeth onto my leg in the deepening darkness. His bite is hindered somewhat by my thick uniform pants, but it still tears and bleeds. I might die, being eaten. His jaws clamp and grind at the tissue and bone, bringing such pain. He is dragging me across the wide metallic table, toward the waiting mouths of the rest of them. If I fall off the table, they will never let me live.

This is the only way, but I've never killed anything before, or even tried to. My knife blade flashes, burying with depth into masses of fur. It yells and bites down even harder, and some new rage comes over me, then another stabbing of my bloody blade, and it lessens its grip. I'm almost to the ledge of the long table. I jab again, another pierce of my knife into its side and it stops, and its jaws are let loose, and it falls off the ledge by its own weight.

And I am no longer an immediate interest to them. Their yelping is eerily quiet. The tall one, whom I kicked before, he walks up to the stabbed beast and nudges it with his nose, sniffing at it. Then the others follow its lead, and they are pulling at the animal's dead carcass, and growling. There is a fight over who will get to keep it, disgustingly.

They don't seem to care about me any longer. Maybe I

could sneak away. I inch toward the edge of the table, nearer to the door, but the tall one leaps back, growling and lunging at me. I stab into its neck, and he pulls away, howling with a gurgling sound in his throat. And now they are afraid of me; I've injured their leader. They bark and scream, running out of the door, and leaving the pieces of the dead animal's carcass that they had not yet devoured.

And their howling rings out through the empty half-men building, until they are gone. But I haven't won, not really, my leg and cut finger are wet with blood. I wrap the length of my old blindfold around my calf and I try to hold the wound closed on my finger, until the wet flow finally stops. But by then, my body can not possibly stay awake. And I collapse, back upon the table.

21

The night wind blows the edges of my hair. I am there again, outside the School, watching the crowd of militants, with Delta, and the Disciplinarian holding his caged bird, and they are staring back at me through the grated fencing. Then suddenly, the wind blows stronger, whipping up the dirt around my feet, and the Disciplinarian's already subtle malicious grin grows more apparent. He is looking beyond me, at something, and I turn to see what could be making him so happy. It is Tau, his uniform shirt flapping strongly in the rushing breeze. He has the sight of his gun trained on me.

"Did you think I would let you leave?" he says.

And the blowing dust around my feet feels now more like wet, coarse sand.

■　■　■

My eyes shoot open. Something is licking at the sore on my leg, something mangey and hairy, with sharpened teeth and a gritty tongue.

"Ah!" I yell, shoving it away and knocking a metal container from the table on which I'm laying.

My whole body shivers from the shock of it. Does every animal in this city want me for a meal? I've never woken with any creature that close to me before. I've never woken with anything ever licking at my sores. And I've never felt so weak, or felt like I would vomit so uncontrollably, but somehow I keep it down.

If they were going to be killing things, the Common shouldn't have stopped at half-men only. Why not slay all these other useless beasts, also, while they're at it?

There is a heat in my skin. My forehead is warmed to the touch but not burning, and every muscle aches. And I cannot explain the reasoning: whether it is the onset of this renewed level of physical weakness, spilling over into my emotions, but for the first time in many years, since infancy, I am truly crying. And in an unstoppable inexcusable way, laying weak and bruised and hungry, on a table in the half-men weaponry, just sobbing, like I could never do in front of Theta, or if the watchers were monitoring me.

"Chi, why did you leave me?" I mumble and cry. Then pounding the table—"Why did you leave me!"

But I know deep down that it wasn't his fault. It was Tau's, and the Common that made Tau and all those like him. Although, I can't let myself be afraid, or be purposefully weak. And so, I slide from the table, carrying my knife with me. The pain from putting weight on my leg sends shivers through me. Though in the corner, there is a long pole with a rectangular, cushioned, mushy piece at one end, perfect to use as a crutch, which I use to help me out of this massive half-men quarters, down the stairs, through the shattered doors that crumple under my feet, and out into the lighted and desolate ancient half-men city.

And straight ahead of me, at the other side of a wide deserted transit route, is water. And not just any small plot of water, not a river like they have in the images of the Leader's City (with its flowering trees and impressive mammoth white buildings on either side of a flowing river). No, this is not a river at all. It is something less contained and grander. Then the breeze from off the watery expanse hits me: it is that same smell that I'd had hints of yesterday, when I'd taken off my blindfold, a scent that was like the smell of what tears taste like, but more wild and raw in aroma.

This big water seems to stretch on forever, in some places, though in other parts there is land at the opposite side. Not so far away from where I stand taking in the sight of it, there is a greyed metal path across the water that leads onward to the other land. But it is not a golden path, and Chi specifically wrote gold.

Though then my eyes catch something on the horizon line, something that from this distance looks like a string of gold stretching across the water and arching upward toward the clouded blue sky.

"Ha!" I laugh and exclaim. I found it, near where the air is wet, just as Chi said. And all I have to do is get there, and I'll be safe from the Common. That's what Chi said, and he's been right about this, so far. So that golden path has to keep me safe, somehow—I'm not sure how, but somehow it can, and all I have to do is get there.

There's enough light left today to find it, but I have to keep walking. And so, I hobble on my padded crutch toward this first darkened grey metal path, across the water, leading to the other land. And if my forehead doesn't get any hotter, and if I can keep walking until nightfall on a cut and scarred leg, then I can get to the distant golden path before the dark falls around me, and there I'll be safe.

And I hobble, and hobble, and the more I do the greater the pain feels. Striking in constant intervals, the bottom of my crutch pole ticks on the hard path. My teeth grit. There's a dizziness in my vision, and my chest is pounding. With every step the heat in my forehead is only getting worse.

The crutch pole slips. Too much weight on my slashed and bitten calf. In comparison to all the pain I've felt since I left the School, this is like the prick of a thorn, but it's just enough to be at my breaking point. My shredded leg cannot hold the weight. And I collapse. Skidding on the ground, my crutch pole and knife slide away and out of my reach. I hit the hard path below me like a stone, smacking my knees and palms. My head is a small fire. The ground is my bed for hours, maybe. And I've only made it halfway across the darkened metal path to the other land over the water.

And beyond that, it would be hours more of walking, on good legs... but with these battered limbs I could never get there at this rate, before night fall. And by then, who knows what wild animals would find me?

Instantly, the thought flashes in my brain... I'm going to

die. I am—there's no way to avoid it. In my frailest moments, usually after a "bad dream," if it was an unsuccessful retractment, and especially tragic or bloody, I would sometimes think of what it would be like. But I thought that when death would happen to me, it would be at the hands of the Common, and not like this.

"Ha." I chuckle to think that I wanted to get away from them: from the Common, from the School, but now it seems like I literally can't live without them. I thought the Common would kill me, but now it's just the empty world that will do it. In the thirteen years of silently hating their control over every part of my existence, at least they didn't kill me; at least they fed me my meals, and kept me safe within the walls of the School. And I won't pretend that it's because they cared for me. They needed me, that's all.

Though this empty world, it doesn't need me. It doesn't know that I exist; it's just filled with vicious animals, and death after death, with me as only an extra number in the tally. One more insignificant credit to mark off its list. It doesn't matter... I don't—*Blip.*

What was that?

Though aside from that first noise there is another, a rumbling across the path, coming from the other land at the opposite side of the water. It's coming up speedily, and the rumble grows in volume.

It is an oncoming transport, and it is almost on top of me. The wheels screech, stopping where I can almost touch them.

Blip.

"Alpha!" A male voice leaves the transport, running to kneel beside me. "There are drones all over the place, scanning for you, and this is where you decide to take a nap?" he says.

My eyes blur. He's not much more than a shape. But as he reaches to lift me up, it strikes me that I know his voice. My scattered mind snaps back to reality.

"Let me go!" I yell in a mumbled voice, and I hit my scraped palms against him, but he easily holds my hands back. This is Tau's voice.

My fingers reach up to strangle at his throat, but he throws me into the side seat of the transport, before I can get to him. And he leaps into the operator's seat.

Blip.

And some instrument with moving needled gauges lights up and signals a warning.

"They're scanning for you," he says, "same as I was, and they're almost here."

Squeals, as our transport wheels spin away, and we are blazing across what is left of the greyed metal path, toward the other land across the water.

Blip!

And as the transport instrument sounds again, the gunfire begins, shooting from the sky and striking all around us. A bullet hits the metal of the transport, but it doesn't seem like they can lock onto us, not with the sporadic nature of Tau's maneuvers.

We are to the other land, passing by half-men displays with strange shaped symboled writing that must mean something, but I cannot focus on it, not with the glare of the sun in my eyes, and because of our immense speed.

"I hate you," I say, grumbling with all the strength I have left. Our wheels bump over debris and broken bits of walls. The bullets are coming at us again—a well shot one breaks the window near my head, and shatters sharp pieces all around me.

And in the madness Tau is laughing at me, simply laughing. "You're ridiculous," he snidely says. "Hate the Common; they're the ones shooting at us," he adds.

The transport turns so sharply that I slam against the metal transport wall, and against the finely sharpened fragments of the window. A spray of ammunition flies past us, bullets hitting into tree trunks and branches all around us. We are past the buildings of the city, in an area of overgrown green. Up ahead is the golden path, which is massive now that it's so close, and is stretching across another large expanse of water.

Tau hits a button, and firm yet padded straps wrap around me, and also around himself. We are now onto the golden path, but the bullets are still following us from the sky. Chi was wrong; it isn't safe here.

Clang. Clang. Clang. A rapid succession of bullets into the front of the transport, and there is a plume of white steam, and whatever has been powering the transport seems to have died, but it doesn't matter, as we are turned sharply, and are headed toward a break in the pathway railing.

"There's probably a better way to do this," Tau says aloud, bracing himself in his operator's chair.

My head is still spinning, and this isn't helped the moment we are in the air. The weightlessness stirs an uneasy feeling in my gut. Wind whipping in through the broken window beside me, and the expanse of water below us is coming at an unstoppable speed, and accelerating. Closer—closer still.

I might be too disoriented to scream, or else it seems too unreal, so that the idea to scream has become unattached from reality, like a forgotten dream.

And I turn to see Tau, who is not screaming either, and for the first time that I've seen, he is scared, or nervous. Looking out of the front window, the water is coming, and we break against it, like the bullets that broke against the sides of our transport.

Instantly, I snap against the restraint that is wrapped around me, jerking with so much force that it feels like it could break my bones. Icy cold water floods in around my feet, stinging at my legs, and then to my waist.

Tau strikes a button releasing our seat straps. The water, colder than anything I've felt, and burning against my partially opened wounds, continues to rise. We are sinking, dropping into the water that seems to fall below us in a haze, forever.

The water level still rising, Tau's hands grab at my uniform collar, pulling me into the rear of the transport, where a pocket of air is forming.

Air that tastes like tears fills into my lungs.

"Are you crazy?" I say frailly, even as he has to be the one to keep my head above water.

"Can you stop hating me for one second, while I'm trying to save your life?" he replies. Then adding in a softer, whispered breath that echos in the rising water level, he says, "You witless little brat."

How dare he? He's a killer, and I can hate him if I want to hate him. And even if he does call drowning me "saving my life", it doesn't mean that's what it is.

If I had enough of my strength left in the shivering cold murkiness, I would try to strangle him. But there is a flash of light in the water, that steals my attention. This light shines through our transport windows as we continue to fall into the wet darkness. The speed of the light is astonishing, coming so quickly and drawing blindingly nearer. Until it is almost on top of us, so that it is very obviously not just a light but a person, holding tightly to and being pulled through the water by a bullet-shaped motorized device that is propelling him, and unbelievably this person is breathing air, underwater.

In the glimmering glow of his underwater light, there is the gleam of a knife, and the butt of a knife handle is being beaten into the back transport window, as we continue to sink almost unendingly, into water so cold it burns.

The inner portions of my ears pinch and throb. I am screaming as the back window continues to be beaten and cracks in fine dark splinters.

Air bubbles seep from the broken cracks in the window, as Tau reaches over, taking ahold of my nose, and telling me to blow "so that the pain will go away," which sounds ridiculous, but it works. In that, the immediate pain goes away, but there is an ache that still lingers on.

The man breathing water stabs his knife blade through the widening window cracks and begins to cut. We have almost no air left, and once the window breaks out, it is gone entirely. Water falls into my mouth, choking me almost instantly. We are pulled from the transport, which falls faster without the remaining air inside of it, sinking deeper into the dark clouded blackness.

The water breather shoves a bubbling mouthpiece through my lips, and after choking and gagging out this fowl liquid, a bitter tasting dry air fills into my helpless lungs.

My hands grip onto anything I can hold, as the water breather kicks his long, webbed feet, gradually sending us out of the cold depths. A fist beats at my arm. It's Tau, and he's frantic, without warning pulling the mouthpiece from my lips. In all my thoughts to breathe, I must have forgotten about him. There must only be one extra hose to breathe by, since the water man will not share his. And so we trade air, rudely ripping the mouthpiece away from one another when we feel like the other has had his fair share. But Tau always takes one extra breath; I'm sure of it.

We reach the water man's illuminated underwater bullet-shaped transport, and start to move horizontally through dark haziness. The cold liquid passes over my skin at an incredible rate, traveling at such a speed and for so long that I soon can no longer even squint to see, since the water burns my eyes so intensely.

And in all of this traveling below the cloudy waterline, my skin starts to forget its chill, and it pretends that it is warm, but there's no way that it could actually be. How could I be this weak and tired? My hands progressively lose their griping power, until they release altogether. Though the water man immediately catches me, pulling me onward, and onward.

Until I must hold my nose and blow, multiple times. And until I can feel how dark it is all around us. And when it would be impossible, we surface in a new pocket of air, though still below the water.

A new air strikes at my face, and I no longer need the bubbling mouthpiece. Somehow we are both below the water and yet above it, in a new world below the surface.

Muscular hands snatch ahold of me, and I am dragged onto a metal floor, and this is the last thing I remember.

22

"He's awake. Get the others," a female voice says.

My eyes flutter in a bright and blinding light. Then, darkness.

■ ■ ■

My squinted eyes, which are no longer burning, open with a misty blur. The same female voice—I'm sure—is saying, "For real this time, check his pulse," she orders. An old hand reaches to feel my neck, at the vein. My eyelids are pulled wider open. A glaring beam is shone into them.

"Alpha, you're safe here," an older woman's voice says. But I feel anything but safe, as my head and vision turns to show that I have tubes and needles stuck below my skin in multiple places.

I am shouting and kicking, and trying to pull at the rubber wire in my arm, but multiple hands withhold me. And then the prick of another needle into my body, as if they had not had enough jabbed into me already, and the world goes black again.

■ ■ ■

I awake once more, but this time there is only the one female medical rank, who has been there in all my iterations of half-waking. She is seated in a chair away from me, and looking down, while she is making markings on some portable writing surface, and while she grips onto a tiny pointed writing instrument, which she uses to make her lines and scratches.

I gaze at her for some time. And all the wires and tubes are removed from my body except for a few, and my leg has been properly wrapped. Maybe it is safe here, or at least safe enough to talk and to ask questions.

"What are you doing?" I ask, finding that my voice is hoarse and fragile, as if it has not been used for many days. I've startled her. She closes her writing tablet, leaving her handheld writing instrument folded up in between it.

She smiles at me. "I'm writing in my *notebook*," she says, as if I should understand what that means.

"Why?" I ask, and I'll worry later about what a notebook is, once I know why she's writing in it.

"So I can remember what's happened?" she answers.

My face must be obviously uncomprehending.

"Why would you need to do that?" I say. Since all we see and say is monitored and recorded, what difference would it make to write it out ourselves?

"For *History*," she answers.

"For what?" I ask, and she shakes her head at me like I am an infant, and possibly unintentionally I glare at her for this.

"I forget what they do to you..." she mutters, before starting again. "For History [like I should know what this word means], for a record of past events, for our memories," she says.

I grin at her, this peculiar medical rank.

"But our memories are stored with the watchers," I say. "Why would you need to write down anything?—" She stumbles over the end of my words, interrupting them with her own.

"And what if you'd wanted to keep your own memories for yourself?" she asks.

But I don't say anything else to such a strange girl.

"And what if we'd all, collectively, wanted to keep our memories locked away, in places where the Common couldn't touch them, and alter them"—she takes in a breath—"...that would be History," she says.

Then my body begins to cough, and it won't be stopped until she has given me something to drink. And once the coughing ends, I ask when I am able, "And where would we keep our memories, where the Common wouldn't find them?" I say.

She smiles at me again, with a glimmer in her eye. "In notebooks," she answers, before coming to pull her chair up nearer to my bedside.

"My name is Sarah," she says.

I give her an odd look, on purpose. "Your name?" I say. "...like, 'the name for a flying, chirping animal with wings and a beak is a bird,' or 'the name for a small, black insect that lives in the ground is an ant'?" I say.

134

She blinks quickly, making tiny side-to-side movements with her head, likely in unbelief, as if my question were not a reasonable one. Then she oddly touches the back of my hand as she answers. "Yes, and the name for a *me*, the girl sitting in front of you with the brown hair, is Sarah," she says.

I sit up more straightly in the bed, letting my back rest against pillows, but being careful with my injured leg to move it gently, since the wound which they have stitched and mended is still healing.

"So, your *designation* is Sarah?" I say, still cautious of this strange girl. Though thinking that I am beginning to understand her new use of terms, I ask, "How many Sarahs are there here? What is your number?"

"No, we don't have any numbers here, Alpha, only names. And yes, there are other Sarahs in the city, but none of us has a number."

"Then, how can you tell each other apart?" I ask, since this haphazard naming convention seems to already have multiple flaws.

"Alright, yes, well we all have first names here. Mine is Sarah, which I share with several other girls..." My face must look suspicious, since she is speaking to me more methodically. "And then each of us has a separate, *family* name, which is shared by close relations, or a 'last name' as we call it. And so, with these first and last names we are able to tell each other apart... My last name is Robins."

Even through this slight medically induced haze they must be pumping into me, by way of the few tubes left in my arms, this is starting to make sense.

"So your name is"—hoping I have it right—"Sarah Robins?" I say.

Her face lights up so brightly. "Yes, that's it."

There is a slight pause, as the next question seems to flow out naturally. "But how are these 'family names' given —who assigns them to you?" I ask.

She looks unbelieving. "It's your family who would give it to you, Alpha... your *parents*," she says, as if I should understand all these new words.

But there is a blankness in my expression that she must be able to see. "Tell me you know what a family is, Alpha," she says, choking back what might be a rush of tears, that would pour from her eyes.

Normally, I would lie to save my credits, but I don't think that should matter here.

"Why, should I know?" I ask.

And more quickly than she was made happy, a few moments ago, she is bursting with sadness, sobbing in short winded gasps, and holding her hand up to her mouth to show some ounce of discretion.

"What's the matter, Sarah Robins?" I ask, never seeing someone cry so much, or so freely, in my whole life.

She is trying to compose herself, and speaking in stuttered increments.

"I just—I hate what they do to you there," she says.

"Where? At the School?" I ask, trying to understand what she could mean, and whom she hated.

"Yes, at your School, in that whole Common," she answers, wiping away tears from her still seeping eyes. "I hate them. I hate the way they steal from you, and try to squash you into these boxes, and label you with designations, trying to make you all the same... their blind little *puppets*. And I hate them," now she's raising her voice, and crying aloud, "I hate them." Her words echo in the metal-walled room, as she turns her head away, possibly trying to regain herself.

"But they haven't stolen anything from me," I say.

She turns back with an earnestness in her voice. "They do, and you don't even know they're doing it... They steal your words, and your thoughts, by not even teaching them to you. Which is the worst of it all, that you won't even know what a family is, to know that they have stolen it from you."

And she must be able to tell by my lostness, that she should continue her explanation.

"A family, Alpha, are those people you are closest related to," she says.

"Similar to? In what way?" I ask.

Her eyes shift, as if to think of something else. "No, wait, let me start that again..." And she goes on to explain the construction of a family: wherein male and female progenitors, or fathers and mothers as they are generally called, they birth at random, either males or females, who would then be related, as a family unit. And these new persons would be brothers, the males; or sisters, the females; but around the part at which she introduces the special cases for aunts and uncles, and grandparents, and cousins, it all becomes a distorted mess.

"So do you have any brothers or sisters?" I ask, attempting to keep her on track.

Her eyes sparkle in a visible manner. "I only have one brother, who's still alive," she answers. " ...and his name is Alpha, Alpha Robins."

That's odd, and my face shows it.

"Strange... and are there many other Alphas in this city? Is that a common name?" I ask.

"No," she says, holding out the word, as if to imply that I am close to the truth, and expectantly leading me to ask my next question.

"Then, how many are there?" I ask, but somehow I seem to know her answer before the words even leave her mouth, and I am right about it.

She smiles so deeply, it looks like she could cry again. "There's only the one, Alpha, in the city. And I'd never met him, before today."

For a second I try to place whether this is merely a convenient and purposeful lie, but it must be the truth: I've never seen someone so happy to tell something, and how could she pretend to be so happy, or lie so successfully, so that it must be the truth.

I have a sister, Sarah Robins.

23

"What do you mean, 'I can't leave'?" I say.

It is the day after my first meeting with my *sister*, which stretched out in a long conversation until the drugs finally pulled my eyelids shut. And I'd almost begun to think this new, unfamiliar girl was on my side, until she came back in this morning with "bad *news*," as she called it.

"Well, I'm sorry, Alpha. It's not my decision," she answers. And I'm fuming with determined animosity. Who does she think she is to keep me locked in these medical quarters?—when I could get up and walk out, presumably, if they'd let me.

"Don't be like that," she tells me. "The sensors in your head are still active, and we only have a handful of these signal sealed *rooms* [which is their word for personal quarters], and the others have been taken up. If you were to leave, you'd put us all at risk. And we can't risk the lives of the whole city, just because you want to get out and stretch your legs."

She's no longer smiling, and looking fairly serious, with a tightened expression, so I should stop pressing her.

I rest back against my set of pillows, and let my recovering leg be delicately propped upon a cushion.

"Fine, how long do I have to stay?" I ask, with defeat seeping from my voice.

She takes a small step away from my bedside, glancing over her shoulder at the solid metal entry door, and speaking less distinctly. "The doctor is on her way. I think it'd be best if she were to explain it to you," she mumbles.

The doorway to my quarters is not one, but actually two doors, made to be an air-locked seal, as if I were a quarantined patient. Not more than a few seconds after she speaks, the outer entry door swishes open, then footsteps in the joining corridor, then the inner door breaks open.

It is the doctor. Her pressed grey straight hair falls far down her back, and the wrinkles on her face, might have at one time been pleasant to look at.

She stops by my bedside, glancing at Sarah to acknowledge her before returning her attention to me. A stitching on the old woman's uniform shirt reads, "Dr. Smith."

"Hello, Alpha." Her voice is a soft rasp. "You've come a long way to see us, haven't you?"

She might be expecting a response, and it would be against their protocol not to answer, but I also don't like being locked up, so they'll just have to deal with my lack of cooperation.

The old doctor glances down at a writing board in her hand, that has my new name, Alpha Robins, scribbled across an attached writing sheet that must bear some information about my condition.

"Doesn't he speak?" the doctor says to Sarah, without looking up from her writing board.

"Yes, but not when he doesn't want to, ma'am," Sarah replies.

The age-worn doctor glances up, staring at me with her eyebrows lifted, and she speaks to Sarah again, though never taking her glare away from me. "So he's just rude then, is he?" she asks.

"Sometimes, ma'am," my sister answers.

"Well, we can fix that," the doctor quickly replies, as if it were a medical condition that needed treatment. And she grabs my bandaged leg, applying just enough pressure to make me wince.

She speaks slowly, keeping her grip firm. "You've come a long way to see us, haven't you, Alpha?"

The corners of my mouth lift subtly. What's the old medical rank going to do? I bet she could be demerited or de-ranked for even trying something like this. Instantly, her boney fingers dig down slightly more into my padded bandages, then she releases.

My eyes open wide and jaw clenches as a reflex. And taking a deep breath, since I'm not going to win this one, I answer, with a grit in my voice, "Yes."

"Well, that's a start," the doctor answers, scribbling something down onto her writing sheet.

And I don't let her finish completely, before I ask, "When can I leave?"

Though it is apparently not a simple question to answer, as she sits at the corner of my bed to give her explanation, which is this: I have active sensors in my head, which the Common has been scanning for, for weeks, so hence my quarantined room and added precautions.

"If you were to step one foot out of those doors, they'd be sure to find us with their deep scanners, and a single torpedo would be the end of us," the old woman explains. "And frankly, the fact that they have found neither yours, nor Tau's bodies in the wreckage, or picked up a latent signal with their scanners has probably caused enough trouble for us as it is."

Which leaves only two options for me—to either stay locked up in quarantine, indefinitely, or to have my internal sensors dealt with.

"What does that mean, 'dealt with'?" I ask.

"It means... we have to take them out, or destroy them," the doctor replies.

And specifically, this would mean a supersonic pulse into my ears, while unconscious, to break my audial sensors, but the eyes would be a more delicate procedure, in which a flexible video monitoring tube and laser are *fished*, as she calls it, behind each eyeball. Though she assures me, that while this would be incredibly painful to feel, that I'll be locked in a heavily sedated, forced sleep by that point, and I wouldn't be able to feel anything, until I awoke after the surgery.

But as if this were not a downside enough, there is more. This procedure is not always successful, which when I press her on it, means that while there is a one hundred percent chance of destroying and removing my visual sensors, there is still a one in four, or five, chance that I might never see again.

"What!" I stammer.

"It's an inherent risk, Alpha. The nerve endings behind the eyes are just too sensitive," the old medical rank replies.

At least at the School, they didn't torture us like this, cutting us apart, trying to make us deaf and blind. There, they'd only borrowed our vision for themselves, though at least they'd left some for us to use, as well.

"And what about Tau? Why doesn't he have to do the same thing?" I ask.

And Sarah speaks up, standing at the foot of my bed. "He's already gone through the procedure." And as she says this, she's perhaps nervously rubbing her hands together, which cannot be a good sign. Maybe they don't know what his outcome will be yet. "Why do you think he hasn't been here with you, since you arrived?" she asks.

Because, he's plotting his kill shot for me—which is what I'd like to say, but don't. And say instead, "I hadn't thought about it."

The doctor, peering over her collection of notes, begins to speak again. "Well, he should be fine to be moved around by tomorrow morning." Then she seems to have gotten an idea. "Alpha, wouldn't it be nice if you boys could share a room? And he could explain in his own words, how simple his surgery was," the doctor says to me. Then turning her head to slightly address Sarah as well, "And I'm sure you'd both be happy to see how well he's recovered," she adds.

Sarah looks partially more comforted, which is fine for her, but not for me. And especially after I ask when my supposed procedure would take place. "Tomorrow morning," Sarah answers first, since maybe she thinks I would take the words better, if they were coming from her.

Tomorrow morning? Am I really going to let them shove laser tubes behind my eyes?

I can see it now. 'Oh, good morning, Alpha. I hope you've enjoyed your sight, 'cause you won't be needing it any longer.' And I've only recently got out of my previous blindfold, and now they want me to put one on again, perhaps forever.

I shake my head with tiny side-to-side movements. "Not interested," I say.

The doctor glances at me quizzically. "Not interested... in what? In the procedure, or in seeing Tau again?" she asks.

A mocking short breath leaves my mouth, followed by a quick word. "Both," I say.

"Don't be that way," Sarah says, and starts to plead with me, but the old doctor prevents her.

"No, wait. It's his decision," she tells Sarah, which is the first rational thing either of them have said since this conversation began.

"If he wants to live and die in this cramped, tiny room, that's his business," she adds, as she stands to leave. And giving a gentle, perhaps mocking tap on my good leg, she adds, "But if it were my choice, I'd rather be blind and free, than a prisoner with full sight of my surroundings... forever."

Which sounds an awful lot like a threat, because it probably is. If I don't go through with this, then this old medical rank will make sure I never set one foot out of this room again, and that means never having a chance to go back for Theta. And if I have to go save her as a blind person, then that is what has to happen. The first time around, I made it all the way to the giant water while blindfolded— I think I could make it back the way I came.

"Fine, I'll do it," I mutter.

"Yea!" Sarah says, congratulating me for my good decision, as she describes at length the highly adept skill of the doctors, and how I shall be "just fine." And then Sarah wraps her arms around me presumably as a sign of affection, and it hurts. It almost burns my skin, because it's so unnatural and uncomfortable.

■ ■ ■

The whole night is an awful mess of non-sleeping, and in the morning a group of masked and gloved medical ranks burst into my room, one by one, through the airlock seal. And they all take their turns prodding at me with gauges and needles, until it is time to begin. Though in all of it, Tau has still not been brought into the room. I was supposed to see him before my procedure, I explain to an unfamiliar medical rank, but they tell me that Tau was not ready to be moved.

I don't want to do this anymore, but I can no longer struggle. The sedative starts seeping into the tube that's stuck into my arm. The room drifts in and out of focus, and they must think I am more asleep than I really am, because the last thing I can almost see and feel are the braces set in place to hold my eyelids open, and the feeling of my right eyeball shifting out of place, and then a black nothing.

24

I awake in a sweat, in a panic. The inside of my head, and the space behind my eyes feels like someone's taken a fire to them. I am wrapped in a thick layered medical bandage, like a blindfold—they must not want any light to come through. And my words and moans of pain, all blend into the same gargled, uninterpretable sound.

There is a deep voice, familiar, though vastly unexpected. "Don't move, Alpha," he says. "The next few days are critical. Don't scratch an itch, or touch anywhere near those bandages. Don't even move your head, if you can help it... but stay absolutely still, to give yourself as much chance as you can get for proper healing."

And I try to do as he orders, though not moving only makes me focus on the pain, all the more.

"It hurts, doesn't it?" he says. "I know it does, 'cause I've felt it, in every way, the same as you feel it right now... but it'll go away, eventually. It only lasts a few days. Just remember, only a few days of endurance, for a lifetime of sight."

The space behind my eyes feels cracked and burned. And I wish I could pour water through my head to help the pain go away, but I shouldn't even move. Chi said so. That was his voice; I'm sure of it.

The drugs they're pumping into me must be even more powerful than I first thought, 'cause it's impossible: Chi's dead—I heard the shot with my own ears.

But it's a comfort to hear his voice again, even as a passing dream. Though then his hands reach out to touch my arm, and I almost leap out of my skin. Those are his hands. Those are a laborer's hands. I remember how they felt from when we were palm-writing, coarse as sand or dry stone.

I must be going crazy, absolutely crazy, or else... this is what life is like after you've died.

"Chi? But you're... are we—" I begin to speak in pained whispers, not able to form full sentences. Though he must know what I am meaning to say, and so he interrupts my words before they're completed.

"Oh, stop it. I'm not dead, and neither are you," he says.

And he pulls my hand forward, letting me feel the bandages around his torso. "Feel that," he says. "That's where the bullet pierced through. It was a perfect miss: never even broke a bone."

And his words drift and flow, until I am again lost in an unconscious haze.

▣ ▣ ▣

Then I reawaken, what must be for real this time. The pain is still obvious, but lessening, and the relentless blindfold still covers my eyes. And it was good that I'd imagined that Chi had told me not to itch, or else there would be nothing to hold me back from digging under my bandages, and possibly causing inalterable damage—if what is said in dreams can be believed.

For a long while, I am as still as death, not moving a muscle, like Chi had told me to do... but I cannot hold this rigid position forever, and when I adjust my head on the pillow, and move my restless feet, my bed makes a squeak, which alerts a nearby voice that I loath in an instant.

"Are you awake?" Tau's voice asks, not more than a few feet away from me, and from the angle of his voice he must be laid out on a bed as well.

But I don't answer: he doesn't deserve it. Though he's considerably persistent, so my non-response doesn't seem to matter.

"They wheeled my bed in here. They said it would be good for us to be together while we're recovering," he adds.

Even with my eyes closed and covered, I know I am making a snide grin. "Why? So it'll be easier for you to kill me once they take your bandages off?" I say.

"What!" Tau gasps. "Is that what this is all about?"

"Of course," I answer. "You shot Chi. I heard you. What would make me think I'd be any different? But I'm not going to let you get away with it. I'll tell them what you did, and they'll have you retracted, or they'll take away your citizenship. It's what you deserve."

Now he's laughing at me, softly at first, but then growing louder; that arrogant beast is laughing.

"You're so dumb." And he laughs all the more.

That petulant creep thinks he can talk to me like that. "I am not," I say, with the anger spilling out of my voice, so he can hear it.

"Fine," he says like he's appeasing me. "Well, at least you're not very observant. First of all, you think I couldn't have shot you from a mile away, or when you were hiding under those leaves and dirt in the forest?"

He saw me? Why wouldn't he have shot? He could've gotten both of us at the same time.

"Alright, well why didn't you?" I ask.

His voice is no longer laughing at me, and seems to be sincere. "Because I didn't have to," he says, "...but I did have to shoot Chi. I had to take him down before the other militants got to him, and would have wounded him more than I did."

So he didn't want Chi to suffer? There're a lot of other ways he could have gone about that without killing him with one shot. And when I explain that to Tau, this is his response, "I didn't kill anyone," he says. "Why do you think I'd practiced so hard, shooting their target dummies until I'd killed everyone of them a thousand times over? And until the militant trainers stopped making up new tests for me, and until I'd shot more times, and more accurately, than they'd ever wanted me to."

How should I know why? And that's what I tell him, and he takes a moment to respond, as if he's settling on the answer, himself.

"Because..." he finally says, "I realized a long time ago, when they first handed me a rifle, that they could shove a gun in my hands, that they could force me to shoot, and they could see where I shot, and exactly how I did it, but they couldn't pull the trigger. It wasn't them aiming the rifle; it was me. It was the only, one thing at the School the Common had no control over. And so I practiced killing, over and over again, so that when the time came, it would be me who'd decide whether I'd kill or not."

Then Tau goes on to explain, how the younger, inexperienced militants loaded up Chi's body into the rear of his transport, everyone else thinking the old man was dead, or nearly dead. So that afterward, when their bumbling search party had stopped along the return route to check through the forest again, Tau was able to easily shoot out the other transports' wheels, and rescue the only barely conscious Chi, taking him to where Chi had said to go, in dying whispers, "to the golden path over water, where the air smelt like the taste of tears."

"We found the golden path after sunset, and they found us, and blindfolded us again, taking us through the tunnels, buried deep underwater, until we got here," Tau explains.

"So you... saved his life?" I ask, utterly surprised that my hatred of Tau might have been illogical, and still, however, slightly confused as to whether or not Chi was actually alive, and if that had been the real Chi who'd come to visit me, or only a dream of him.

"No, technically. I brought him here, but it wasn't me who saved his life. His heart stopped when we got here, and they had to bring him back," he says.

All this is swimming in my head. Tau is not a murderer.

And from all his stories, and the cursory evidence, he seems like someone I can trust, someone to add to my oddly growing list of people whom I can be sure are not against me.

There are five on this list, maybe four (since Sarah only says that she's my sister, and there's no proof of it): I can trust myself, and Theta, Chi, and possibly Sarah, though time will tell, and now Tau. It is a strange feeling to trust so many people; it is like having your heart stretched thin and vulnerable. Though perhaps they'd feel the same way about me, from their perspectives, and so it might be an even trade.

The words are hard to come by, but they do come. "Thank you," I say, softly. My words are barely a whisper, but I know he can hear me.

We wait in silence for a few minutes, until he interjects, "I hope you know, this doesn't change anything," he says.

What is he talking about? His voice sounds so serious, though there's something in the underlying expression that would seem almost joking.

"...I'm still going to kill you when they take my bandages off," he says. Then he laughs, and we both do. We laugh at a joke we've made, just between the two of us, and no one else knows it is happening. There is no one to watch us, or to monitor our words. And we can laugh without fear of being caught, or punished, and there is no other laugh more meaningful.

25

We talk in between times of rest and sleep, and dulling pain, and Tau speaks more about my rescue, and about what he knows of this underwater city. They call this place Logos. It was built upon the remnants of a *research* station. Though when I ask what the half-men could have been searching for, here below the water, Tau is uncertain.

Since its early days, the whole city has grown outward from its initial bounds, and underwater tunnels were added over time, so that they could access the station in secret, without having to expose their underwater location.

But we did that, I tell him, when we crashed our transport into the water. The Common would certainly find our empty transport, and our bodies would be absent from the wreckage. "They'll find the station now, won't they?" I ask.

Though he is unsure about this. And when Sarah comes to visit us, she explains that their city's unusual location has made them undetectable, thus far, to the Common's air drones and thermal scanners, that cannot detect our heat, so far below the water.

"So we're safe?" I ask.

Sarah's voice wobbles with what could be uncertainty.

"Safe from the Common, maybe," she says. "But Tau and I disobeyed direct orders, when I helped him through the tunnels, so he could find you."

He broke orders to come find me? "Orders... from whom?" I ask.

"From the *elected* officials," Sarah explains. Though she then has to explain her words. An *election* is what happens when the people get to choose who will lead them, and they can choose from amongst themselves. There is no Leaders' ranking, here, no class of people who will always lead. It is a choice.

"And will you both be retracted, because of me? Will they revoke your citizenships?" I ask.

However, Sarah tells me that that is not how it works here... but they are both completely uncertain about what will happen to them.

And we all continue to be unsure, until the day the doctor comes to remove Tau's bandages, and he can see. He can see on his own, without his visual sensors, but he does not see good things.

"Come with us," I hear a man's voice say to Tau.

Tau speaks loudly to describe what is happening, for me. "There are three militants here, with guns," he says. "They're taking me with them."

The sound of boots knocks the metal ground as they leave; and also neither Chi, nor Sarah, comes to visit me for the rest of the day. And when I ask my medical attendant, later on, about Tau and Sarah's situation, she says that she has not heard anything about their judgements, but that she could not tell me anything, even if she had.

And the world is much darker, as the days and nights pass on in cycles, until the doctor comes to unwrap the bandages from my eyes. Light, blurry at first, then seen more clearly. There is the doctor's face. She looks satisfied with her work, and is pleasantly smiling at me, but just beyond her is presumably the same set of three militants in blue uniforms; their hands are all tightly griping the barrels of rifles.

"Alpha Robins, please come with us," the center militant says to me.

What happened to Tau and Sarah? At first glance, this place doesn't seem any different from the School, or from the Common. I have to do what they say, and they have guns to make sure of it. Though when I try to follow them, my legs buckle, and I collapse to the ground, and they have to lift me into a wheeled chair. I have not walked in days, in more than a week. My legs must have forgotten their natural ability; so that very literally, there's no way I can escape from them.

▪ ▪ ▪

I am wheeled through the city. Arched metal corridors split off in various directions, like veins from our larger central path. My chair wheels hit all the grooves in the floor, and the dips in the worn metal plates thump in repetitious increments.

My dilated eyes, that have remained forcibly shut more often since I left the School than they have been allowed to be opened, they are still having trouble tracking movement, of which there is a lot. There are people dressed in whatever randomly, or oddly assigned uniforms the city has provided for them. These people dart between hallways, within arm's reach in front of me, and behind me. Though as soon as they catch a glimpse of my face, they stop in their places, whispering to near bystanders, or gasping on their own.

My wheels beat continually on the uneven metal floor plates, that look like they could have been collected from any assortment of rubbish piles, and placed together to give only the appearance of a floor, wherein each tile could have come from a separate garbage heap. In fact, all the walls, this whole place seems to be loosely sealed together with scrap and parts. What a terrible way to build a city.

A drop of water falls from the ceiling and hits my lap as my chair is pushed along. And what an inconceivable way to build a city, underwater. Even one, solitary, meagerly aimed bomb could sink this whole place; I'm sure of it.

As we pass a nearby corridor, an infant male, roughly five or six years of age, gawks at me with extra wide eyes.

"Why do they look at me like that?" I say to the militant who pushes my chair.

"Because they've never seen you before," he says.

"Yeah, well I've never seen them either," I answer.

"Yes," he says, "but you're the only person here they've never seen." And he adds, "We don't get many visitors."

156

Another drop falls, and splashes on the center of my forehead. "I can't imagine why," I say, out loud, but mumbling the words, semi-intentionally.

And as I say this, we've arrived at the end of the long central hall, and a set of doors swings open for us to enter by. At first glance, it's clear to see we've come into the technological hub of the city, but technology in loose terms, if you'd not known what else to call it.

There are large black wires set on tables all around, and strung into the backs of absurdly bulky and cumbersome display monitors. And none of these display monitors are the same, and some of them have brightly colored backings, though some of them have no backings at all. Even my simple display monitor, on the surface of my desk at the School, must have at least twenty to thirty times the output capability of one of these mangled devices.

Why would these technology ranks appear to be working so intently, with such inadequate equipment? And what could they possibly be doing?

As my wheeled chair glides by a close display monitor, on the screen a gridded circle is swept by a singular solid line, and each time the line makes another rotation, a row of dots moves gradually nearer toward the center of the circle. After we pass that monitor, a young man standing in the middle of the room, who seems to be in control of the whole group of technology ranks, he calls out to another man seated in front of that nearer monitor, and this lesser technology rank does not turn away from his work at the monitor, busy analyzing the strange circle and spinning line, and dots on the screen.

"Let me know if they get within a half mile," the head technology rank says to the other man at the monitor.

"Yes, sir," the lower technology rank answers quickly.

My chair is pushed over bundled wires, and out of this room, and into another: into a room with six men and women (four men and two women), who could not be mistaken for any others but the city's elected officials. And they are all seated on one side of a long rectangular table, with seven seats total, and its center seat is left empty.

A man sitting to the left of the empty chair begins to speak, and his voice is firm but not harsh. "I wish we'd had more time for pleasant conversation, but given the circumstance, we will begin," he says, staring directly at me. He glances to his right and left, perhaps to see if any of the other officials would like to make a statement, but none of them do, and so he continues; and in the low lit light, there is a subtle reflection on his balding head.

"Why are you here?" he asks, letting all the cordiality he seemed to have before, melt away.

Because three militants with rifles came barging into my medical quarters, and forced me to come with them... is what I'd like to say, but don't, since he's obviously asking about why I came to their city, generally, and not about how I came to this room, specifically.

"Chi brought me here," I answer.

The man replies, almost instantly. "And how did Chi know how to find this place, who told him about us?" the man asks.

It's something I'd never really considered, and maybe I was foolish to never ask about it. "I don't know," I say. "We never talked about it."

"So, then the two of you spoke about leaving, while you were at the School?" another man with dark curled hair at the end of the table says.

"No... not really," I answer.

And when asked what "not really" would mean, I'm forced to explain that we never shared our plans aloud, but that we either used the process of palm-writing, instead, or else we spoke in code, which once I describe what it means to "speak in code," they seem to be appeased, and continue their questioning.

The serious-voiced man is flipping through individual pieces of writing material, and appears to be pressed for time. "We've heard that Chi was shot, and you were left alone, is that true?"

I nod a "yes."

"And after this, how did you find your way to the *bridge*, without any help?" he asks.

"Bridge?" I ask, since I can't answer his questions, if I don't know the meanings of their many arbitrary words.

A gentler sounding woman, with tightly pulled back hair, seated at the opposite side of the empty center seat, she speaks up, since she can obviously tell I don't understand his question. "Alpha, how did you get to 'the path over water,' without help?" she asks.

The whole group has their eyes locked onto me. It's tremendously uncomfortable, but at least this is only an interrogation of words, and not a torturous one.

"I walked," I tell her. "I just did what Chi told me to do... and I found it," I say.

"And were your eyes closed the entire time?" the first man asks.

"Yes, sir."

The man at the end of the table who'd spoken before interrupts. "But Tau reported, that you did not have a blindfold on when he found you, is that true?"

And of course that's true as well, and that fact does make me appear to be a liar. "I waited until Chi said it was safe to take the blindfold off, until the air smelled like the taste of tears," I say.

And it takes me a long while to fully explain to them, in a way that will satisfy them, at what time I had my blind-fold off, and how far away from the golden bridge I was when that occurred. And once I've done my part, they continue to argue amongst themselves about the finite details of my account, going on at length about the strength of sig-nal jammers, and other things that I don't fully understand.

In all this, it seems their overall concern now, is that the Common could have been allowing us to escape, and that we might have unknowingly been leading them here. Though unfortunately, after all their questions it's hard to say if I've made them feel any better. But since there's no way to know for sure, if the Common was able to track Tau and me, once we crashed below the cold water (what they call the *Ocean*), they begin to ask me other questions.

Namely, why did I leave the School?

160

And I tell them my whole story: about the late-night retractment, and my progenitor, about re-evolution (which causes them to smirk at me when I say this, perhaps I am mispronouncing it), about Theta, and Delta, and the Disciplinarian. How I was helped by the Schoolmaster, and how Chi and I escaped at night, when it was no longer safe for me at the School. And about how he and I walked for days, until he was shot, and about my survival from that point on.

And when I have finished, the woman official, who'd spoken before, says, shaking her head, "You poor thing..." And then she continues, saying, "Alpha, do you know why your father was captured? Has anyone told you that?" she asks.

"No," I say.

She has already started to tear, wiping drops away from her face, and strangely smiling even while she's crying. "He was trying to rescue you... and—" she says, but the head technology rank from the other room shouts loudly, interrupting her.

"Half a mile. Lights out!" he orders. And at once something triggers all the display monitors, and every single light to be switched off. We are in complete darkness, but I've been in darkness so often lately, that this doesn't even bother me. And nothing in my body flinches when this happens; it's like my natural state has become darkness, and light is what's strange to me now.

The head technology rank's voice is projected through a public address system, coming through an audio speaker in the ceiling. His voice is barely above a whisper.

"This is not a drill," he says, almost silently. "Absolute... quiet," he adds, letting the words drag on for emphasis.

And everything is quiet, presumably every citizen of this city waiting in utter darkness. Nothing moves, and it is only now in the pervasive stillness that I can hear the city walls creak and moan. They might have always done that, but it was regularly so loud that I'd never heard it before.

And the only thing that is not darkness, is that singular display monitor with the line rotating within the gridded circle, and a set of three dots that are for the moment positioned at the exact center of the circle. Though there must be something odd and perplexing about this particular instance, because the lead technology rank is breaking his own orders, and is speaking with the man at the display monitor. There must be something unprecedented or unusual about the data that shows on that lone screen, or else they would be silent like all the rest of us. And they continue on at length, until it is safe again to speak and to have the electricity switched back on.

The lights shine with a blinding irritation. There are running footsteps into the room, and the lead technology rank bursts through the open doorway, and address the six elected officials, even while our eyes are still adjusting to the returning light.

"It's not a regular signal ping," he says, not explaining what a *signal ping* is, possibly assuming we all will know what he means.

Though the elected officials seem to understand. "Then what is it, Andrew?" a previously quiet, female official asks.

"Alright," he begins to explain, taking in a readying breath. "You know how the drones will usually send out a signal, just to see if it will get bounced back, something nonsensical usually, like some *high-pitched frequency*, nothing audible to the human ear, but something that only a set of active audio sensors could hear?"

The elected officials are nodding their heads, acknowledging that they understand the process.

"Well, this time it's more than that... it's also a message," Andrew adds. And without a warning, or being asked to do so, he motions to the man at the near display monitor, who then projects the Common's hidden message across all screens at once.

But it is not a written message as I'd expected, or something from the Leaders—it's her. It's a recording from a visual sensor. It's someone's recorded memories, as he or she watches Theta seated in a wooden chair, against the background of a blank white wall.

I recognize that chair. It's the same one I sat in when I was called to the Disciplinarian's quarters. And that means, that this visual feed must be from his eyes staring at her. Shivers run up and down my spine. If there is one thing that I'd never wanted, it would be to see the world from inside the Disciplinarian's head. Ugh...

The Common must have known I'd be able to pick out that chair, and this location, and they've done it all to spite me.

She looks terrible. Her reddened hair is in dirty curls, matted and unkept. Her uniform is filthy, like she hasn't washed it in weeks. She doesn't deserve any of this, and before this she'd never even received a legitimate demerit. She was perfect before I started making trouble, and now she's only being beaten, likely, and misused, because I'm not there to take it myself. I was a coward to leave. I should have known they'd do this to her.

Air struggles to fill into her lungs, and she stares ahead blankly. Thick ropes tie her hands to the arms of her wooden chair. Theta is being punished for all the things that I did, and she's in their control, fully.

"Alpha," she says, with almost no life in her words. "This will serve as your final warning, if you are indeed still alive."

She would never say this. The Common must be in her head, telling her what to say.

"Unless you surrender yourself immediately, I will be sent to a retractment. And I will lose my citizenship, forever..."

She takes in another audible, painful breath.

"My citizenship for yours... But know, you can never *get away*," she says, emphasizing "get away." She doesn't want me to trade myself for her. Since she must know it wouldn't matter, regardless. They'd just as soon kill the both of us, if they could.

"This is your chance to do what is required," she adds. *Required* is anything that the Leaders have decided must be done. It is the name for things they have asked you to do, and even the name itself leaves you no choice. "This is your final chance," she says. "You have six days."

And with those last words her face is frozen upon each display monitor, in a weak and awful state, her eyes piercing through the screen at each of us. She's not normally this frail, and I'd like to explain that to everyone here, for her sake, but it seems so obviously the case that I don't mention it. And instead, I say something else that is plainly seen.

"They're hurting her," I announce, with an infantile expression in my voice that is unflattering.

"I would be surprised if they weren't," the serious-voiced male official, who is seated near the empty center chair, says. "It is only in their nature to be unkind, and ruthless, and all the baser parts of man."

"We have to help her," I say as forcefully as I can, considering my own fragile state, from my seat in a wheeled chair.

"No," he says.

"No?" I say, disbelieving. How could they sit there and do nothing to try to save her? Or at least if they can't save her, then they should at the minimum try to pretend that they might, for my sake. It's meaningless to say that the Common is ruthless, when they all seem to be exactly the same. These elected leaders are no different.

The first lady who spoke, the one with her hair pulled tightly back, begins to speak again. "Alpha, you're fortunate enough that we've even agreed to take *you* in, after you'd exposed the city to so much irreparable danger"—then she speaks more casually and quickly—"and it's only for the reason of your father's position that we've even allowed it."

My face gives the same confused look that it gives to Sarah when she says something, and I have no idea what it means.

"What? Did my father have some high ranking? Is that why you're not punishing me?" I ask.

For a second, the woman with the tightened hair seems surprised that I would even ask the question. "No, no, we don't... we don't have rankings here," she tells me as she glances toward her right, toward the empty chair beside them all. "I wonder what else no one's told you, if you don't even know this. No, your father... did not have a ranking, like you mean it; he was chosen for the most important elected office in the city. He was our mayor," she says, and she glances toward the empty chair again.

Then the first man speaks again. "Yes, and as acting Mayor, I can say that we cannot risk the resources, nor the manpower, endangering the city, to go whisking away on some blatant suicide mission."

He takes a pause, then speaks again, this time with a calmer tone. "I'm sorry... there's nothing we can do to save her," he says with some spark of empathy, but not so much that it would be significant. "All in favor of non-engagement, say 'Aye,'" he says looking to his right and left, to address the other elected officials.

"Aye," they all say with varying levels of reluctance.

"It's unanimous. The ayes have it," he says, and he slaps the table top in some formal way with the palm of his hand, perhaps to signal that they have made their decision.

All this saying "Aye", and hitting tables must be what Sarah called a *vote*. And they've made their choice starkly clear. I have no way to save Theta from retractment, since the elected officials won't get involved, because it would risk the city's safety, a city that is so haphazardly built and fragile as it is.

And as I am wheeled back to my medical quarters, I can't help but think about how strange it is that Chi risked so much to bring me here to this city, where it is safe, and now all I can think to do is leave. I mean, what good is it to be safe, if you can never go out and face the world as it really is? It works out fine for them to vote against saving Theta— they're not her, and if she were able to vote I think she'd give a much different response. Yet since she cannot vote, I'll have to be the one to speak for her. I'm going to find a way to rescue her from the Common, and I'm not about to let six people I've never met before tell me otherwise.

My chair beats on the warps and divots in the metal city floor as I am pushed through the central hallway toward my room, and another large drop of water falls, splashing into my lap from the ceiling. I let out a subtle smirk that maybe only I'm aware of. Just because they call a place like this "safe," doesn't mean that it is.

26

When I arrive again at my medical quarters and the interior second airlock door opens, there is Tau, seated on his bed, and staring at me with the same expression he usually has stuck onto his face—overconfident, and presumably smug, like he has always half a mind to make fun of you, but he is normally good enough to keep it to himself, except for right now.

"Look at you, getting pushed around in a wheeled chair, like a regular Leader rank," he says, seeming playful in his joking, and not as condescending as he could have been.

The militant rank pushing my chair stops near the foot of my bed, and my voice strains as I both struggle to my feet, and also try to explain myself to Tau, "I haven't walked in days," I say.

"So... you've just decided to give up on it?" he replies.

"No," I answer, with my legs throbbing from that small walk, but at least I could do it. "I fell over when they came to get me." Our doors open and shut, as my militant escorts leave the room, and we are now completely alone. "I tried—" I start to say, before he cuts me off, as soon as our doors are closed.

"What about Theta?" he asks in hushed voice.

That sneak, he was only teasing me to avoid suspicion.

"They won't help her," I say. "They say, 'It's too dangerous for the city.' "

"I know," he says, "as I was leaving the confinement hall, her video was playing on the display monitor. My militant guards said the same thing. They said, 'Haven't you done enough damage already? We can't risk another rescue.' "

"Well, if you knew, then why did you ask me about her?"

"Because that's not what I meant—I meant what are we going to do to save her?" he asks.

I hold up my emaciated leg by the thigh, to show him how weak it is.

"I can't walk, remember?" I say.

A knowing grin flashes upon his face, and he motions his head toward the door, to where our militant guard just left from. "That's what they think... but you can walk, I just saw you."

In a second, the idea comes upon me as well, and I can see what he's getting at: if they think I can't walk, then they likely aren't worried that I'll escape, which means now, tonight, is my only realistic chance for leaving, but it has to be soon, before they think I've had time to recover.

My legs shake and burn as I attempt to stand. And feebly moving my lower limbs, the weight shifts from my left then to my right, but my aching knees buckle before I can walk any further. There is a smack on the rattling metal floor that would give us away for sure, if it happens again.

169

And Tau hurries over to lift me off the ground. "Can't you fall any quieter than that?" he jokes, though with some seriousness lingering in his voice. "Keep going," he says, letting me stand again under my full weight. "If you're going to save her, then you're gonna have to learn to run... and you better do it quickly."

Four steps this time, and I fall again, though Tau catches my arm before my knees hit against the ground. And over and over again we walk the room in circles, and we lay in our beds when the medical rank comes to fed us our night-time meals, and to check on my condition. Which, as far as he's concerned, is that I still cannot walk at all, and I make a great show at helpless weakness when he bends and stretches my legs and feet for a nightly therapy.

And when he leaves, the lights in our quarters dim to simulate our curfew time. My head is laid on my pillow as we wait for an appropriate chance to sneak away. If this were any other day I would already have fallen into an exhausted sleep, but this is so much more important than any regular day. We have to escape, and there won't be any sleeping tonight.

But unexpectedly, there are footsteps softly striking outside our quarters. Then the outer door opens. No one ever comes to check on us, after the lights have dimmed. They must have heard us practicing, or our medical rank as tipped them off, and they've realized our intentions.

A swooshing sound, the inner door slides open, but it is not a militant, or a medical ranking like I suspect—it's Sarah.

She is wrapped up from head to toe, in a thick uniform, like she is headed somewhere where she will need the extra warmth. "Good, I haven't missed you," she says.

"What makes you think you'd miss us?" I say, casually keeping our true intentions hidden, which makes her give a noticeable look of disbelief.

"You're still leaving tonight, aren't you?" she asks.

Thoughts flood through my head of all the ways I could lie to my sister, but Tau never lets me get to them. It's as if he'd almost preferred for her to come along with us.

"Yes," he says, his voice stirred with his familiar overconfidence.

Silently, she cheers the fact that we are leaving, and that presumably she'd be allowed to join with us, although we'd never agreed to that. And the worst of it is now there're three of us—just fantastic. I wonder if everyone is as bothered by their sisters as I am. Three of us makes it harder to escape without getting caught, harder to travel. A party of three is not ideal, and she should know that.

But there's still one part of this that doesn't make sense. "Who told you we were leaving?" I ask, glaring down my nose at her.

"Chi did," she answers, as if I should have known that. She comes to sit at my bedside. "He said that there was no way you wouldn't try to help her, and he wishes he could come along, but this is something we'll have to do on our own."

I'm sure Chi's wounds would make it difficult for him to travel with us, but how can I trust this girl I've only just met? And she must see this distrust in my eyes, since she punches me squarely in the arm, sending a twinge of pain pulsing in my body, as if I wasn't mistreated enough.

"Oh, stop it, you brat," she says. "I'm on your side."

She's got a lot of nerve to strike me in the arm, and then say she's on our side. "You can stop hitting me, please," I grumble, as I rub the sore sting from my arm.

But we don't have time for these infant-ish quarrels—we need a plan—which is what I announce to the group with some certitude, knowing we don't have time to fool around, saying, "We've only got six days... we need a plan."

"We'll need a transport," Sarah says. "Primus is over..."—she pauses, possibly thinking over the distance in her head—"two thousand miles away from here, and that's where they'll hold the retractment, for sure."

"And we'll need weapons, or at least I will," Tau says, as if he's the only one who's worth anything with a weapon, which is almost entirely true, so I let it go.

And Sarah says that they keep the weapons near the entrance to the underground tunnels, and beyond the tunnels are the transports. "But the city's only got four of them left"—she glances at Tau—"so please be careful this time," she says.

Only four? Only four what... tunnels, weapons, transports? She probably means transports, since we sunk the last one, and one would hope they'd have at least more than four weapons.

"I'll be as careful as I need to be," Tau answers, in his own casual way, but Sarah gives him a look.

"You'll be careful, this time," she repeats, slowly.

"Fine," Tau answers. "We'll bring it back safely... nothing to worry about."

So there we have it—weapons, and a transport, but I still have to hobble through the underground tunnels to get to them, and Sarah says that those tunnels can go on for miles. It's one thing to walk in circles around my tiny quarters a few times, but that doesn't mean I'm healthy enough yet to walk for miles on still weak legs in darkened tunnels. And so Sarah goes to find me something that might help, and she comes back a few minutes later with a comfortably padded crutch.

"Thank you," I say, when she hands it to me, and I hold it for a few minutes feeling the sturdiness of it, and the cushioned arm pad. This is not something the Common would have ever given me, simply because I'd asked, just because I'd needed it.

"It's weird, isn't it?" Tau asks me, seeing my response.

I nod, a silent nod of recognition.

"What's weird?" Sarah asks.

Tau pulls his fingers through the front of his hair, before he speaks. "At the School, every time you get injured, you get demerited or de-ranked," he says. "And if it's really bad, and they can't use you anymore, they'll take your citizenship."

Sarah looks at me, while I'm still holding my crutch. "That's awful," she says.

"It's just weird to get something for nothing, simply because I need it," I say.

She leans down, and puts her lips against my cheek. I shudder at the intrusiveness of it, and wipe the lingering wetness from my face.

"What was that for?" I say, quickly and in an accusatory way, which is what she deserves for being so awkward, and disgusting.

But her answer doesn't make any sense. "You needed that too," she says.

Though honestly, how could I need something like that? And the place where her lips met my cheek still burns with an uneasiness.

"I think I'd rather have you punch me," I say, which catches her by surprise.

"You are a brat," she scoffs.

27

When we leave the medical quarters, the city corridors are dimly lit all around us to simulate their nighttime. The end pad of my crutch rattles the flat metal floors more than a normal footstep might, though only slightly more. But there's nothing that I can do about it, and at least I can keep up, as Sarah leads us through winding halls with ever contracting walls and ceilings.

We turn into a hallway, and Tau uses a militant hand signal, holding a tightened fist in the air, which I guess means to stop.

"What is it?" Sarah whispers.

"Shh," Tau answers with an almost silent shush.

There's nothing to be heard. Maybe he thought the end pad of my crutch scuffing the ground was someone following us, but the only things audible are the ever faint and persistent moanings of the city as the water outside is perpetually trying to break down its walls.

We continue on, and pass through a circled doorway and sneak to the end of a long, straight, low-roofed hallway. At the end, there is a door with a wheeled handle which Sarah turns to open, and we come into a completely black room, and she closes us in before activating the room light.

My eyes blink and water as they acclimate to the light, but when they adjust, there's nothing I can do to keep from smiling.

Weapons, glistening in bright light, shining off the barrels of rifles and stacks of ammunition in crates and organized upon shelves. With all this, maybe we do have a chance of saving Theta. But instantly my mind flashes back to my single day of militant training, and to the target dummy I couldn't even shoot, without Tau to help me pull the trigger; and if I can't even fire at that, how can I ever aim at a real person? And would Theta even want that? Is her life worth all the bullets it would take to save her?

My eyes are glazed, and slightly overwhelmed, as I reach for some gun to take, and it freezes in my grasp.

And Tau breaks my trance.

"Hey," he says to snap me back to reality. "That's a shotgun, infant," he says, being especially arrogant. "You'd never get close enough to use that," he adds, taking the gun from out of my hands, and replacing it with a thin long barreled rifle with an extended scope. "The further away the better, right?" he says.

I should have known better, and I feel even more useless than I did before. "Yeah, of course," I say.

Sarah is busy searching through various crates of ammunition, and through sets of elaborate eyewear. And while she's occupied, I lean over to Tau and ask if he'll pick out the rest of my equipment, since I obviously don't know what I'm doing.

He nods in agreement; and as he helps to strap a double handgun harness across my chest, and clips of ammunition belted around my waist, he whispers so that my sister can't hear it, "You'll do fine."

Sarah's rustling through crates finally ends. "Here they are," she says, with an excitement on her face, and delicately carrying a pile of new ammunition clips in her arms that seem to be special by the way that she holds them.

"What are they?" I ask, still trying to adjust to the new weight of guns and bullets draped around me.

"They're stun bullets," she says.

Tau is pulling apart a new rifle for himself, inspecting the stock and barrel, and every inch of it, but he's given enough peripheral attention to us, to make a comment. "Doesn't that miss the point of a bullet?" he adds, as he's locking his rifle barrel back in place.

Her voice harshens as she tries to make her point. "No," Sarah says. "These are better than real bullets, 'cause you don't have to kill anyone."

An honest smile fills onto my face. This is what we'd needed all along, a way to save Theta, without creating more murder for ourselves.

I pick a stun bullet out of the pile in her hands, and I feel the polished metal casing between my fingertips. They're the same as any other bullet, so you'd never be able to tell them apart.

"How long do they work for?" I ask.

"Maybe an hour," she says, "but I've never shot anyone before, so it's just a good guess."

Tau flings the strap of his extensively examined and reassembled rifle over his shoulder. And he adds to the conversation while he's loading his gun with real, killing bullets. "And what about when they wake up in an hour, and they're trying to kill you again?" he says. "They sure won't be firing stun bullets at you." He fits the last bullet in the chamber. "Don't fool yourself. I was a militant rank for over ten years—to them, you're nothing but a target dummy who needs to be shot."

There's nothing to say; he's right... but if we only think of them as target dummies for ourselves, then are we any different from them.

"I'll take some," I say to Sarah. Her face lights up again with excitement, as I take several handfuls of stun bullet ammunition clips and add them into our already over-weighted munitions bag.

"Tau?" she says, offering him the remaining bullets.

Though he only takes a few select rounds of ammunition, tossing them into his pack. "Thanks," he says, like he might never use them anyway.

Sarah scowls at him.

"You'll thank me when you're still alive after this," he replies.

A footstep rattles outside the weaponry room door. Tau reacts with a flashing speed, picking a handgun out of my double side holster, and aiming it at the doorway; aiming a loaded handgun, with real killing bullets, at a citizen of the underwater city—not a Leader of the Common, not a mindless militant, but a regular citizen, and one that I recognize. It's Andrew, the lead technology rank who was first to tell us about the signal from the drones, and about Theta's hidden video message.

Andrew's face is pale, but he's making a show of being unfrightened. "What are you planning to do with those?" he asks.

Tau steadies his aim onto Andrew. "You never saw us —" he begins to say, but Sarah interrupts him, stepping between the trajectory of Tau's gun and this foolish technology rank.

"We're going to save her," she says, like she knows this intruder well.

"Are you so sure?" Andrew asks, giving a distrusting glare at Tau and me. "They've been *brainwashed* by the Common, Sarah. They're not capable enough to even *cook* a meal for themselves, and you think they can travel across the *continent*, break into Primus undetected and save this girl, who might even be dead already. It's a blatant trap... and what if they, instead, take these guns and murder everyone in the city?"

"They wouldn't do that," she says.

But Tau still has my handgun trained upon the forehead of this technology rank, which is indirectly proving his point.

Gently and gradually, Sarah reaches her hand out and pulls Tau's aim down, until the sight of his gun is aimed at the floor.

"You think you can trust them, but you can't," Andrew adds.

I adjust the weight of the rifle in my hands. "She can trust us," I say, being as determined as I can. If we were back at the School, I would tell him to review my memories, to see how trustworthy we are. But it's a completely different world here; it's much more wild. And who could trust anyone in a place where we all keep our memories hidden, and where trust is only blindly hoping someone will tell you the truth.

"Is that right?" he taunts. "Alpha, you know nothing about yourself... you know nothing about the *birthing farm* where you were born. You've never met your mother or father, and you've only just met Sarah a few days ago." He turns to Sarah. "He's not your brother yet, Sarah. He doesn't even know what that means."

I want to glare at him, but a part of me knows he's right.

"But anyway, it doesn't even mater," he goes on to say. "This is a ridiculous mission. Even if you steal another transport, which I'd imagine would be your plan," he says, ending his statement with a glance at Tau, "you'd never make it to Primus, and even if you did, by some bizarre chance, you'd never make it past the city's drone net, or the constant scanners, or the army of militants, and it only takes one,"—he holds up his pointer finger for emphasis —"only one person has to see you and it'll trip the facial recognition scanners. It's statistically impossible to survive a mission like this, Sarah, and you know that," he says to her. "Your father couldn't even get by them... and he was a lot more prepared than you are."

He's right. I can't stand his condescending attitude, but he's right. The only one of us who could last more than five minutes against the full force of the Common would be Tau, and even he'd eventually run out of bullets. We can't kill the whole world to save Theta. And so we're going to have to do our best to hide, and who better to help us than someone who knows what we're up against.

I pull the extra handgun from my dual-sided holster and offer it to him. "Come with us," I say, holding the gun out to Andrew, but he doesn't take it.

He looks past me, addressing Sarah. "It's hopeless... it's suicide," he says, adding a strain to his voice.

"Please," I reiterate, holding the gun nearer to him to get his attention. "If you'd wanted to turn us in, you would have done it. And so there must be a part of you that hopes we can win.

"If you stay behind, you'll know you had a chance to save our lives, but you didn't take it," I say, and hold the weapon up nearer to him. "Please," I offer again, and he takes it.

"I'm not doing this for you," he tells me. "I'm doing this for her"—pointing toward Sarah—"and for your father."

Why does it matter what he does it for? As long as he can keep me alive for long enough to give me a better chance at rescuing Theta, he can help for whatever reasons that suit him.

"But, if I'm going to help you, then Sarah can't enter Primus. She has to stay back with me, " he orders.

Sarah gasps. "You can't tell me what to do," she says, protesting.

"I can if you need me," Andrew answers, finding a spare holster of his own to place his new gun into.

"Fine," Tau agrees, speaking for us all. And since I don't want for Sarah to place herself into any more danger than she is already in, I nod in agreement, as well.

Sarah must see how finely Andrew's assistance hangs on a thread. She is visibly stirring in anger, incensed with us boys for making all her decisions for her, but she eventually relents, and waving her finger at us with indignation, saying, "This is the last time I don't get a vote on something, is that understood?"

"Of course," Tau says, and I immediately agree, in turn. And Andrew does as well, though in his reluctance it's hard to say if he will keep that end of his deal.

There's no way yet that this technology rank has moved into the category of persons whom I trust: he's only just slipped from the category of outright distrust, so that he stands somewhere along the middle dividing line. He's not, at the moment, turning us over to the elected officials, but he's not presumably on our side either. He's helping us for his own reasons, and we have to be alright with that.

28

There is no room in the tunnels to stand up straight. I'm hunched over my crutch. The weight of my pack presses down on my back and wearied legs. It is filled to the top with meal rations, and extra uniform layers, and piles of added technological items, all of which Andrew calls "necessary", but none of which I can deduce a purpose for. But I had no time to ask, as we loaded up our packs, and our hands with weapons, and as we descended a ladder into the tunnels below the city—below what Sarah, and the elected officials have called the *Ocean*, the name for this large collection of water above us.

The straps of my pack dig into my shoulders. On the roof of the tunnel ahead, lighted boxes periodically flash vidid blue warning beams. And I know what these are for, from the first time I asked Sarah about them.

"What are detonators?" I asked, when she told me what those luminous boxes were.

"They're bombs that'll blast the tunnel if there's been a security breach," she said.

And that's all I can think about as my head lowers under another similar detonator.

I'd rather not drown in a sealed underwater tunnel. And even though Sarah has deactivated the city's perimeter system, like she did when Tau came to save me the first time, it's still hard to believe it will work a second time, even if Andrew is fairly sure it will. And so we hobble through the dim, enclosed tunnel. My legs teeter with every step and I would be useless without Sarah's crutch. The air in the tunnel is an old dampness, and we travel by way of lights worn upon our heads.

At the head of the line, Andrew is leading, with Tau following closely after. They are engaged in a serious discussion, evaluating Primus's known defenses, and strategizing ways to break through what would seem to be an impenetrable barrier of drones, and scanners of all shapes and sizes. But I am relegated to the back of the line with Sarah "keeping her eye on me." We continue on in strict silence, until she decides to break it with conversation.

"I'm proud of you," she says, with an unanticipated tenderness.

"What for?" I say, giving her a look that I'm sure she can't see in this darkness.

"You... you escaped the Common, and now you're willingly going back—that's brave of you," she says.

Every word echos slightly off the walls of the tunnel.

"You'd sacrifice so much to save this girl; she must really be a good *friend* of yours," she says with a peculiar inflection in her voice.

If this is what sisters do, simply prying into your life at all chances they can get, then I don't think I'll like having a sister at all.

"I'm sorry—I don't know what you mean," I announce, as plainly as I can, hoping that will end it.

"I bet you do know what I mean... you little liar," she says. Her voice sounds almost like she's joking with me, but I can't understand what for.

"No, I'm serious," I tell her, if it'll get her to stop teasing me. "I don't understand... What's a *fiend*?"

A sad breath comes out of her nose and mouth, as if she's been instantly deflated. "You mean friend?—Alpha, you don't know what a friend is?" Her voice is strained with concern.

And when I explain that that's not a word we had in the School, she tells me that a friend is someone to whom you can tell all your secrets, someone whom you can trust without reservation, a person who is not overawed when you are at your best, and is not turned away when you are at your worst.

And what she says settles for a moment, imprinting with the steady thud of my crutch pad on the tunnel floor. "Is it possible for someone to be more than a friend?" I ask. Which is what I think is a reasonable question, in case there are words I've not yet learned that might describe Theta even better, but Sarah can't even give a simple answer without mocking me.

"Oooowwwooo," she says, as if I could know what she was teasing me for.

"You're ridiculous," I say. "You make absolutely no sense—"

Tau and Andrew are stopped ahead of us. "This is it," Tau says, interrupting our conversation, to warn us that we've reached the end of the tunnel.

I can't wait to feel the outside air again. Andrew spins a wheeled handle at the center of the end door, which unseals and opens, giving us a view of the world above water and above ground. But it's not exactly that, like I'd suspected. Instead of the open world with its partially crumbled and deteriorated old buildings, it is yet another system of tunnels, but older and more dilapidated than the one we're currently in.

"We're still underground?" I say, as a general statement to the whole group, and Andrew responds.

"It helps to disguise the entrance to Logos... we can crisscross through these network of tunnels, and pop up anywhere within the Ruined City above us that we'd like."

He leads us through the door and seals it behind us. There is a dried sandy crust lining the lower portion of these still very dark ancient tunnels. My crutch pad slips and skids, and I nearly fall on top of the rifle in my hands, but Sarah catches me. These degenerated tunnels are not as easy to walk in as the previous ones.

"Were these tunnels built to hide from the Common?" I say to Sarah.

But Andrew speak up. He seems to be amused by what I've said, although it's impossible to know why.

"These tunnels weren't meant for people," he says, and he might be chuckling to himself, although he's so far ahead that it's hard to make out clearly.

186

That self-important snob.

"What is he laughing about?" I whisper to Sarah, assuming that that noise he'd made had been chuckling.

She pauses to whisper in return, but maybe loud enough so that everyone else can hear it as well. "These are *sewage* tunnels," she announces.

When once the purpose of a sewage tunnel is fully explained, I can't wait to leave, to be out in the real open air. We twist and turn through these winding filthy pipes. We continue on, and coming nearer is a long crack in the ceiling that fills with bright and real sunlight. Has it really taken us all night to make it through the tunnels?

But Sarah says that "nighttime" in Logos is not a true nighttime, which is how it could be daytime in the open world, and not there, underwater, where sunlight has no real bearing, either way.

We reach the sunlight and my legs find the rungs of a rusted metal ladder that is broken in places, and bends disconcertingly under my feet. My thigh muscles are almost so lifelessly weak that I cannot lift them, and the heftiness of my pack is pulling me away from the ladder. My fingers slip, and Tau grabs at my pack before I fall.

"You make it to the top, and I'll carry you the rest of the way," he offers me. Like I would ever ask for something so demeaning, though there's no way I'm going to turn it down.

My calves and ankles ache; one more step up the ladder. Only a few more strenuous feet and I won't have to move under my own power again, until we reach the transport.

Another step, and the sunlight glares in my face—another step and my hands find the outside world. My head and body slowly emerge, like I was a dead person coming back to life.

Tau grabs me by the waist and lifts me up onto his shoulder, along with the full weight of my pack and ammo, and with my rifle still strapped around me. There's no way I'll tell him to stop. I couldn't walk again today, even if I had to. My muscles are seized in place and burn with a remarkable discomfort.

By the way Tau carries me, I cannot see where we are going, only where we've been. This portion of the Ruined City is perhaps the most demolished. Though the one thing that can still be found, all over the ground and some that still hang above doorways, are these unexplainable stationary display signs. They all have similarly bizarre, lined drawings covering over all of them, but nothing that makes any readable sense. Howbeit, they can't just be drawings for drawings sake: by the structuring of them, they'd almost seem like words or letters. This must be an ancient form of half-men writing; it's the only thing that could explain them.

"They're Chinese," Tau tells me, but he has little more reliable information than that, and this information was passed along from Andrew, who might only be playing with us again.

What's a Chinese? If I ask, he'll tease me again for not knowing, and Tau, who is trying to establish himself as an expert on military matters, doesn't ask either.

We walk on for another long mile, with Tau still carrying me hoisted over his shoulder. With the added weight of my pack and ammunition, and weapons, I must be nearing one hundred and seventy-five pounds, but still he doesn't show any weakness, and if he's tired he's not mentioning it.

His feet crumble over a massive pile of broken building. And we are led into the break of a wall, into a room that is nearly intact, with towering shelves stacked five levels high. A thick layer of dust lays atop everything, over every box and crate. There couldn't have been anything here that has been moved in ages. Every step kicks up new layers of dust, and at the far end of a long line of shelves is a transport, hidden under its own layer of shabby dust, and with boxes stacked haphazardly around it.

This can't be the transport. It looks like a relic, and who could say if it even drives anymore?

"Is this it?" I ask.

"What, you don't like it?" Andrew answers. He's shoving aside boxes and opening the driver's door which is unlocked.

Tau sets me back on my feet. This is all a part of a disguise, he explains. Saying that, they throw dust and debris all over the transports to make them look old, but a careful eye will show fingerprint divots in the dust, indicating the transports are meticulously, yet secretly maintained. "This will get us there," Tau insists, which I'll just have to trust him on, since he has more experience with transports than I do.

Andrew crawls into the driver's seat. The front lights are

switched on, shining through a grimy layer of ashy dust. It's a working transport, hidden under rubble and ruin, and hopefully well maintained enough to carry us the over two thousand miles to Primus, across who can know what inhospitable landscape, on an almost hopeless mission. But I'm not going to think of it like that; it's only hopeless if we give up. And so, I'll hold on to whatever lingering hope we might have, for Theta's sake.

29

My eyes blink in and out of consciousness; and every time I come back to my awakened senses, the Ruined City is further and further behind us, toward what will soon become the setting sun.

I'm resting on the back row seat of the transport, which was kept clean inside, unlike its dusty exterior. Sarah is seated to my left, and my head leans drowsily against the window glass.

We can't drive at night—our dirty *headlights* would become too visible by the pale moonlight, so that we could be seen for miles. And with this knowledge, we speed away from the city, traveling by way of an old half-man route, trying to make as much ground as the transport, and the bumps and cracks in our chosen path will allow. But every sizable dip jolts my head upon the window glass, and I reawaken, but too tired to find a better sleeping configuration, and so it repeats on loop each passing hour, until we halt for the night, beneath the shade of an unimaginably wide tree, and as the evening sun finds its place below the horizon.

It's "nighttime shift," Sarah says. It's an extra tiredness from the differing schedule of Logos, and that of the real world. Though I would just as soon guess it was from not sleeping at all last night, however you would define night.

Though now that I've been in and out of sleep all day, I'm unable to rest when I should. We park beneath the shade of a giant tree, and pull out blankets from our packs to wrap up in, but my mind, which had finally a chance to rest, is unfortunately filled with questions.

Andrew and Tau haven't moved in the past quarter-hour, though it's hard to tell if they're truly asleep. My head turns toward Sarah, and my mouth fills up with questions, though I try to be quiet about it, to not wake the front row.

"Sarah..." No answer, only slightly louder this time.

"Sarah?" I say.

She turns in her seat, and half yawning, moans out a "Huh?"—which is possibly my cue to ask a question, if she is even awake enough to answer.

"If we're really related, how could you grow up in Logos, and I didn't?" I ask.

She yawns again and stretches, and tries to answer my question with her eyes closed and turning to face toward me, with her cheek leaned against the back of the seat. "I was a part of the Common," she says, "until I was six."

"You were barely older than an infant. How could you escape?" I ask.

"Um..." She pauses for much longer than would be reasonable.

"Sarah," I say with a quick whisper.

And she begins again as if she had never paused. "I was rescued during my transfer from the infantarium... me and my whole convoy." She yawns for a considerable amount of time. "Father intercepted the transports and saved nineteen of us, including Andrew." She pauses. "It would have been twenty, but one of the boys died during surgery, when the doctors tried to cut out his location sensor."

And she speaks again, saying, "He was always sad when he thought about that [probably referring to our father], and I don't know if he ever forgave himself for that... it was like he sacrificed that boy's life for my own."

"There's no way he could've known that would happen," I say.

Sarah breathes heavily, and her words exhale in a tired stream. "No, but every time we go against the Common there's always a *price to pay;* there's always a loss." She inhales with noticeable exaggeration, and begins her spew of words, again. "That's why we stopped fighting them— the elected leaders voted a long time ago for disengagement —they're just too big; nothing we could do to them would be worth anything, and they'd kill us all with one bomb, if they could."

She's right—we're nothing to the Common, to the Leaders. We're like ants to them.

Sarah's body is completely limp, laying against the seat, but I still have questions. "Sarah, wake up," I say, but there's no answer.

Andrew stirs in the operator's seat. "Let her sleep, Alpha," he grumbles.

Fine, I'll let her rest, but there's no one who says I have to give that same opportunity to Andrew, and especially not after he's laughed at me.

"Andrew... Andrew?" I say.

"What?" he asks, with an exhausted sharpness in his voice.

"You're so much older than Sarah, how could my father have saved you in the transport convoy?" I ask.

He chuckles, but not as demeaningly as last time. His head shakes as he begins to speak, "I am older than Sarah, but not 'so much older,'" he says. "The reason is, because I wasn't an infant... I was a first-year militant, out of a School, a separate School from the one you went to. And when your father raided our convoy, all the other drivers fought back, but I didn't... I dropped my weapon and surrendered, and your father let me live."

That's why he's helping us. That's why he didn't turn us in.

We wait for a few moments, wrapped up under our blankets, until I have another question, but it takes three times saying his name before Andrew will acknowledge me.

"This is your last question," he warns. "Make it good."

Of all the questions flooding my mind, this one seems oddly the most important. "What's revolution?" I ask.

He breathes out a surprised breath, as if my question had been unexpected. "What do you think it is?"

He's probably only asking this so that he can tease me again, but I'm beginning not to care.

"It's like, like re-evolution—like if you were already evolved once before, but you tried to do it again."

A big grin on his face twinkles in the moonlight. "That's good," he says. "I'd never thought of it like that... but no, it means, when you fight a strong power, to *overthrow* them..."

Overthrow? He must be searching for another word to replace "overthrow", since he might have correctly guessed that I hadn't known it.

" ...to, ah... to beat them, to win against them. It's a *war*," he says. Though he then has to explain the concept of war, which takes a few minutes but I think I have it.

A *war* is an event, in which one group fights another, for a considerable length of time, and for some overall reason. It's vague, but it does make sense.

And when I ask Andrew if my father had wanted to fight a revolution, his surprising answer is "no."

"No?" I say. "Then why talk about it, if he didn't want it?"

"Well, he didn't 'want it,' which is what you said—but he did think it was necessary to save Logos. He'd say in speeches all the time, 'We can't bury ourselves underwater and expect the world outside to change for the better. Anything the Common does not control it seeks to destroy, and we are at war, even if we never fight them.' "

My imagination plays out in my head, what the man in the retractment would look like, saying those things about the Common. But if even he was shot to death, why would we be any different? We're not any better than he was.

"Do you think we'll make it into Primus?" I ask.

No answer. I must have already generously used up my one remaining question, but I have to know.

"Andrew... Andrew, please," I say.

"You don't want me to answer that," he says. "Now go to sleep."

He's right. I don't want to know. He would say there's no chance we could ever make it, and he would have his good reasons for it.

The transport is quiet for hours. My blanket is pulled up to my neck, and I wait to be tired again, which eventually does happen.

30

The morning sun pours through the windows as we climb to higher and higher elevations. Our ancient half-men route is frequently scattered with rocks and immovably large boulders, which we always find a way to squeeze past. Except for once, as Tau and I have to strain to shove a considerably-sized stone out of our way and down a steep embankment.

Our early meal is a reconstituted powder, thickened with water, and eaten with the most unnatural metallic device, which Sarah calls a "spoon." The mixture sloshes in my mouth, almost gagging my choking reflexes with each slurp. What is this runny mush? It's not a nutrition square, and it's not a liquid, exactly, and it's not as thickened as nutri-mix. Instead, it's a waste of perfectly good liquid water, turning it into a dripping sludge. The dribble falls down the side of my cheek; and what is worse, Sarah has heated this filth, so that it's not only unpleasant and impossible to eat cleanly, but warm and drenched with so many overpowering flavors that it makes me almost literally sick.

"You don't like your soup?" Sarah asks, as if I could like it.

Our transport travels onward, passing through the highest parts of these rocky mountains, which seems a good enough name to call them as anything.

Is there a way to like this mess?

"Don't you have anything else, any nutrition squares?" I ask, after I slurp and swallow another labored bite. The contents of this *soup* slide around in my unsettled stomach.

Sarah insists that she doesn't have any nutrition squares, or nutri-mix either, that that's not what they eat in Logos. Though, I'm quick to say that I was given both nutrition squares and nutri-mix while I was in my medical quarters.

"That's because they wanted to make you feel comfortable, but that's not what we typically eat in Logos?" she says.

I don't know how people in Logos can suffer to eat this drool.

"Well, it's disgusting," I announce, with a line of soup dripping down my face.

Sarah gazes at me with an unimpressed expression. "It's supposed to be *creamy potato*... most people love it," she adds.

Then, Tau speaks up, bringing a quick end to my complaints. "I think you did your best, under the circumstances," he says.

But he must have been exaggerating his appreciation for this terrible soup, because only a few minutes later our transport is stopped, and he's vomiting on the side of the half-men route. And a minute after that, I'm joining too.

The acidic nature of my regurgitated soup burns in my

nose. And I drink more than my allotted water rations, just in order to get that awful taste out of my mouth.

Tau and I are composing ourselves, standing outside the transport, overlooking a high vantage point, as we stretch our legs, and try to recuperate from that vile soup. I take a swig of water and swish it between my teeth, then spit out the remnant over the ledge.

But Andrew is carefully watching our whole experience, and he snatches the water bottle from my grip, spilling some of it himself.

"We're not going to have enough water for the *desert*, if you keep spitting it out," he says.

He deserves to be hit. To punch his nose with my fist would be the easiest thing to do.

Instead of violence, however, I'm yelling, uncontrollably, "I don't know what a *desert* is—you never tell me anything, and then you laugh at me for not knowing," I yell. I would almost shove him to start a fight, but my hands refrain.

"Then ask a question, if you care so much," he replies.

"How am I supposed to know what questions to ask! You never use words that I understand, and so how am I supposed to ask any questions?" My hands move in exasperated motions as I try to make my point clear. "I don't know the questions to ask, because I don't know the words to ask them with."

Andrew is silent, holding his lips tight, very visibly thinking over what I've shouted at him. He blinks his eyes shut for a considerable amount of time, and when he opens them again, he speaks more gently.

"You're right." He shrugs his shoulders. "I'm sorry... I'll teach you *English*," he says.

I glare at him, unamused. "What's English?" I ask.

Sarah has run out from the transport, to see if she can sooth this situation.

And Andrew speaks again, sincerely, "I'll teach you the things you need to know... in order to ask questions," he says.

Excitedly, Sarah throws her arms around Andrew's neck, pulling him close to her, and she thanks him for softening to me. And then she does the same for me, wraps her arms around my neck and squeezes. Maybe there's a word for what she's doing.

I want to kick her away from me, but I finally take her mistreatment, begrudgingly. Her arms grasp around me more adamantly, as I slightly push her back. And so I again take it without fighting. There is a word to describe this situation... "surrender." She's beaten me, and I've lost my will to fight any longer. Maybe this is what all sisters do, look for ways to make you as uncomfortable as they can, until you lose your will to fight them.

31

Gritty sand whips across the front glass of our transport. Our route, hidden by years of blowing desert sand, is only barely visible, if you could call it visible at all. The only way we can tell that it might be an actual route is that there are less shrubs and bushes growing in a straight line ahead of us, and which continues on for miles and miles and is lost in the distance.

The sun beats on our transport, heating us up inside till we are sweating uncontrollably. Why did I ever spit out even one drop of water? So wasteful—Andrew was right to stop me.

The only good thing in all this, as Sarah explains it, is that our transport will never run out of fuel, as long as we're in the desert, since it has panels that contain a light collecting material on its roof, and which create fuel for the transport from the light of the sun. If Andrew had said it, I wouldn't have believed him, but since it was Sarah who said it, it must be true. Fuel from the sun? How could any-one believe that?

Puddling drops of sweat pool on my forehead. My hand wipes them away, but they quickly return.

"So... this is a desert?" I ask.

"Yeah," Sarah says, wiping a soaking hand of sweat from her own forehead as well.

"Pretty terrible, right?" Andrew answers.

Is that a true question, or a simple statement? It's hard to tell, so my mouth stays quiet and I don't answer. But instead I ask the relevant question, "How long does this go on for?"

"Maybe..."—he scratches his chin, probably thinking through his answer—"fifteen hundred miles. I've been told there are a few breaks in it, around larger *lakes* and rivers, but other than that, it's an unending wasteland for miles and miles," he says.

And likely because of his agreement to tell me more about the world, he explains to Tau and me about the true history of the desert and where it came from.

Long ago, the *Pre-Commons*, or the people who lived before the Common, they built great *farms* (places where meals are grown), but because of the massive amounts of open land required for these farms, the Pre-Commons removed all but a few of the natural plants that would typically grow in this region, and they replaced them with other plants, used for their food, that needed to be handled with extra care.

The people who were in charge of these lands were called *farmers*, and they lived here and cared for these food plants for centuries, until the Common was formed.

Howbeit, the Common, and its Leaders, despised the farmers. They considered their labors menial and ignorant, and so the Leaders of the Common made plans to forcibly confiscate the land from the farmers. And so, the Leaders sent out messages, this was before the days of implanted sensors, and these messages said that all the land, including all that the farmers had *owned*, would become the *property* of the Common, to be shared by all.

"Yeah right, 'To be shared by all,'" Tau scoffs. "When the Common takes something they don't ever give it back."

"And did the farmers fight the Common for what they had?" I ask.

The wind blows a hard blast against our windows, and for a moment nothing can be seen, except dust and sandy winds. Once it settles, Andrew answers, "Of course they did," he says.

They were the first to fight against the Leaders, and they were the first casualties of a *war*, or a succession of battles all for a singular purpose. This war that the farmers first fought, and then later those in the cities, it was called a *revolution*.

"So, is that where my father got the idea from?" I say.

"Yes, exactly," Andrew replies.

This revolution was fought for years, and continued on with lesser and lesser affect, as the Common solidified their powers. In the end, the total dead reached into the hundreds of millions, though by then the Common controlled everything, including the land of the farmers, who were all but dead.

But the Leaders, and specifically their newly assigned labor ranks, could not care for the farms in the same way that the farmers had done. And so their food plants quickly perished, leaving vast stretches of empty dirt, which then spread and grew, until the majority of the land that the Leaders had taken from the farmers was by then a useless wasteland.

"And that's the reason why you ate nutrition squares at your School," Andrew says, finishing his explanation.

"Because they killed all the other food?" Tau asks.

Andrew nods his head in agreement.

This must be the first time I've heard a detailed story of the past, or a *history* as Sarah calls it, and I didn't have to question its honesty. It sounded so true. There was a certain assurance in Andrew's voice, and a method in the words that he chose. It was nothing like our lessons in instructors' courses. Maybe there was nothing I've ever heard of past events that was completely true, until now. Years of my life, wasted with lies. Which makes me ask a new question, based on what I've learned.

Our path over the desert sand is a slow and repetitive journey. The sun is falling lower behind us.

"Were the Pre-Commons the same as half-men?" I ask.

Immediately Andrew forces the transport to a halt, and he turns to look at me. This is the most serious I've ever seen his face. His eyes stare into mine, with imperative.

"This will be hard to hear," he says to me and Tau, giving us his full attention. "There were never any half-men. The Leaders were never evolved from anyone. They only made up the stories about half-men to help explain away their actions. The Pre-Commons were all real people, just like you and I, though in a lot of ways better than us, I think. The Common murdered whole cities and families, anyone who stood in their way, millions and millions of real people, who were just as fully human as you or I."

The transport remains inexhaustibly quiet.

I knew it. Somehow I'd always known it, but I never let myself believe it, fully. It was the Leaders who were the real half-men, and not the people whom they killed. This is the true history of the Common, built with blood, and I hate them even more for it.

Under his breath, as the night creeps in around us, as we are stopped along an almost unnoticeable ancient buried route, Tau whispers, "Good thing I brought real bullets," he says—and who would blame him?

As brutally hot as the desert can be during the day, at night it is just as unsympathetic, and cold. Only after wrapping up securely in all the extra layers of uniforms I've brought, and after pulling my blanket over my ears can I stay warm.

In the morning my insufferable soup is barely swallowed down, and kept down. If this is what regular food is like, then I'll have to get used to it eventually, even though the flavors are so potent that they burn in my mouth, and churn in my stomach.

Sarah congratulates me for finishing my early meal for today. "See, it wasn't that bad," she says.

I have to stop this before it starts, before she thinks she can give me whatever dreadful Logos food that she wants. "Just because I'm not vomiting, doesn't mean I like it," I answer.

It's the first light of morning. We're standing outside the transport, finishing our meals, the only extended time during the day when we're not scheduled to be sitting, and I'm leaned up against the body of the vehicle, holding my empty bowl and spoon in my hands.

"You'll like it eventually," she says to me.

"I will not."

Sarah pauses, with her soup spoon stopped halfway between the bowl and her mouth. She stares at me, and the tiniest corner of her eyebrow raises before she begins to eat again.

The sun rays are quickly rising and warming the whole world, soon we'll have to leave.

"We need a plan," I say to the group.

After a second, Tau emerges from the opposite side of the transport. He says that we're going to need to show that we're serious—because of the high profile of this retractment, they're undoubtedly going to take her to the Stadium in Primus. And they're not interested in her retracting her treasons against the Common, so they won't allow her to speak, he says. Instead, they'll bring her onto the stage, so that the Leaders, and everyone with a visual sensor can see her slaughtered.

"But they won't do any of it, if they see a few of their fellow Leaders die," Tau says.

Sarah snaps at him. "We're not going in there to kill random people," she orders. She's adamant, but Tau seems to have already made up his mind.

Andrew interrupts. "Whatever we do, it can't compromise the safety of Logos," he adds. "That's their main prize.. they want Theta, to get to you," he says looking at me, "to get to Logos."

All their words and thoughts stir in my head: A few precise and public murders would never be enough, if it is like Andrew said, that the Leaders had killed millions of people just like themselves, in order to gain power. In that case, they're not going to care about a few of their own being shot, and who knows if it's even something that would concern them at all.

It's all those drones and militants, and the unnumbered amounts of visual sensors scanning for us through hundreds of thousands of pairs of eyes, that are the real problems. If we can only rescue her, just to be captured again before we leave Primus, and if we're all murdered in a retractment of our own, then what kind of plan is that. The Common is too big. You can't beat them. They'll win no matter what we do... and they'll never stop until they kill her. That's the only way this ends—it's with her death. That's it!

"We have to kill her," I blurt out.

"What?" Sarah says. Her face contorts at the thought of my bizarre statement.

Tau steps closer, and with concern says, "We're not giving up on her."

I have to better explain myself, before they think I've gone crazy. Shaking them away from me, I take a step from my spot leaning against the transport. My empty bowl and spoon move in my hands as I speak. "The only way this ends is with Theta's death—if the Leaders think they've killed her then they'll stop. And they'll assume that Tau and I are dead, because we never came to save her," I say.

Andrew speaks, looking out of the corners of his eyes at me. "How is *killing her* any different from not saving her? If you wanted to do that, we could have stayed in Logos," he says.

"It is different," I announce, reaching into the transport for our ammunitions bag as I stumble over myself, trying to make my point clear.

"But how?" Sarah asks, before I can find what I'm looking for.

There it is. I pull a bullet from an ammo clip, holding it between my fingers for all of them to see.

"Because... stun bullets," I say.

Sarah snaps at me. "That's a real bullet, Alpha."

My face reddens. These things all look the same.

"Alright, but I do have a stun bullet in here somewhere," I reply, skimming through the bag until I find an actual one. "We shoot her with this, and they'll assume she's dead, and we can save her after that."

"But they won't think she's dead if they don't see any blood," Tau explains.

The day is getting too hot for us to be standing around without shade for much longer.

"Then you shoot her with a real bullet, and I'll shoot her with this," I say, holding up my newfound stun bullet.

No one is saying "no," or telling me how much they

hate this idea, so maybe this is our plan now, incredibly basic, but better than the nothing that we had.

"Well it doesn't matter what we do, if we don't get there in time," Andrew announces, drawing us back to reality.

And filling into our seats, and with a newly developing plan, now the desert doesn't seem so wide, or Primus so impenetrable.

32

The sand passes by us, without break or end in sight. It is as if the desert were the ocean and the rolling *dunes* its water. And we drive on forever, sipping cautiously rationed drips of actual water, when we can. The inside of our transport is seeping with the stench of our sweat. And the sun with its unrelenting, unsympathetic rays is only, as the sun descends, somewhat hindered by the plume of dust that follows behind us.

Our false sun at the School was never so hot as this real one. It never truly burned your skin with its light, or brought so much sweat to your face, or made your eyes squint. Andrew says that's because the Schools are built within climate controlled domes, for optimal learning environments. But that the glassed dome above the School had its downsides as well, in that it obscured the true sky and sun so much that it would be obviously noticeable, and because of this, a false sky and sun were superimposed upon our vision using our visual sensors.

"And that's why the climate and the sunsets were always perfect... because they weren't real," Andrew announces.

"I think this might be a little *too* real," Sarah adds, below her breath, wiping a palm-full of sweat from her face.

Though I might be the only one who's heard her, since no one says anything in response—and Andrew continues on.

"And they imposed the image of the trees around the perimeter of the dome, so that no one would question, 'what's beyond the forest?'" he says.

"And why wouldn't they?" Sarah asks, speaking loud enough for us all to hear.

"Because no one ever does," he answers. Then looking at Tau and me—"Did you ever question 'what's beyond the forest?'" he asks.

My mind flashes back, and I can't remember a time when I ever did ask that question, if even only to myself. Tau and I both shake our heads to show that we'd never asked.

"It's a trick the mind plays on itself," Andrew explains, as we continue on through an endless desert. "It fills in unknown bits of information, making assumptions based on what it's already seen. And the Common knows this, they're masters of this... and so no one ever asks 'what's beyond the forest?' because they assume, illogically, more forest, more trees... when the trees that they saw in the first place weren't even real to begin with."

His statements, about the falseness I'd come to assume was fact, stir up inside of me.

The desert sands pass by my view window, seemingly endless in all directions. "And how could we be sure that this desert is real, and not like the forest around the School?" I say.

"Hmm..." Andrew makes a noise, like he is pondering

my question intently.

"Well, it's obviously real," Tau explains from the front passenger seat, then disgustingly turns back to wipe some of his neck sweat onto my forearm so that I can feel it, before I pull away, making a gagging sound with my mouth.

"I don't think that was necessary," I say, but he only shrugs at me.

Then Sarah leans in, quickly stating, "And we've all had our visual sensors removed and our audio sensors broken, so they can't put pictures into our heads anymore."

Everything they're saying is so obvious, and of course I know this. They're all treating me like an infant, all of them except for Andrew, who hasn't said anything for over a minute. Maybe I was naive to ask that question, when the answer seems so obvious.

After a few minutes more of silent travel, Andrew speaks up. "You're beginning to ask the right questions," he says.

And we all look bewildered. He can't be serious. I bet he's teasing me again, but his voice sounds too honest.

The route continues on before us; stretching onward is an unending horizon of desert. Andrew clears his throat. "First of all, let me say, from all accounts, all the data we have on it, and from our own private experience"—he takes a sip of water, before speaking again—"this is a real desert, Alpha. It obviously is. Somethings are what they are, and it's not the Common trying to fool us. There are real things called deserts, and the sun and sky, and even though the Common has their false versions of them, they're only mimicking what actually exists, and so this is a real desert.

Although, the premise of your question is a good one." He takes another sip, in the sweltering heat. "We have to assume that everything is a lie, and work backwards from there, until we find the truth."

"That sounds exhausting," Sarah says, then adding, "and plus, we don't have any more working sensors left in us, for them to track or to lie to us with."

"You think that's the only way they can lie to us?" Andrew says. "Everything they ever taught us in our Schools was purposely untrue, or altered in some way."

"It's just like the forest," I say loudly, gathering their attentions, and intentionally speaking over Tau who was about to say something.

All their eyes are on me, for an explanation. "It's like the 'what's beyond the forest?' question," I say, with the whole transport quiet around me. "That's the wrong question."

Sarah looks at me, seeming puzzled. "Why's that?" she asks.

"Because the whole question is based on a lie," I reply. "There is no forest."

Tau makes a sound with his throat, and we all stare at him, being drawn away from our conversation.

"Can I say something?" he asks, his tone implying that he was offended that I'd spoke over him.

No one responds to his statement, though he doesn't actually wait for us to reply, saying poignantly and forcefully, pointing toward a spot on the nearing horizon, "What's that?" he says. "Is that a lie too?" he asks, possibly as sarcasm.

On ahead of us, he is pointing toward a descending swirling mass of clouds and dust. It is growing by the second and surges with exponential strength as it strikes the ground, directly blocking our path.

There are cracks in the sky, explosions of light and power that rattle the window glass of the transport, and rumble with a trembling boom I can feel inside my chest.

The transport stops sharply. All around us the desert sand is being blown, not away from the swirling mass, but toward it.

"I don't think so," Andrew says, looking over the driving wheel of the transport, with widely opened and terrified eyes, just like we all have.

▨ ▨ ▨

We are almost flying over the newly half-exposed ancient route through the desert. The piercing grainy winds whip around us, constantly striking the sides of the transport, and sweeping clean the forgotten path beneath the sands.

Everything is being pulled toward the cycling mass behind us. We are turned around, and headed back the way we came. Bundled and balled desert branches tumble and break across the front of the transport. And the smaller desert plants around us are being pulled up by their roots, and still the twisting cloud of sand and fury grows in strength and velocity, and we are traveling at our top speed, trying to get beyond its reach.

"What is that thing!" Tau shouts, looking back through the window glass, at the swirling destruction that is chasing us.

"A Tor-na-do," Sarah says in her loudest voice, being purposeful with every syllable, to get above the noise of sand and wind.

Then she beings to speak, giving time for each word to sink into our ears, so that it can be properly heard. "In Logos, we have a few *papers*, scavenged from hiding places within the Ruined City, papers that the Common hadn't found and burned. And in one collection of them, there's a story about a girl and her *dog*, who get sucked into a tornado."

"And what happened to her?" I ask. "Did she live?" I say as the tornado hurries to catch us.

"Yes," Sarah says. "But... it's not a real story; it's a *fiction book*." She must be able to tell that Tau and I don't understand, and so she explains, "It's a made-up story, that people read for fun... so no one was quite sure if these tornados had actually existed."

Well, we picked a great time to prove that they do, and Tau agrees with me.

"I'm pretty sure they exist," he says.

Then the truly terrible happens, and my stomach sinks to floor when I hear the sound, faint at first.

blip.

Something high-sounding strikes in my ears, making its way past the chaos of sounds around us, but no one else seems to have noticed it.

Blip. Once more.

"Did you hear that?" I yell to Tau, nudging his shoulder.

He must see my newly frightened eyes, by the cautious way that he asks, as if he already knows the answer, "What is it?" he says, letting the words drop slowly from his mouth.

Blip. My face twitches and I peer out my side window towards the sky, trying to find it, before it finds me, like that would matter.

Tau sees this and bursts into action. "We've got a drone!" he shouts, removing his harness and leaping toward the rear seats. His hands fly over the equipment, nearly ripping open bags, and he has his rifle halfway assembled by the time Sarah can ask, "Where? Did you see one?"

"No," Tau answers locking his rifle barrel in place. Then she glances at me, as my hands are covering over my ears trying to block out the sound.

Her mouth makes the shape of the words, "Oh, no."

Our seconds pass and they feel like minutes. There have been no "blips" since I plugged my ear canals; maybe it won't find us, and we'll be able to outrun the drone and the tornado all at the same time, but it's not likely. And I'm sure Andrew, and Tau and Sarah have all figured that out as well.

The butt of Tau's rifle beats against the back window glass. The glass cracks and crumples, and is pulled away from the transport without ever touching the ground, being carried through the air on toward the swirling funneling cloud.

Tau is laying flat on top of our bags of supplies, with his rifle pointed through what had once been the rear window. His eye is in the gun sight, searching the sky above. The clouds crash again with power—it must be impossible to see anything but wind and sand. Then, Tau's mouth yells out some warning, and Sarah covers her ears like I am.

A blast of gunfire rings through the transport, ricocheting off the enclosed metal frame. Another shot. Then Tau is shouting again and his face is angry. With such a near perfect aim as his, he must have grown so used to not missing, that anything less than perfectly on target would be infuriating. And he won't quit shouting, even as he fires another round into the violent sky.

Tau is yelling again and repositioning his aim, while Andrew is responding with his own answers, as if they are in a heated argument.

Suddenly, the tires slam to a halt, skidding for a distance atop the ancient sand-covered route.

Andrew's face is livid; this must not have been what he'd wanted. And there's only one logical explanation for it:

It must be a cold and dangerous calculation. Presumably, Tau might be able to adjust for either the blasting winds, or the jostling transport, but not for both, not at the same time.

We come to a stop, and no one in the transport says a word. Without us moving forward, the tornado is quickly gaining ground. Tau steadies the barrel of his rifle in between two fragments of glass left over in the rear window frame, and his marksmanship finds an exact point. Maybe

only one more shot left to us, before the winds of the tornado become too great.

A single blast rattles from our transport toward the sky.
Tau is cheering, and after a few seconds the wounded
drone dips into view, and is sucked into the murdering tornado's swirl.

We begin to drive, but the back tires of our transport are
lifted off the ground. Tau rushes over the rear seat, and
clips into the restraint harness between Sarah and me,
before we are all taken up, like the girl in the made-up
story, except that this is real, and we feel the force of it as
we are pulled into the dark and frightening clouds. And we
spin, and spin, and spin, and spin with a screaming that
seems to be unending.

33

Though it does stop.

Where are we? I can't recall a landing, although there must have been: the immediate ache in my neck and back indicates that there must have been one.

The night is upon us, and the desert cool has easily found its way through the broken rear window.

How did we survive? My safety restraint pulls at me in a strange way, as if it's keeping me from falling. And it is— I'm hanging by the seat harness, my legs and feet dangling. The transport has been driven directly into the ground, and the front windows are all buried. And sand has fallen through the broken rear window, leaving Andrew half-buried in his seat.

No one else is moving. Are they all dead? Or just unconscious like I was? The nighttime shadows make it hard to tell. I grab at Tau's hand beside me, and shake it violently. "Wake up," I say. He does not respond, and so I shake him all the more. If he is alive, he'll be happy I revived him, and if he's dead, then he won't care how rough I am with him.

His head snaps up, and he pulls his hand away as a reflex.

"Stop..." his dry voice protests.

It takes him a few seconds to adjust to our present situation, but when he does, he's much gentler with Sarah as she awakes; and lastly, we all kick at Andrew and at the back of his chair until he comes to his senses.

We are hung by our seats, trying to come to terms with what the tornado has brought us.

But even adding to the conversation about our condition is more work than I would like. Everything is drained of water, my lips and sandy mouth, and tongue, are their own deserts.

Though this is our consensus at the end of our weary dangling conversation: All our bags of supplies were blown out in the *storm*, and we won't last through tomorrow without shade and water. And we won't last at all in this desert, unless we can leave it quickly.

Andrew says we need to dig out the transport, but Tau argues that it would be better for us to look for our supplies, and none of us can come to an agreement.

"Well, if we're going to do something, we'd better do it before the sun comes up," I protest, and they all agree.

Fingers fumbling with the manual release clasp, my belt unbuckles, and I slam against the seat in front of me. And we wait as Andrew shovels the sand away from his body, until he's loose enough for us to pull him free, but it takes so much energy from us, and everything is more painful, and every muscle burns without water.

In the end, we climb upward, over our seats, and out the shattered back window, being careful to keep ourselves from being cut by the bits of glass still lodged in the window framing.

The chilled desert air hits my skin as my face and limbs emerge. My feet hit the hill of sand that we were buried into, and my shoes sink in deep, under layers of unsteady granules.

Being stranded in a lifeless desert, with nothing, makes you assess the things you still have: my uniform and shoes, an ammunition belt clipped with real bullets around my waist, with a wearable head light attached to it, and a single stun bullet tucked inside my pocket.

Tau has his own ammunition belt as well, and his rifle, that he managed to keep ahold of. Sarah has a half-empty water bottle, and Andrew and Tau say they have nearly full bottles of water, but those are buried under layers of sand in the transport. However the rest of our supplies, along with my almost empty water bottle, blew away in the storm, sucked through the open hole in the rear of the transport, and possibly scattered for miles across the wind torn desert.

Nearly as soon as our feet have touched the sand outside the transport, and we have taken account for our resources, they are arguing, again.

"We have more water in the bags," Tau protests, motioning out toward the open wasteland. "We need to find them before the sun comes up, when we'll need them."

"And we could find them better with a vehicle," Andrew snaps.

"You can't drive that," Tau exclaims, pointing now toward our half-buried transport.

"We will, once we dig it out," Andrew answers.

But nothing can be decided on, and so we handle it "*democratically*," as Sarah suggests, meaning that our choice goes through a *voting* process, in which we all get a say.

"At least we know we have two more bottles, buried in the transport. I make a vote for staying," I announce.

Andrew and Tau's votes are obvious, while Sarah oscillates between the two opposing views, giving the best reasons for each idea, and speaking her thoughts aloud. Though in the end, she looks at Tau, and with an honest expression says, "I'm sorry, Tau. I see your point, but if we don't dig out the transport, we'll never be able to leave, and it won't matter how much water we find."

And without another word, and without actually making a definitive vote, she trudges through the cascading sand at the front of the transport and begins digging. Then, one by one, we join in with her, pushing away mounds of sand, as new loose sand quickly falls in to fill its place. This is a nearly impossible task, but it has to be completed by sunrise. There is no other choice.

■   ■   ■

My stomach aches and twists in knots because it wants water, but we aren't having any of Sarah's half-empty water, until we find the full bottles, that are buried under several feet of sand in the transport, if they're even still there.

The night ticks on, and the skin around my fingernails is cracked from constant digging. Another swipe of my hand and my fingertips hit into hardened grooves at the base of the vehicle.

"I found a tire," I call out.

"I've got one too," Sarah says, digging across from me.

My face smiles at the thought of another wheel. Am I crazed to think this could actually work? Maybe. But no one talks anymore about this not working—we've made our vote, and it has to be successful, or else the desert has trapped us.

The light of the real sun is beginning to return, slowly stealing all the deep shadows that we could hide in. We have to uncover the engine compartment by morning; there's absolutely no way we could keep digging once the sun starts to burn.

Tau unlatches the driver's door, and shoves his hands into the pile of packed sand, pulling out armfuls of it. And which in turn covers over some of my tire which I'd worked so hard to unbury, but it's a necessary inconvenience: we need to find our two full bottles, before the heat begins to grow again.

Andrew is digging out the underside of the transport, which is not as perpendicularly vertical to the ground as it had once been, and which is now slightly at an angle as the rear wheels are slowly falling back toward the sand.

The desert is silent all around us, preparing itself for

morning. And then, at the identical moment, Tau is mumbling something to himself: most of it is indistinguishable, but what I can clearly hear are the words, "Oh, no... sand." And at the same time, Andrew is shouting horrible things, presumably at the transport, as if it had done something to personally offend him. "You stupid, stupid *car*," he's shouting.

Clank! He kicks at the underside of the vehicle and continues kicking at it, yelling out in frustration, "Ahhh!" before collapsing backwards onto the shifting desert sand. A strike of distant sunlight breaks over the horizon.

We leave what we are doing, coming to the rear of the transport, and seeing Andrew laying flat on his back, and panting.

"What's wrong?" I ask.

"Yah," Sarah interjects, "you mind using your words like a grown-up, instead of beating up on our only means of transportation?"

"It doesn't matter," he grumbles, still lying flat on his back like he's waiting to be buried by the drifting sand.

"It's broken, isn't it?" I ask.

Andrew glances at me, not lifting his head from the ground.

"Yes."

"I knew it," Tau says like an accusation, while shaking his head, and glaring at Andrew.

It seems like an inopportune time to go around blaming each other for things that aren't our fault. And Sarah gives Tau a look, and he stops shaking his head, almost instantly.

"Can we fix it?" Sarah asks Andrew, very deliberately. Causing him to finally sit up and to explain to us what's wrong, as I'd asked initially.

The *axle* is broken. The axle, which is a long metal bar between the tires that makes them spin, driving the vehicle forward; Andrew says it's "shot", though not literally shot —all it means is that the axle is tremendously broken, as if it were shot. And if the axle is broken, the wheels won't turn by any other means, and the transport won't drive, and he says it's impossible for us to repair.

Though if we can't fix it, then maybe we could make another one, which is what I suggest to Andrew, but he only laughs at me like he used to.

"I wish it worked that way, Alpha," he says finally. "But there's nothing we could use to replace it."

At this, Tau argues that we should go out and look for the supplies and water, like he'd suggested last night. But Andrew refuses to take a vote on it.

"You go out there, in the sun, and you'll be dead in a few hours," Andrew protests.

"So what?" Tau argues. "If we stay here in the sun, will it be any better?"

Andrew doesn't answer, but just stares blankly at the broken axle.

Sarah says we have two bottles buried in the transport, if we dig them out, we'll be alright, but she doesn't sound convinced, even by herself.

"We only have one extra bottle," Tau interjects.

We instantly stare at him.

"The sand on your side of the transport was wet," he says to Andrew. "Guess you didn't tighten your bottle lid, did you?"

Andrew snaps back at Tau, claiming he did close the bottle lid. And they fight back and forth, about something that could be easily discoverable.

And so I leave during their argument, thrusting my hand into the damp sand near the driver's seat, where Tau had been digging, and pull out a newly emptied bottle with a cracked cap.

And I return, throwing it down between them. They fall silent.

"Are you done? We're gonna die of thirst, figuring out who's right," I say. Then turning to Andrew specifically, I add, "You said we need shade to survive... Well, let's rebury the transport and make some shade." My attention shifts toward Tau. "And we can wait till nightfall to go look for the other supplies."

No one is objecting. All their eyes are fastened onto me. Since when did I become the one to make the plans?

"All in favor?" I ask, which is what you say before before voting.

And each one of us raises our hand. Then my hand reaches out to help Andrew off the sand. And Sarah is again the first of us to begin, hurrying toward the holes she'd just made, and quickly filling in all of her progress from last night.

Yet as pathetic as it is to have wasted so many hours, at least covering something is much easier than uncovering it.

226

And before the sun burns too hot, we are huddled under mounds of sand, within the shadowed protection of our transport, sharing cautious sips of warm water, and knowing entirely that these last drinks, this bottle and a half of water, might be the last water we ever taste. No sips have ever felt more vital than these. It is like these bottles are our life, and each drink, though necessary, is slowly killing us.

34

The heat—the heat has wrapped around my skin, draining every bit of its moisture, and leaving it rough and coarse like the sand that still lingers on the floor of the transport. And our lips are becoming cracked ridges, that sting with every tiny sip from our last remaining bottle. But the sun is subsiding, and the heat is not as insatiable as it had been during the middle of the day, when we poured through our water rations without as much caution, and while we slept taking turns, so that one of us was always awake in this terrible heat, while the others lay unconscious, or dreaming of better places than this.

I have been awake this final time, watching the true sun fall and color the sky red and fiery orange. The sunsets at the School could not compare to this. Those were placid. There was never any heat in the day, nothing that made you cheer at the sight of a setting sun. Sure it was nice to look at; it was an ideal repetition of familiar colors in regular formulas and sequences, but nothing in the Common's fake sky compares with a sunset that is worked for, that has taken the full amount of your efforts to be achieved: brought about with suffering, and dried out skin, and thoughts of giving up. After a day like today, I appreciate sunsets for what they really are... rest.

Though the worst torture of today, worse than any the Disciplinarian could give, has been guarding the water while everyone slept. I very quickly reached my limit of four sips, and this bottle was the heaviest weight in my hands ever since. Even once, I loosened the cap and set the rim of the bottle to my cracked lips, but Sarah, at that moment, stirred in her sleep, and I never tried it again. In fact, for the last part of this hour I haven't even been holding the bottle, since the pressure to drink it only increased with it grasped in my hands. And I haven't looked at it either. Which is why I've been so intent on the sunset, which is better to look at anyway since it reminds me of Theta, and why I have to make it through the desert—to pretend to kill her, in order to save her life.

The circle of the sun strikes the edge of the horizon. My fingers fall into my pocket, and retrieve our one and only remaining stun bullet, which might continue to be our only one, unless we can find our bags of supplies tonight.

Sarah stirs in her sleep again, lying beside me, and she awakes, frail and dry words exiting her mouth, "Yea..." she says with rasping voice. "We made it."

I tuck the bullet back into my pocket.

She sits up, and we watch the sun fall lower, twinkling its colors in our eyes.

"Do you think we'll find anything?" she asks, and I know she must be referring to our lost supplies.

The sun shines its last beams across the desert and it is gone. We've made it to another night, but who's to say that we'll be able to find ourselves in a similar position tomorrow? What if this was the last sunset that we will ever see? What if the desert heat and unstoppable wind has swallowed up all of our water and supplies, and has left us with nothing?

And if we perish, what would Theta have said about us risking our four collective lives, for her one? It's ridiculously impractical, but I can't imagine she would ever be mad at us for deciding it. And, maybe sometimes there is a greater risk in being practical; it's too much like what the Common would choose to be comfortable with. The Leaders would never give up four lives for the sake of one. It's not what they would think of—it's not a direct ratio, one citizen's life equal to that of another—with consideration only ever given for age, and usefulness, and viability.

But what if we can't count people in the same way that we count everything else? What if the mere attempt to save someone's life is worth just as much as the actual success of it? Inside my thoughts, in some inescapable part of me, it seems like risking myself for Theta's rescue is something I'm required to do. I only wish Sarah hadn't come along to willingly endanger herself with us. She tilts the whole calculation on its side, so that the logic of what we're doing begins to mix in my brain, and gets lost.

"Alpha..." she says, like she wants to get my attention. "Do you think we'll find anything?" she repeats.

Oh, I'd forgotten she'd said that.

I reach for the head lamp tied around my belt, and click the light on and off.

"We have to try," I say.

Tau moves with a groggy moan. "Try what?" he asks.

"Try not to die," Sarah answers, with a smirk growing on her face.

"I'll second that," Andrew says, without even fully opening his eyes.

A grin finds its way onto my face as well. It seems like the worst of all times to make a joke, but if not now, then when? We're running too short on time to not be smiling.

The grin fills out on my face. "All in favor," I say as if beginning a vote, as if we could vote away death.

And everyone raises their hand, with some chuckling or outright laughter. Sarah is giggling, until her laughing becomes soft sounds of pain, and she punches me in the arm.

"Stop making me smile... it hurts." She pats her fingers on the corner of her mouth, showing tiny drips of blood on her fingertips. "It makes my mouth bleed."

"Sorry," I say, though knowing it's not my fault.

And we step outside the transport, into the night air, and take turns drinking the last sips from our final bottle. Every taste of water is evenly portioned, and there is just enough for one extra drink, which we give to Sarah.

That's it. That's the last of our water, and the seriousness of what we're doing sets in. If we don't find water tonight, we shouldn't expect to ever leave the desert, which even that is a nearly impossible thought.

With no axle on the transport, there's no way of driving it, and any attempt to escape from the middle of this desert, on foot, would be terrifically ridiculous.

So what's the point in even trying to find our lost water? Because we have to, because of Theta; maybe this plan was ridiculous all along, and the tornado only helped to prove it to us. Who are we, against this unending desert, against the unstoppable Common? They're both too big for us, yet maybe we have to make ourselves so terrifically ridiculous to even have a chance at it.

And then we separate: Sarah with me, and Andrew and Tau together. We will circle the wind torn desert until sunrise, and then head back to the transport, with whatever supplies we might find. If there's danger, or if we need help, I'll flash my head light until Tau and Andrew can come for us.

"And if there are two gunshots, it means to come find us," Tau adds, holding up our only rifle.

"Then what does one gunshot mean?" I ask.

Tau locks a new bullet into the chamber of his rifle. "It means someone or something's dead," he answers very plainly.

"Not one of us, I hope," Andrew says, with a cautious awkward grin on his face.

Tau smiles. "Probably not," he says, but maybe as a joke. I'm almost certain he's joking. Though, I'm not even sure if he'd resist shooting me, if it came to it. Maybe I should rethink his place on my list of people I can trust, which brings a slight relief to me that I'm searching instead with Sarah, who doesn't have a weapon, and whom I more generally trust.

We separate. Within a minute, they've disappeared along the hazy dark horizon. Sarah says I should save the battery on my head lamp, which is apparently a good thing to do. And so it is clicked off, and we walk in the blinding darkness, until little by little the blackness of the desert is not so absolute. My eyes can see in darkness, and the void of the night sky is transformed into a billion tiny points of light.

And these smallest stars shine their gleam onto the sand, so that almost every place has pale light on it, though there are still small valleys of shadow.

Ahead is a large black lump, that almost looks like a shadow, except it's sticking out of the sand like a stone. My hands find it. There's a soft canvas on its sides—a bag.

We dig it out and my fingers tug at the zipper, which is hard to move because of the grains of sand lodged into its seams. But it opens at last, nothing but hard metal: the pieces of a rifle and some "tactical equipment" that Andrew made us pack.

Nothing useful like water or meal rations, but we can't just leave it here either, and so we drag it back toward the transport.

Where is the transport? My mind is jumbled and not as clear as it once was. Sarah says the transport is just over this next hill, and it is. Good thing she'd been staying attentive, and was not as distracted as much by the stars as I had been.

My legs and back muscles ache. We leave the overloaded bag outside the transport, and walk off into the night, though not as quickly or as surefooted as before. Everything drags and the joints of my bones creak and feel sore. And we traverse dunes of sand, and search around desert bushes for nearly a half-hour without conversation, until Sarah speaks, under the falling starlight, and in the deep silence of barren night.

"Alpha," she says, "has anyone told you why our father was captured?"

I glance at her, and continue to walk. "All I've heard was that he tried to rescue me, but I never got anymore than that," I answer, after considering what little the elected officials in Logos had told me about my father.

He was trying to rescue me, she explains, but not only me...

Whom else could there be?—the thought goes across my mind as she says the answer aloud.

"Our mother," she says.

And maybe because of this new information, or maybe because our limbs are too weary to continue on walking, we collapse upon a tall hill of sand, and she continues her explanation.

"You were always under constant direct surveillance, Alpha," she tells me. "It was more than just the automated scanners that everyone gets. You had a dedicated watcher on you at all times, ever since my escape... if there's one thing the Common doesn't like, it's someone getting the best of them, and so they made it nearly impossible for us to launch a successful rescue mission, for you. And so, he decided to try first for our mother in Primus."

She says that he'd talked about it, and had planned the operation for months, and that he'd made it into the city, but after that he had to break communication, and the last they saw of him was at his retractment.

Her face shows swelling anger. Her eyes are determinedly set. "They blasted a signal from their drones, all over the Ruined City and down the *coast*, and it was strong enough for us to get in Logos... all that effort, just so they could make sure we'd watch him die."

She balls up her fist and punches the sand repeatedly, with her eyes shut. Her expression is furious; she must hate the Common as much as I do.

I lean in closer to try to get her to open up her eyes, after she stops pounding at the ground.

"Did he find her?" I ask.

Her shoulders shrug. And in a helpless way, she answers, "We don't know..."

The desert stars are beginning to fade away. Sarah's words resound with truth, but still somethings don't make sense, and the most glaring of which I ask her about.

"If they put a watcher on me, why wouldn't they put one on our mother? They must have guessed he'd try to save her," I say.

An area on the horizon is beginning to lighten. The murderous sun will soon be up again, and all we've found are worthless weapons, and no water.

She stares at me with an aching expression, as if she does not wish to say what she is about to. "Because the Leaders don't put watchers on their own," she says.

On their own? It takes a half-second, then I get it.

Sarah looks distraught when I say it. "She's a Leader?" I ask. My thoughts are a mess with unbelief. How is that possible?

But Sarah simply nods her head with a "yes" motion. It's true. I can feel that it's true.

The silence is broken.

A single gunshot.

Is that it? We wait. Someone's dead. I shouldn't have agreed that they go searching on their own. I should have raised a vote against it.

Blast! A second gunshot.

Breath falls out of me with a sigh of relief, both from my mouth, and audibly from Sarah's. She must have thought Tau killed someone as well. Though it's not exactly a relief for us, because now we have to go find them, and try to hurry before the sun gets too hot. Though as for now, we still have the night, but not for long.

35

"We're leaving," Andrew shouts.

We've circled the desert, following our tracks until we came to the transport.

The sun breaks over the horizon, and Andrew is standing on top of the roof of the transport, pulling off a single solar fuel panel, and he's yelling out some nonsense as we arrive; and it's easily seen that his erratic mood is a mixture of excitement and weary exhaustion.

"He shot off the antenna, that lucky freak," he says.

"Antenna?" Sarah says, though Andrew is still fumbling with the solar panel and has likely not heard her.

"Bet he couldn't do it again, if he tried," he mumbles.

This is infuriating. "What antenna?" I say, climbing up the mounds of sand, and onto the roof alongside Andrew.

"Can you turn that for me?" he asks, pointing toward a twistable latch near my foot, which is the last part needed to dislodge the panel from the roof. It's obvious—he won't be able to concentrate enough to answer my question, until he's finished this absurd task.

Turning the latch, the panel is loose, and Andrew's eyes look less distracted.

"We have to get this back," he says, speaking his thoughts.

"Stop!" I exclaim. "What antenna?"

He finally settles his attention on me, long enough to give an answer. "The drone... don't you understand? The drone," he says.

At once, he steps from the roof, and begins to walk away. He's only about half of himself by now; this is clear. Sarah and I chase after him, and forcibly take the panel out of his hands, because he's not in a condition to carry anything at the moment.

"How much farther?" Sarah asks, since the panel is heavy for our weakened muscles.

He points into the distance ahead of us. "Over there," he says, which is not an answer.

"What's the panel for?" I ask.

And he explains in incomplete sentences, that the drone's panel was damaged in the storm, and this new one must be used to replace the original, although he never actually finishes his line of thought, and so this last part has to be inferred.

The unblocked heat burns at my skin, blistering what was already red and painful. We almost stumble with the panel, but don't drop it, and continue on over lifeless desert for another mile. Why are we trusting Andrew to bring us to the right place? He's completely irrational. What if he only made up this entire story, in his illogical state? What if we're following a mad man through the desert?

Another hill, another hill, and we find it, and also find Tau slumped below a drone wing, hiding in the shade. He looks even worse than Andrew does.

The drone is uncovered from the sand, and its driver's area is opened, with Tau's rifle and our tactical bag (the one we found buried in the desert), lodged behind the operator's seat.

"I thought drones didn't have drivers. Don't they fly themselves?" I say.

The question is presented to Andrew, but he's in no condition to answer, while he's distracted, preoccupied with the task of removing the damaged panel, and replacing it with our new one. So I help him hold the new panel in place, while Sarah answers the question for him. She explains that they used to be built as solely unmanned vehicles, until the people of Logos started overriding the militants' signals, and confiscating drones. After that, the Common put manned operators in all the drones near the Ruined City, and along the *coast*.

But they must not have thought we'd get through the desert, so this one didn't have an operator in it, even though it was made for one.

"So, we have our own drone?" I say.

She smiles big and full. "Yes"—she giggles—"looks like it," she says.

The solar panel is secure. The interior lights and display monitors re-engage.

Suddenly, Sarah's arms wrap around me with excitement. Her tenderness is unsettling, though I can bear it more than I once could. I swallow hard, and shut my eyes until she stops.

Now that the drone is ready, Andrew's mannerisms are more stable. He reaches for something under the shadow of the wing, and places it in my hands. It's my nearly empty bottle that was lost in the storm, with scrapes and dents on the outside, but still intact, and with an eighth amount of water in it.

The familiar sound of water sloshes in the bottle. It would be so easy to take it, but it feels uncomfortable to do so, knowing that I don't really need it, not as much as others. My eyes turn to Sarah, and we both share a similar expression.

I glance at Tau, lying beneath the wing, and she nods in agreement. So we rush over to him and kneel in the limited shade. His face is dried and cracked. His eyes hang drearily open. The cap is unscrewed, and very delicately we force him to take minuscule sips, until the whole bottle is emptied.

His eyes open wider. His mouth twitches a grin. He's smiling at us. These tiny sips of water have awarded us more time, but not long.

We have to leave, but there's only one chair in the *cockpit*, which is what Sarah calls the driver's seat. And that's reserved for Andrew who is the only one of us who knows anything about these flying things.

Sarah says she can squeeze behind the *pilot's* chair, which leaves Tau and me with nowhere to sit, but evidently they'd already thought of that late last night when they first found the drone, and so they'd cut the harnesses out of our transport before we heard the two gunshots this morning.

Tau has the cut harnesses grasped in his hands, and he lifts them up to Sarah, who begins wrapping the straps under my arms, and fastening me to the drone, so that I will dangle below the tip of the wing.

"What if I fall?" I ask, while she's busy with her work.

"You won't fall," she answers.

"But what if I do?"

Though she insists that she's tying a "double knot", and so it would be impossible for me to fall. Though, I don't think we're sharing the same definition of impossible, at the moment. Instead, what she likely means by "impossible", is that if I don't let her tie me to the wing, then it would be impossible for me to live, and she's probably right.

The straps are pulled with force, and dig into my chafed skin. This will hurt.

Across the drone, at the tip of the other wing, Tau is lifted to his feet, and strapped up with the same amount of care. It's weird to see him without his gun in his hand; he's been clinging to it ever since the tornado. He's even slept with it. And it's strange, also, to see him so weak, with his face blistered and cracked more than ours, and with his eyes sagging closed, when he had just as much water as we all had; we rationed it—we kept track.

Sarah fastens his straps, checking her knots several times over, and then whispering something into his ear.

No... wait, he didn't have as much water as we all did.

After the tornado, we split the remaining bottles between ourselves: half of Sarah's bottle, and Tau's nearly full bottle. Which would mean that he's probably had less than half of a full bottle to himself, while I've easily had more than an entire bottle on my own. I guess when you're merely trying to survive in a desert, the evenness of portions is not a highly kept priority.

I don't know why I hadn't thought of it sooner; maybe because it didn't affect me. I had enough water, so it was easy not to think about how much Tau got. But I'd imagine he's been feeling it ever since we crashed into the sand dune, ever since we started digging out the broken transport two nights ago, probably while he was voting that we go find water, but none of us listened... we'd drank our water, so it was easier to make those sorts of decisions, to waste time uncovering a worthless transport, when we weren't as thirsty as Tau.

But, in the end, it's probably his fault for letting us take all his nearly full water bottle, splitting it between the four of us; I know I would have said something about it, if I was only getting a half-bottle of water to drink. I would have said something. So it was his fault for letting us take it... and even though we voted to share the water, he's to blame for not stopping us. He had the only gun—he could have done it.

My skin is warming in a more direct sunlight. We'd better leave soon. Across the wing, Sarah finishes her work, and then crams herself behind Andrew's pilot seat. Andrew is already in position and ready; but with Sarah jammed behind his seat, the protective glass over the cockpit cannot shut, so he'll have to fly with it open.

The propulsive engines at the center of each wing tilt up and down as Andrew looks behind himself, checking their movements.

In the end, the engines are left in a downward position. Then they're engaged—hot air and sand spray up around me, blasting into my face. My lips seal shut, and I won't breathe for fear of swallowing mouthfuls of blowing dust. This is like the heart of the tornado, all over again.

My feet lift—the toes of my uniform shoes leave the ground. The harness straps tied around me squeeze at my sides. We are risen off the ground. Now we are higher; now we are higher still.

The dunes and desert bushes around us are smaller and less significant. We are higher. Away in the distance is the wreckage of our transport, crashed into the sand, where no life could survive. As we climb higher, the air is moved from burning, to warm, to moderate, and now pleasant.

The engines tilt again and we fly horizontally. The uninhibited wind passes quickly over my face, and the heat of the desert falls away behind us. If these straps hold, if Sarah's knots are secure, then this burning wasteland will find a place in our past events: it will be a part of our history, something else for Sarah to record in her written notebook; that is if we can ever return to Logos.

But as for now, we are flying, and that is all that can be functionally thought of.

We fly for hours, and the world below us turns from wind blown sand and desert bushes, to parched grasses interspersed with feeble trees. Then far ahead, color—a color not seen since we came to the desert. Green. It is the vibrant green of living grass and full-leafed trees. And splitting between the two variances of color is a mighty dividing line of water, what I know to be called a river. This prominent gap of water cuts the landscape into two, on one side a place of brown and wilted death, and on the other side, an area of green and growing life.

We are descending, toward a wide grassy field near the edge of the river. The engines point downward as we float to the ground. Though the landing still jerks and pulls at the straps, which scrape my skin and tear already tender flesh. But it doesn't matter, I would rather choose to be cut and bleeding, and alive for it, than to be in perfect health and dead.

Sarah leaps from the cockpit, and Andrew comes stumbling behind her, and for obvious reasons they go to Tau first to untie his straps, and he falls onto the grass like a lifeless stone. Then they come to me, and make me readjust, Sarah says, to take the weight off the knots. The harnesses let go, and I fall to the grass. Overhead, the drone wing protects me from the still warm sun, and Andrew drops beside me in the shade.

Sarah is the only one of us who's had enough water, and who has also not hung from a drone wing for hours. And so she commits to bring us water.

She takes an empty bottle, and is gone for not even a minute when we hear a yelp of pain. She's not in view, but her voice speaks clearly. "I'm alright," she says from down by the river's edge. "The water burns," she explains.

What does she mean? Perhaps, this is hot river water. Assumably, it would make sense to have warm water at the edge of a desert, but any temperature water is better than none at all.

"Is the water hot?" I ask her, while she gives the full first bottle to Tau, making sure that he drinks it all. Yet she never turns to acknowledge me—maybe she hasn't heard me, but she's gone before I can ask anything else.

Thirst, as mighty as this river beside us, is surging in my veins. It is uncontrollable. I cannot wait for my turn, when Sarah will bring me water. My body pushes off the ground. My feet hit heavily with aching steps. Andrew mumbles something as I leave—maybe he wants me to fetch some water for him also, but I don't have an empty bottle, just dried out hands and blistered skin.

Sarah hurries past me with a newly filled bottle, making her way toward Andrew. "...little sips at first," she says, as she passes.

My feet tread onward, down to wet sand near the edge. My fingertips drag over the water; it's cool to the touch but the sensation of water tingles against my skin. It is unlikeable, and uncomfortable, but bearable. Thirst. A feeling rushes over me—not only my lips need water, but my whole body. It is not enough to simply drink it.

My feet move and stumble forward. I collapse into the coolness of it, past my head, but it is a deceitful coolness. Every inch of my body where the water touches screams in pain, like sharp burning needles blasting from every crack and pore. My mouth lifts above the water, and I'm screaming for real. It is like my skin, which has been drained of all moisture, is now fighting the liquid that would help it. I'm screaming and gulping water, almost too weak to keep my head above the surface.

Something splashes into the water, and grabs at my uniform shirt. It's my sister. She is yelling from the pain, herself, and pulling me back to the wet sand at the edge, throwing me onto my back.

She drops to the ground beside me. Her voice is harsh. "Didn't I tell you, little sips?" she says.

My eyelids flutter. Her face is both angry and concerned, but something inside of me, something also uncontrollable is laughing.

I am overcome with laughter, as my lower legs which are still in the water begin to develop a tolerance to the stinging sensation.

I am still laughing. "I did my best," I say, chuckling as I speak.

The sand grits in my hair and the water tingles against my feet, but it is bearable.

"You had me worried," she says. "I thought you were drowning."

My eyelids are closed, soaking in the deliciousness of the water all around me. "I couldn't help it... I was too thirsty," I announce, before reopening my eyes and seeing her expression.

She scowls, though there is some care beneath her scowl which still shows through. "You are a brat," she says, smirking, and then flicks my sun scorched earlobe.

"Oww!" I howl. "I almost drown, and you're flicking me," I say.

"Well you deserve it," she says. "And this," she adds, reaching her hand into the river, and splashing my whole face with water, which burns at my skin, but even in its burning, it's still spectacular, because it's there.

"Oh, yeah... do I?"

My hand finds the water, and we are both splashing each other with handfuls of unending cool water; water that burns, but in its burning it refreshes, and washes away the dust and dryness of our desert selves.

36

We've had all the water we can possibly drink, but no food. It is the warmth of the day, and we are seated beneath a shaded tree by the edge of the river. My uniform shirt and shoes are off and are drying in the sun. Idly, my fingers pick through the grass and over the ground for twigs to break, or for tiny stones to toss into the water.

"The retractment is tomorrow," I say. No one moves from their positions, but Andrew speaks, saying what I already guessed, that we can use the drone to sneak into Primus, which he explains is roughly a two hour flight from here, but we can make up that distance tonight, and he can have Tau and me within the Central City before sunrise.

Though in the end he adds, "But Sarah stays here... It's the safest place for her; she's beyond their long range scanners, and there's no reason for her to go any farther." He seems adamant about this.

And Sarah is lying at the edge of the shade, letting her lower half dry in the sunlight. She turns to us. "But I want to see them get into the city," she protests.

Andrew shakes his head. "No," he answers.

"But that's not fair. Why do you get to go, and I don't?" she says.

"No," Andrew says, emphatically, without an explanation.

Sarah tries to raise a vote over this, but still he says no, and adding, "Didn't I tell you before we left, that I'm not taking a vote on this?" he says. "No..." he repeats. "None of you can fly the drone without me." He looks around at all of us. "If she goes, then I won't go." And his voice is strict and resolved.

Tau, who looks like he is sleeping in the grass, speaks up. "I don't know why you're so surprised—it's what we agreed to before we left," he says, as if he's addressing Sarah by his inflection, though his eyes are still closed.

"But I thought you'd *both* stick up for me," she says, over-emphasizing the word "both," like it's somehow our fault that she can't go. Then she turns to Andrew. "And what makes you think you can push me around?" she says.

He gives a deliberate pause and a stern gaze at her. "I'm not *pushing you around*. I'm protecting you."

"Well, I don't need it," she answers, with a harsh spite in her words. "It's not your job to protect me," she snaps.

Andrew shuts his lips tightly, and uses a clenched fist to cover his mouth, as if he's withholding a rising frustration. And he finally speaks, "Your father is dead... it's not what we wanted, but now it's my job to protect you."

Her eyebrows raise, and she glances away, staring out over the river, and she won't even look at us as she speaks, answering Andrew, "You're not my father... No one asked you to be."

After some moments, she twists her attention toward

me. "And what, you're not gonna say anything, Alpha?" she says.

Her eyes are glaring with expectation. She looks at me like I should speak on her behalf. What does she want me to say? Andrew's right, or at least he has a claim to tell her she can't go.

My shoulders shrug.

"We agreed to it," I say.

At my remarks, her face makes a grimace, as if she's just endured something awful. And she sighs loudly, and stomps away, toward the waterline.

■ ■ ■

She's gone for over an hour, and by the time she returns we're unpacking and assembling our supplies for the mission. Everything from the tactical bag is laid out in the grass: knives, thermal scanner camouflage, glasses for improved night vision, undetectable communication headsets, and lastly, my rifle that Tau had picked out for me, but unfortunately no extra stun bullets, and most disappointingly for my stomach's sake, no food.

Sarah comes walking up from the river. And she stands over our collection of equipment, blocking our remaining sunlight as it falls below the horizon behind her.

"I've decided not to go," she announces.

Andrew is inspecting the communication headsets, which takes all his attention. He speaks through each attached mouthpiece, systematically listening for it to be relayed through each headset.

"Well you don't really have a choice," he says, not looking up.

"Shut it, Andrew," she exclaims. "I'm agreeing not to go, will you just take it?"

There is a twitch of relent on his face, and he softens his expression. "Okay," he says. "...Thank you for agreeing," he adds.

At this, Tau returns to guiding me through the step by step process of assembling my rifle, and we almost have it finished, when Sarah speaks again, holding up some mushy cluster of items.

"I know we don't have any food left... so, I found these on a thorny bush by the river. There was a bird scavenging for the fallen ones from the ground, so I thought they'd be alright to eat."

She holds up the finely clustered dark purple and black items, that ooze a liquid into her hands. And under close inspection, there is a purplish hue around the cracks of her lips, showing that she's already tried them.

"What are they?" I ask, staring at the wad of mush she's brought for us.

"I don't know," she answers, "but the birds eat them."

"Birds eat a lot of things," Tau remarks, as he takes over the task of assembling my rifle, since I'm now clearly distracted.

It's uncontrollable; my fingers pick a mushy item from her hand, and the tip of my tongue touches its oozing liquid. A tingling sensation stirs within my mouth—a taste I guess I've never really felt before now.

"It's sweet," I say.

I almost have it in my mouth, but Andrew interrupts, "You shouldn't eat that if you don't know what it is," he warns. "It could be dangerous."

The item leaves my awaiting mouth, and I hold it between my fingers examining it. How could this little glob of mush be dangerous?

"Don't listen to him," Sarah says, leaning in to whisper. Then she says, loud enough for Andrew and for all of us to hear, "And you know what's also dangerous?... Dying of starvation." And she smiles to herself, and flicks another dripping thorny bush item into her mouth.

Andrew comes to stand beside us. "How long ago did you start eating those?" he asks Sarah.

"About a half-hour ago," she answers, and another one goes into her mouth. They look so good—I can almost not help myself. As a reflex, the mush item in my hand approaches my readied lips and mouth-watering tongue, but Andrew stops it, grabbing at my wrist.

"We should wait, at least, till dark," he says, assessing the height of the sun above the horizon. "If she's not sick by then we can eat them."

Who says he can tell us what to do? It was easier to watch Sarah go through the same struggle, when she wanted to come with us to Primus, but now he wants to decide what we eat?

"I say we vote on it," I announce, while his hand is still clasped onto my wrist.

Tau, who has been quietly working on what should have

been my responsibility, sets my finished, meticulously assembled rifle down, and steps toward us, taking his own clustered mush item from Sarah's dwindling pile. He throws it into his mouth, with a firmly planted contented grin on his broken and cracked lips.

"I vote we eat them," he says, through chewed bites.

"Tau," Andrew protests, with wide-opened surprised eyes. "We—"

"Listen," Tau says, interrupting. "It's a good plan—I get it." He picks up another item from Sarah's hand. "I just don't care," he says, plopping it into his savoring mouth.

There is only one remaining item left in Sarah's open palm. I reach with my available hand and take it, then offer it to Andrew.

"Here," I say. "If we get sick, we'll stop eating them."

He's been outnumbered, and beaten in a way. He nods in agreement, conceding this small loss, and he lets go of my hand. But there is a part of him, up around the eyes, that seems to be satisfied with his reluctant choice.

He points his finger around at all of us. "I'm gonna blame you all, if I get sick." But there is a underlying joke in his voice that cannot be ignored.

And we both eat our thorny bush, mush items together, with Sarah and Tau's clamoring cheers in our ears. And we are finally together: we are fed together, or sick, or in danger together, and we never had to take an actual vote—it just happened. We chose to enjoy this sweetest food together, and if danger will come from it later, then let it come.

37

Though there was no danger in our newfound food. There was only sustenance; which makes it good to know that the world is not a ravenous murderous creature, always out to get us—sometimes there is food, for food's sake. And in our case, we've found some of the sweetest things in and amongst the thorns, that are good on their own account, and not a trick, or a trap, or a hidden danger.

At present, the night has come and we are flying, dangling from the tips of the wings. My night vision improving goggles make the world green and grainy, but with them I can see every sinking and rising tree-covered hill, and each tiny passing river. My rifle is strapped to my back, and a tactical knife is hung onto my belt, and we have an awful, ridiculous, horrible plan—a plan that I came up with.

When we left Sarah in the open field by the mighty river, she said into my ear, "Come back for me... you're my only family now."

What does that even mean? A few weeks ago I would have had absolutely no idea, but now it's coming into view in blips, like a distorted visual signal. From what I know, it means that there's an obligation: an unspoken requirement that I would give up what I would want, when it would benefit her more—like giving her extra sips of water even while I'm absurdly thirsty myself, or in telling her I will come back, when it would be easier to just escape with Theta, and be finished with all these extra obligations that complicate my plans.

A voice speaks in my ear. "See that bright spot in the distance?" Andrew says, speaking into mine and Tau's headset communication links.

With the effects of the night vision, it is such a blinding white spot that it's hard to make out any detail at all.

Andrew doesn't give us time to answer. "That's Primus," he says.

"I never thought it'd be so big," Tau replies.

Though the closer we get, the more blinding and incomprehensible the city becomes. I'd have to take off my goggles to see anything, but Tau still has his on. How is he not blinded like I am?

"Is there a way to turn these glasses off? I can't see anything," I say.

"Yeah, just tap the side of them," Tau answers, which I do, and in the moment my finger touches the casing of my goggles the city before us becomes clear.

"Have you had them on this whole time?" Andrew asks.

"Yeah, why?" I answer.

He sighs at me, and speaks with condescension in his voice, "'Cause your batteries are probably dead by now."

My nose snarls. He thinks he can treat me like that? It's not my fault. No one told me how to work these things.

But Tau interjects before there can be an argument. "We've only got a few hours till sunrise. It'll be fine," he says.

There is a pause, then Andrew replies, "Then you'd better not get caught in the dark."

"We won't," I say, making a promise: another promise today that I can't be sure to keep... but it serves its purpose, and ends the conversation.

And as the city approaches it continues to grow, larger and larger, sprawling out in every direction, and at the center of the city are sets of brightly illuminated tall white buildings. And we are crossing the edge of the beginning of the city, the first lights of Primus.

"Not a word, now," Andrew says, his voice whispering through our headsets.

We pass the initial barrier of lights. We are far above them, hidden in the sky and potentially out of view. From our perspective, it looks like the city is enclosed by a deeply dug pit and a metal fence structure, covered at the top with bundled wire. And after this fence, there is an open area of around two hundred feet, then a second fence with bundled wire, and after that the rows of tightly packed citizens' quarters begin and stretch on for miles. And between us and the citizens' quarters are lower flying drones, likely scanning the ground below them, and maybe never thinking to scan the skies above, but if they did, they would only see another innocuous drone. Andrew said that our new layer of thermal camouflage below our uniforms would protect us from their scanners, but there's no reason to test those assumptions, so we stay well above them.

And as we move toward the center of the city, the pathways between quarters widen, and there are broken up areas with fountains, and open lawns, and trees, and the quarters that remain are phenomenally much larger, and more intricate.

Behind one tremendous quarters, there is a lively gathering with flashing colored lights, and persons joined up into pairs and engaging in synchronized movements. The event seems so elaborately configured that it is hard to take it all in as we pass. It seems like this would be the type of event during which to have loud conversations, and unsquelched laughter, and it might be that sort, but because of our immense height, and my headset which blocks out too much of the outside noise, it is impossible to know for sure. There might be laughter, or conversation, but I cannot hear it.

How could the Common permit this? What about curfews? Won't they be demerited, and lose their ranking? What will they say when they—wait, the amount of drones in this area has greatly diminished, and the grandness of these quarters is beyond anything that the Common would allow for its citizens. These are Leaders. These are Leaders' quarters. This is their world of elaborate events, with bright colors, and laughter. We've flown far beyond the tightly packed and well segmented drab citizens' quarters, far from the places with no open lawns or ornate fountains. The Common permits this event, after regular curfew hours, because to a Leader everything must be permitted. To them there are no curfews, or demerits, or rankings. In their eyes, they are as high above us, as I am now above Primus. It is another world to them, and they cannot hear us, just as I cannot hear them now.

Our drone makes its gradual descent, toward the brightly lit collection of white buildings, and the retractment stadium at the center of the city. But we stop short of those structures; the drone engines tilt downward and we come to rest on a tall squared rooftop, with a clear view of the entire central inner workings of Primus.

My feet touch the sturdy rooftop. My arms, chaffed and wearied, reach to untie the harness straps that have kept me attached to the wing for hours. The blood in my legs and arms can again move without restriction. But the awkwardness of the straps tied around my body has made my legs useless, or at least useless until the blood can find its natural place again. I drop without a chance of standing, though so does Tau. And the engines blast again with hot air, sending Andrew high above into the night, and out of view.

Breath comes into me in stammered puffs, and I crawl to Tau without the full use of my legs yet.

Palm writing, because we can't speak for fear of drone detection.

"Isn't this too far?" I write, meaning, "Isn't this too far from the stadium?"—but he knows what I mean.

"You want to get closer? Go ahead," he writes and smirks at me.

Our legs begin to settle, and Tau stands, leading us to the roof ledge overlooking the center of Primus: the open-roofed retractment stadium, with white buildings of various shapes around it. The largest white building being far bigger than any normal building I've ever seen, with a tiered, domed roof at the center, and the tallest structure being just a single pointed tower.

And these grand white buildings stand out in cold contrast to the retractment stadium, which is just a flat grey, a dull oval structure with no intricacies in it, whatsoever. And barely visible within the stadium is the stage, and the confessional podium, almost directly in front of us, but at a downward angle.

Seeing the stage, my mind flashes back to the retractment that started all this: The unknown man, who was my father, rushing to the confessional podium, knocking the orator from his microphone, and speaking that one word that changed my whole life, and put Theta into a retractment of her own.

"Revolution." Just a single word that no one even understands, and yet it has the power to kill us all. Just one single word, sharper than any bullet or weapon, and more devastating.

Tau has found his spot on the ledge, and is adjusting the stabilizer legs on his rifle. We only get one shot each, and so it has to be exact.

I search the rooftop for an even spot on which to place my own rifle. This nearby ledge looks ideal, with the perfect angle for trajectory, in my opinion. But I'm not even finished focusing my sight's lens, and here is Tau coming, shaking his head at me.

What's wrong with this spot? It's perfect?—I try to make that clear with hand motions. But he won't tell me; he only shakes his head, and makes some incomprehensible gestures in the air, as he's pulling my rifle from my hands, and leading me to the furthest corner ledge. Then he sets up and finely adjusts my stabilizer legs and gunsight. His movements are so calculatedly precise that it's hard to be mad at him, because I could never do this on my own. After a while, his specifications become so finite, that it would be easy to guess that he wasn't doing anything at all.

But seeing the progression in its entirety, from wide flowing motions to gradually more detailed exact precision, it's only noticeable for that sake when he moves the stock of the rifle only the smallest fraction of a millimeter to the right, or to the left. And when he's finished, I point my finger to this location and palm-write, "Why?"

And he answers by demonstrating how my arms will rest at the exact corner of the roof, with one arm on each ledge to steady my aim, and then he points to the sky and writes, "Also, wind."

Somewhere down there is Theta, locked up and waiting for her retractment. In a few hours, they'll bring her out onto the stage—maybe make a show of a regular retractment—but I doubt they'll ever let her speak; since regardless of what she'd say, she'd still be executed.

At the ledge, Tau directs me into position, and I peer through my meticulously focused scope. It's positioned to the side of the podium, where they will likely make Theta stand while her pronouncement of judgement is being recited. What an incredible distance, and looking through this magnified scope doesn't make me feel any better. Sure, Tau can hit a clean target at this range. After all, he's got about a million points on the militant firing range... but as for me, I've only shot one gun, once in my lifetime, and even that was with help. This plan of ours was at first generally ridiculous, but now seeing the actual distance through the focused lens of my gunsight, it's impossible.

He taps me on the shoulder and moves me to the side as he demonstrates the process: how to properly kneel into position, how to breathe and when to hold my breath, how to gently pull the trigger without jerking my aim. It is a far more indicate system than I ever imagined. And when he's finished, he palm-writes, "Practice."

It doesn't make any sense. How am I supposed to practice without a target? And if I can't fire a single shot, 'cause the Common would find us in an instant? Or if I could, I've only got one stun bullet available, so that by definition I only get one chance at it.

I stare at him, questioning. "One bullet, no target," I write.

"Doesn't matter," he scribbles into my hand. "You miss with your body, not the bullet."

He opens the firing chamber of my rifle and removes our single stun bullet, and then directs me through the proper steps: Kneel, my foot is not in the right position, try again... Kneel, breathe, steady hands, aim, slowly on the trigger, click. The metal lever that would normally strike the bullet engages, echoing a click through the empty chamber and across the otherwise silent rooftop.

My eyes turn to him for validation of my efforts, but he's shaking his head in disapproval, and then makes a pointing motion indicating that I should try again.

Once more: Kneel, breathe, steady, aim, slowly on the trigger, click... still no. How could he be sure of anything, if I'm restricted from actually firing a real shot? This is useless —but maybe if I only get one chance to save Theta's life, then I should continue this ridiculous plan, with all the determination I can give to it.

Again through the steps, click, no. Through the steps, click, still nothing.

And we continue, firing at an imaginary target in the air. The night is passing by quickly; the sun is touching the sky to our right. My arms and trigger finger are losing their strength. At sunrise, the first arrivals into the stadium are finding their seats. It's long been a popular opinion that the only reason the stadium is filled during each retractment, is because the Common requires it. And so it makes sense that it would begin to fill with citizens even before the last rays of sunrise.

Again through the process, another of my attempts: Kneel, breathe, steady hands, aim, slowly pulling the trigger with the tiniest of motions, click.

The sun hits our ledge and Tau's face; he is smiling and nodding in approval. And I collapse against the ledge wall with exhaustion, finally.

I can't believe it's over. Hours of practice, and finally I got it. But he's waving his hand in front of my face to get my attention, then he palm-writes, "Twice." Of all the ridiculous mindless endeavors, why twice? And after several more attempts I finally get it once more—but that's not what he meant, apparently—he meant twice in a row, consecutively. Another half-hour passes by us. The stadium is almost full, as a handful of late arriving Leaders fill into their respected section near the podium. Where are all the rest of the Leaders, like the ones that I saw last night?

This is only a minimal representation of them. Probably just enough to fill up the view of the camera which transmits its image into the visual sensors of all the outside citizens who are made to watch the retractment that's violently imposed on their brains. And what about the Leaders? Only enough of them to fill the camera lens. Another thing that's just for show; they don't even care enough about us to watch us die. To them there must be no distinction in their minds between us and the half-men —only that the half-men were able to fight against them— and us, we can't even fight them with our words. In reality, we are even weaker than half-men.

A stadium, full of citizens, against a dozen and a half Leaders, and several militants. If the half-men would have had this chance, there's no way that they'd let their own get executed repeatedly before their eyes, and not so much as say a word.

Kneel, breathe, steady, aim, "Revolution," trigger, click.

Tau's face is terrified. I'd said the word out loud, and I hadn't meant to. What if the drones heard it? Glancing at the presumably empty sky above us, it doesn't look like they had.

He pulls me away from the ledge, and we find shelter under a metal grating that might obscure us from passing drone surveillance. And he palm-writes, "Good. Twice."

Is that real? Did I really "hit" it twice?

"Really?" I write.

But he doesn't respond at first, and then writes with some reluctance, "No... but almost. Now be quiet."

We huddle in silence trying to stay out of view, staring up at the sky for a few more minutes, but no drones seem to be circling, though the morning sky is ominously calm. How could I have been so careless? Our thermal camouflage will keep us relatively protected from detection, but if the audio scanners of a passing drone catches my voice print, we'll be found instantly. Though nothing, and no one, comes for us. Perhaps we're safe.

This mindless error almost ruined our plan, which is hopelessly flawed to begin with. The plan: I shoot first, then Tau—he says I can't hit a moving target. But realistically, at this distance, chances are that I couldn't strike a stationary target either. Or what if I do hit her, except that at this range, or because of an unpredictable gust of wind, the stun bullet hits her in the face? Would that kill her on accident? How unbullet-like are these bullets?

A voice in my ears startles my senses, completely unexpected. Are we missing the retractment? It'd have to be something drastic for Andrew to break our radio silence.

"There's a problem," his panicked whisper says into our headsets. "Don't say anything. Just go to the scopes."

And Tau and I rush to our rifles—there's no thinking about drones now. My mind floods with possibilities: They could have put militant guards around her. They could have positioned her behind a piece of the building's structure. The rifle is in my hands. My eye peers through the sight, and it's worse. It's instantly worse than anything I can imagine.

My voice is caught in my throat, but Tau is speaking with full force. "Andrew, this is your fault," he says. "We leave her there without thermal camouflage and this is what happens," he grumbles.

There she is, clearly focused through my sight, at the center of the stage. There they both are.

"She was beyond the long range scanners. She was safe," Andrew argues.

"If she was safe, she wouldn't be here," Tau answers.

My scope moves within my shaking nervous hands. It's focused on Theta. She's ragged; her puffy eyes are red and tired. Her face is drained of its regular lively color, but in a way that maybe no one else would recognize, but I can tell, because I know her. I know what the color of her face should look like, and this isn't it. They've tried to mask it by placing new concealing colors on her skin, but I can tell the difference.

And the stock of my gun nudges to the left, and beside Theta is our problem, the complication to our plan: my sister, Sarah Robins, standing in the same location where my father had been when he was gunned down for every citizen to see. But in examining the crowd around them, each citizen's face looks blank, and unimpressed. They don't care. They don't care that I know Theta, or that Sarah is my sister. That means nothing to them. Though, if they don't understand the principle of human names, or the concept of sisters, how could they care about Theta and Sarah? To them, these girls are nothing but unfortunate female retractors, soon to be executed or pardoned, and some in the audience might not care regardless of this morning's outcome, and their blank ambivalent faces make that clear.

From amongst the Leaders, a new orator steps to the podium. She does not have the white hair or wrinkled skin of the standard orator. Her mouth dips near the microphone, and my ears are filled with a terrible, familiar grating. My audio sensors are still active. The piercing voluminous shrill sound being funneled into my audial sensors is overwhelming. They're taking over my hearing.

The new female orator speaks. The jittered movements of my rifle gradually come under control. My breaths are steadying, and my scope finds its place on the confessional podium and the female speaker.

The progression of her voice is calm, and her expression is tinted with an amount of sincerity.

"Hello. Good morning," she says into the microphone.

Tau and Andrew's voices have faded in my ears, since the majority of my hearing has been confiscated by the retractment, but I can still speak, and they should know what I'm hearing.

"I can hear her," I say into my headset communication link. "I can hear her."

In the corner of my vision, Tau is waving his arms and motioning for my attention. His pointer finger presses against his lips. He's very visibly trying to shush me. I must be shouting and not even realizing it. The retractment has taken over so much of my hearing that it must make every shout sound like a whisper.

He's running toward me, with his head ducked below the ledge. He's here, and his finger presses into my palm. "What is she saying?" he writes.

I've been so distracted by Tau—I hadn't thought to listen. My mind refocuses on the retractment, catching the woman's voice partway through her sentence.

"...and so they will not be permitted to speak"—her voice transmits through my audial sensors—"for their treasons and thoughts contrary to the Common have already spoken more than can be borne." My mouth delicately whispers her words as they transmit through my ears. But there is a strangeness in the quality of her voice. My eye goes into the scope, and I can see a similar quality in the expression on her face. She is sad, or else if not sad, then affected in someway. And this is atypical. The Leaders, and the retractment orators in particular, have never shown any semblance of emotion. They are the human equivalent of a blank wall in most cases, but this is different.

She pauses before beginning the pronouncement of judgement, and bites at her bottom lip before continuing, speaking forcefully into the microphone, with an audible apprehension or angst.

"The Common has found them unrepentant." She shutters in a breath, which might not be noticeable to the average watcher, but I have a scope trained onto her, and I can see every subtle movement.

"Their citizenship shall be taken," she says.

I repeat these words aloud so that Tau and Andrew can hear them through the communication link. How strange it is that a regular Leader would care in the slightest about the death of a citizen or two.

A morning wind blows a bit of the orator's hair, and there is something familiar in it, in the outline of her hair on her forehead, and its wood-colored brown shades with lighter intermixed hues. Something strikes in my brain— my father's eyes, they also had a shared familiarity to them, as if I had seen them before, since they were most like my own eyes: This too, I've seen this hair before. This is Sarah's hair, shared by another person. It bears the same shape and shades of colors.

"All together now," the woman's voice says in my ears.

"All together now," I repeat for Tau.

She begins the ritual. "My heart feels the shame of their deceit..." she says.

My mouth is tightly shut. I can't say it, but I have to. It's the worst thing to say about them. What shame? They have nothing to be ashamed of, but these audio sensors don't only receive sound, they transmit it. I have to complete the ritual or else my inaction might flag their system, that is if they haven't already picked up on my voice print. But there are no drones closing in on us, maybe the signal from my audio sensors is being lost in the torrent of other competing signals. Maybe they haven't recognized me yet, but they definitely will if I don't recite it.

My mouth opens in disgust, filled with words that mean the opposite of what I'm saying. I touch my nose before speaking, as possibly the last code between Theta and I.

"My heart feels the shame of their deceit..."

"My voice speaks a condemnation," the woman says.

"My voice speaks a condemnation," I repeat.

"I consent to their termination," she says, and I repeat her words, but they fall weakly from my lips.

We don't have much time. Tau is shaking me, and scribbling in my hand to get my attention. "Who?" he writes.

Who? Whom do we choose to shoot? How do we decide who lives and who dies? Why is that my choice? We only have one stun bullet, and so our plan has to change.

"Both," I write. And then pointing toward myself with one hand, I write into his palm with the other, "T." Then I point toward him, and palm-write, "S," hoping he understands my message; he seems to.

We are running short on time. I hold up my finger to make the symbol for "one," meaning one shot.

He nods that he understands, but writes in response, "No blood—T."

I shrug my shoulders. This is an even worse plan than before: Sarah will not be unconscious, and Theta won't have any blood on her, but what other choice do we have.

Tau rushes back to his rifle, half-heartedly ducking below the ledge, not caring about drones for the sake of hurrying. Just as I was trained, I kneel into position and we wait for the militants to form their firing line at the front of the stage.

The militants' steps are exact and measured, and as they reach their place they turn into position, one-by-one, raising their rifles in anticipation of their orders. A standard execution contains the call for "ready, aim, fire."

"Shoot on *ready*," Tau says into the headset, which I can only barely hear above the sound of the retractment in my ears.

All the dozen or so militants have marched into position, and are awaiting their orders.

The strangely familiar woman, the new orator, she waits to give her final orders, pausing to stare into the distance, but not vaguely into the distance, to anyone else it might appear that way, but from my perspective it seems that her eyes are focused directly and purposefully onto our secret location, as if she is staring down the scope of my rifle. She pauses to keep her gaze on us for a second or two, then she leans toward the microphone to speak.

My sight turns to Theta. Her eyes are closed in anticipation of the pain to come: eyelids so tightly shut that they wrinkle all the area around her eyes and up around her nose. And she is visibly sad, sad in a way that I have never seen from her, but something happens. The lines on her face soften, and there is a confidence now intertwined within the sadness. Sarah has reached out and grabbed

Theta by the hand, and that small attempt of joining their pains together has made a change in Theta's expression, in a way that maybe only I can tell, because I know her. If I am a terrible shot, if the wind blows again unexpectedly, or if my hours of firing at invisible targets has done nothing, then at least she is not alone, at least there is a hand there for her to hold.

The sound of the woman's voice begins in the microphone. "Re—" she begins to say.

"Ready," I shout through my headset.

I have already gone through many of the steps: I am kneeled into position. My breath calms again in my lungs. My aim is as steady as I have ever made it. My finger is halfway through its slow pull of the trigger. This is it, the one bullet.

The trigger clicks.

Blast! The rifle throws itself backward into my shoulder, slamming like an unsuspected fist into me. And at the same moment my gun is shot, Tau's fires as well, as if ours were only a single shot rippling through the air.

"Re-ady," the woman's voice concludes, with quickening pace.

"Aim."

My bullet strikes! Though I was aiming for Theta's upper half, the stun bullet impacts on her thigh. Her balance instantly collapses, and she is falling as Tau's bullet hits, striking Sarah's left upper torso near her shoulder. Sarah shutters with the impact of the bullet, and turns to fall onto Theta.

But they have not hit the ground before the last word is said.

"Fire," the woman orator commands.

And all the militants' bullets explode from their rifles: One strikes Sarah's leg as she falls, and another wisps through the ends of her hair. And when the gun blasts subside, the two girls are lying on the stage, with spots of blood covering their uniforms, and in a way that would seem to any casual watcher to be a thorough execution.

Sarah is lying still, and almost lifeless, having landed on top of Theta as she fell, and both are spotted with Sarah's blood.

Blood. They're both sharing Sarah's blood. The crowds of citizens are rising from their seats and exiting the stadium. Several militants come to escort the familiar woman Leader from the podium. And two blue uniformed laborers come to drag the girls' bodies away, and both girls are taken by the arms and uncaringly pulled away as if nothing were out of the ordinary.

The signal of the retractment in my ears, it is abruptly cut off, and my hearing is again my own.

We did it! Our impossible plan worked. Grabbing our weapons, we retreat from the ledge and huddle for shelter beneath our metal grate again, and we wait. And it will be hours of waiting, until after sunset, when it is safe for Andrew to return. The heat is already on the edges of being uncomfortable. I reach for my bottle of water that is progressively being warmed by the sun, and take whole gulps of its precious liquid. The water droplets drip from my lips.

Tau turns and gives me a look as he loads a new round into his rifle. I know what he's thinking—we have a full day in the scorching sun, and limited shade; I should save my water for when I really need it. I take another sip and twist the cap closed. My face is leaning toward a patch of shade, trying to get the most I can of it, before the afternoon heat comes. But Tau looks like nothing has changed; he's reclined below a set of nearby grated metal stairs, with his gun recalibrated and aimed at the door to the roof.

Why is he aimed at the door? Doesn't he know we've won? It would be much easier to soak in the last amounts of shade, but I'm too curious. My hand reaches for my empty rifle, and I find a place beside him, underneath the stairs.

He doesn't give much attention to me, but keeps his focus toward the door.

"Did you hear something?" I write, making the shapes of the letters on the ground in front of him, and not speaking in case of passing drones.

"No," he writes in return, with one hand still solidly on his rifle.

"Then why?" I write, and point my finger, alternating between his gun and the rooftop entrance.

He writes all his words without taking his stare away from the door. "Because, we shot two high-powered rifles within the center of Primus. Someone heard it."

I hate this. It was easier being slumped in the dwindling shade, thinking we've already won. But now we're trapped on a soon to be scorching rooftop, until nightfall, and what's worse, I'm out of stun bullets.

And even though I have a completely unused belt of ammunition around my own waist, Tau pulls a bullet from his own set, and offers it to me.

"*Will you take it?*" his face seems to say.

There're no other stun bullets to hide behind. If I take it, I could kill, for the first time in my life I could kill someone.

His face makes a more exaggerated questioning expression, and he inches the bullet nearer to me. I have to make a decision. My fingers reach like a reflex, but then I pause. Is this what I want? Am I going to be a killer? The seconds tick away. My fingers grasp the shell casing. There's no reason I have to make my final decision now.

But it might be better to have it, in case I do need it. The clink of live ammunition is loaded into my rifle. I would rather prefer that I never have to make this choice. I would rather that the door stays shut. And I take another sip of water to help ease my nervous stomach.

38

The day is miserable. In actuality, I might prefer the desert to this. At least in the desert we had more shade, but here there's nothing. The roof is a terrible temperature, and it singes any part of my skin if I set it directly on its almost boiling surface.

My eyes scan around for other adequate places to hide, where we would have cover from the drones above us, and a better collection of shade that we might have somehow missed, but there's nothing. And my skin continues to burn, pressed between the heat of the sky, and the heat of the roof beneath us.

Why hasn't anyone come for us? Didn't they hear the shots, or are they just waiting? Or possibly we've escaped their detection, with our thermal camouflage worn beneath our outer uniforms, and our encrypted communication links. Though at any rate, there's only a few more hours left of daylight, and then Andrew will come back for us. Which was our plan, but an easier thing to plan when we'd never spent an entire blistering day on a roof, helplessly exposed to the sun.

Though every time I want to complain to Tau about the burning of my elbows, which he surely feels the same as I do, or when during the sweltering midday, when I almost used the communication link to call Andrew back early, in those times I've thought about the two in our group who are really suffering, Sarah and Theta, who were shot and stunned, and dragged away to the community graves outside the city, which sound better than they are.

Andrew says they're twenty feet deep, dug pits with shear walls, impossible to climb out of; and often times, the Common will throw in the ailing along with the dead, just to get rid of them. In fact, disgustingly, that's one of the reasons why our plan actually has the potential to work, since the Leaders don't typically care to check if the victims of their retractments are dead first, before they throw them into the graves. And there is one story that Andrew told us, and I wish he hadn't, about a man who had only suffered minor gunshot wounds when he was thrown into the community graves. The story says the man was able to survive for a month, by horrific means, living amongst the dead, until a sympathetic militant rank finally ended his agony—and what did the Common do when they found out about it? They shot the militant in the foot, and threw him in as well. And no one ever shot a living person in the graves after that.

It's too much. My mind can't take the thought of it anymore, and I try to shake it from my head, and focus on the door, and only on the door.

I'm glad Sarah and Theta won't have to stay in there for more than a day, but even that is unimaginable. Focus on the door. I would drink, but my water has been gone for a while by now, and my eyes are heavy from not sleeping. Focus on the door, don't speak, focus on the door, on the door, on the...

■ ■ ■

The door, there is the sound of the door. It's open. A hand covers over my mouth. It's Tau's hand, and he's staring at me, and he takes a huge breath through his nose, as if to encourage me to breathe as well, and to above all stay calm.

Footsteps walk out onto the roof. It is in the twilight, after the sun has already sunken below the edge of the world, but we are not yet fully covered in darkness, so the only thing we can do is to be still.

"Come back, Andrew," Tau whispers with the tiniest voice into our communication link.

Across the roof, the noise of those impending footsteps are two militants.

"You're gonna get us de-ranked for coming up here," a young militant's voice says, sounding slightly frightened and thin, like he's only a few months past his graduation. And this first militant is following closely after the footsteps of a hurried-paced larger militant, and he's rushing to keep up.

The larger one chuckles, with an all-knowing laugh. "You're ridiculous. How are we going to get de-ranked for doing our jobs?" he asks.

That voice. The tall one's voice is so familiar. They're armed and searching casually around the air cooling units, and among the ventilation piping with such unsettling thoroughness.

Their feet skid along the rooftop, and their conversation carries loudly.

"They thermal scanned the roofs. They said not to come up here," the more passive militant answers.

I try to follow them with my eyes whenever possible, as their voices and movements trace around to the far edge of the roof and as they are winding their way back toward us.

"No," the more aggressive voice replies. "They said it would be a waste of time. They never said not to come up here." His voice is so familiar, and it rattles within the walls of my brain. Not so far away, they climb a set of metal grated stairs, a mirrored image of the ones we are hiding under. And they search the raised slatted walkway, and around the larger ventilation fans.

"You're telling me that you didn't hear the gunshots coming from this direction?" the more agitated voice asks. I know that voice. I know I do.

"It was an echo," the other militant responds, reflexively, like he were repeating something told to him.

Both of their guns are held in a ready position. Any drastic movement and we'll be dead.

The larger one scoffs. "Echos happen after gunshots, not before."

"It's the—" the first one tries to protest, maybe thinking of another excuse.

"Listen," the larger one interrupts, with an unexpected rumbling anger in his voice. "I know what I heard... and if not then tell me, who shot Theta?"

He called her Theta. Why would he do that? Why not use her full designation?

Their footsteps are almost on top of us, as they pause to speak. This angry militant, the frame of his body, the way he carries himself—I know that voice.

"I shot the other girl," the angry militant adds. "I know I did, but who shot Theta? No one can tell me who did."

"Maybe I did," the passive militant replies. "I shot kind of early. It could've been me."

"It wasn't you... You get a feeling when you shoot someone, like a prick in your gut. It wasn't you. You'd know it," he says.

"Well, if she's dead now, who cares who shot her?"

"I care... It's not fair. I wanted to be the one to do it," he says.

It's not fair. I've heard that before. And now the voice makes perfect sense, and the pervasive hostility in his mannerisms comes into clearer focus, as if he were within the scope of my rifle. He wanted to kill Theta, not just because of her, but because of what she represented, for me and for Tau who got away, and humiliated him. That's Delta. That's his voice, that hates for no human reason, and won't be easily deterred from its anger.

And my mind returns to our fight in the militant training center, and to his hands gripped around my neck, squeezing until he was forced to stop.

The entire roof is silent, as Delta's boots rest directly in front of our eyes on the steps. In Tau's hand is his tactical knife, firmly gripped; I don't know how long he's had it like that. With any swipe he could slice through Delta's legs, but then there's the other militant with his rifle. Though that's not the worst of our problems: We could turn our guns on them and murder, but then our location would definitely be discovered, with nothing to disguise these new gunshots. Or we could use our knives, but even if we could overpower them, and manage to not be shot ourselves, if they saw us just once, a passing glimpse in the corner of their eye, or if they heard our voices make any sound, then the facial recognition and voice scanners would immediately lock in on us, and we'd be encircled by drones and dead within a few minutes.

And so our lips stay sealed shut. The air barely fills into my lungs, until every bit that I do allow in is painful, because I won't permit myself to breathe anymore than the lower limit of my necessity. We cannot risk any minuscule sound, and perhaps they won't check under the stairs. In the time since they first started searching the roof, the light has fallen completely. It's replaced by new layers of shadow for us to hide ourselves in: if we are quiet, and only if we are quiet.

Andrew's voice whispers into my ears, through my communications headset. "Sorry I'm late. I had to wait till after sunset to sneak the girls out."

My neck tenses; shivers run down my back. A heavy breath comes into my nose, that I'm sure they can hear.

Tau glance at me, and grips his knife handle more tightly until his knuckles whiten.

His hand goes up to the step where Delta's legs are, and he reels back for a strike.

The passive militant speaks, interrupting Tau's blade. "Did you hear that?" he asks.

"What?" Delta says, his voice as gritty as the desert sand.

The passive one is leaning over the railing, as if he's peering in the dark to see to the opposite end of the roof. "I thought I heard a drone landing over there," he says, and points in the direction of the sound with the tip of his rifle.

"You can't hear a drone, infant. They're silent," Delta replies.

"No, but you can hear the landing gears," the passive one responds, like he's too involved with the drone sounds to care that Delta is insulting him. "There's a tick, when the metal hits a solid surface." And before Delta can reply, the other militant is walking back along the raised platform toward the unknown sound.

And Delta turns, climbing the stairs again to follow after him. "It's nothing," Delta says, but the other militant is shushing him.

They're gone. Full breaths fill up the deep parts of my lungs, for maybe the first time in minutes.

Tau is whispering, cupping his hand over the microphone receiver in front of his lips. "Two militants on the roof, headed your way. Stay there. Alpha and I will take them out before they reach you."

And Tau lifts his knife up, making a motion to show me

how to stab the blade for a quick kill. But I'm shaking my head the whole time he's demonstrating it, and I'm fairly certain that there must be a disgusted look pressed upon my face.

"No," I say, with more volume than I should.

"Why not?" Tau asks.

"I don't know, just no," I answer.

There has to be a better way than that. And I hate Delta —I hate him for the way he wants to be the one to kill Theta, for the way he wants to get back at us for humiliating him when we evaded his search group in the forest, and I hate him for the way his fingers felt around my throat, but I don't hate him this much, to thrust a knife into him without warning. There has to be a better way. If this is what we do when the Common is not in our ears and eyes, and when the only requirements placed upon us are our own, then how are we any different from the Leaders who indiscriminately kill for their own safety. I left the Common so that I could escape the Leaders' cruelty, and now, am I supposed to let myself become like those people I ran from?

Is there any other option? Anything else in my brain that could save all of our lives at the same time. I should at least give Delta the benefit of those thoughts first, before I allow myself the alternative.

Allow... allow. That's it.

"Andrew, you have to yell at them," I say, cupping my hands over my microphone receiver. "They're afraid to be on the roof because they think their militant leaders will be mad at them... Yell, yell as loud as you can. Say that they will be de-ranked for disobeying orders and wasting search time, if they don't leave immediately."

There's no response in our headset links. We wait, but still nothing, and so we leave our place below the stairs, and rush toward the opposite end of the roof. On the way, I retrieve my tactical knife from its holder.

A shout breaks the pace of our silent, hurried run.

"What are you doing here?" Andrew's voice blasts into our ears.

At the far corner of the roof, Delta's reply is more softly heard, though he's probably speaking in full voice, but in comparison to Andrew's bellowing voice in our ears it sounds like a timid response.

"We were search—" Delta says, but is harshly interrupted.

"You were wasting needed time, and disobeying orders. I should de-rank you right now for this blatant disregard," Andrew says. His demeanor seems to have fallen instantly back into a familiar militant arrogance, so that it's almost impossible, even for myself, to think that he couldn't de-rank them now, if he wanted to.

"See, I told you," the other militant adds.

Tau and I have crept up to where the drone has landed. Andrew has left the pilot's seat and is confronting Delta and the other militant to their faces, but Delta's not backing away like the other militant. His stance is still aggressive, imitating Andrew's.

"You're gonna de-rank me, are you?" Delta says, and

toughens up his chin and smirking mouth. "Tell me, what's my designation?" he asks, with a slow and calculating expression in his voice.

Andrew is blankly still, and, worst of all, unanswering.

My hand firmly cups over my microphone. Tau and I begin to give the designation, but he lets me finish on my own. "Delta 647-40-1," I say, with clearly distinct numbers.

And Andrew steps closer toward Delta's unconvinced face and loaded rifle. He repeats Delta's designation with the same slow and calculating response.

This has broken through. Delta's posture adjusts, as he takes a step backward, and then another.

"I can't believe I ever let you talk me into this," the other militant is saying as they hurry away. A half-minute later the roof door slams shut.

It worked! We rush from our hiding spot, almost jumping up and down with excitement. The girls are here. They are both painfully crammed into the empty space behind Andrew's seat. Their uniform shirts are covered with spots of blood and filth.

We hurry toward the drone, and as Andrew is climbing into his chair we ask them how they feel.

Sarah's voice is frail, but joking. "How do I look?" she says, forcing an even more feeble smile.

"Fantastic," Tau replies. Which is not the word I would have used to describe her, but it elicits a better smile from her, and so it might be an appropriate falsehood in this instance.

Theta's eyes are dazed and partially closed. Weeks of mistreatment and the effects of the stun bullet have made her words ramblingly fragile. "I knew you would come... I always knew it. Even though I told you not to, I knew you would come," she says.

Here she is, at last. Words fill into my mouth, all the best things I've ever wanted to say to her, compressed into one tiny phrase.

But they are stopped with a *blast*.

A gun blast, a bullet whizzes past the top of my hair, missing all of us, but striking the glass cockpit covering and shattering fragments down onto our heads. And as the glass falls, small cuts form over our whole bodies, but the glass hasn't finished falling before Tau turns and fires at an exposed knee at the far end of the roof, near the reopened door.

There is a cry of excruciating pain. The passive militant is twisting on the ground. Then another bullet skims by Tau, hitting the wall ledge behind him.

The wind forced through the drone engines is swirling all around us. Andrew, and Theta, and Sarah are fleeing toward the safety of the sky, while Tau and I run for cover behind an air cooling unit.

Half of my head and my left eye peer around the corner. My partial vision searches the roof for any sign of Delta. Without warning, Tau pulls at my uniform collar and jerks me into complete hiding again. His face is furious. "Never —" he begins to say, when a new bullet hits the corner of our air cooling unit, where my head had been.

We don't know where Delta is, and we can't look for him. And so instead, Tau grabs a large fragment of nearby glass, and inches it around his side of the air cooling unit to get the reflection; a charging, towering militant takes up almost the whole glass. Instantly, a boot comes around the corner, pounding itself into Tau's forehead, and he is sprawled on the ground by the force of the unexpected blow.

Delta's gun is up, and focused on Tau. It raises to his shoulder for the kill. But my gun is raised as well, not out of particular violence, but out of need. My shot fires before Delta makes his attempt. It strikes through his near forearm and clinks against the stock of his gun.

And Tau is on his feet as Delta screams. With one clenched fist, he grabs at the barrel of Delta's gun, and with the other fist he punches into Delta's now open wound. Tau rips Delta's rifle away from him and flings it over the ledge. To anyone who would see this fight it is clearly unevenly matched. After all, Tau had lived as a militant for almost the entirety of his time at the School, and Delta had only had a week of training before his graduation, so that even with Delta's massive size advantage he's quickly overtaken.

Tau slams him to the ground, digging the heel of his boot into Delta's wrist, and with the other boot, he presses it onto Delta's neck.

"How do you like that!" he shouts down at Delta, whose face is turning red. "It doesn't feel good to be choked, does it? ...Does it!"

Delta gargles out an unintelligible answer, and kicks his legs trying to get loose, so Tau adjusts his position placing all of his weight onto a knee at the center of Delta's chest.

"Stop struggling," Tau warns, but Delta won't listen, so Tau has his tactical knife out and sticks the tip into Delta's thigh, not as far as he could stab it, but just enough to make his point. And Delta stops struggling immediately.

"Kill me," the words choke from Delta's mouth.

"I'm not going to kill you," Tau answers. Then he points the bloody-tipped knife toward me, saying, "He doesn't want me to. I don't care, but he doesn't want me to."

And it seems like those unimaginable words alone could kill Delta, as he stares at me with the most unbelieving eyes. "How could you be the one to want to save me?" they seem to be saying, and for that I have no answer. And it's not that I necessarily want to be the one to save his life—I just don't want to be the one to kill him.

Andrew is in our ears, saying that he's coming back, and that a watcher has probably seen us by now.

Our drone descends from the night sky. He's right; there's no doubt that the watchers have seen us by now. We have to fly away from their sensors as soon as we can, if it's not too late already. But something triggers inside my thoughts—the watchers are probably seeing Delta's visual feed by now, and maybe even the Leaders, though if not now, they will see it eventually. In all my years of hiding my thoughts from them, with secret codes, and with swallowing all the words I would like to have said to them, deep down inside of me, now I can finally let them out. And they will hear me; they will have to hear me.

I stand over Delta, and peer into his eyes, through his eyes into his visual sensors, and speak what would certainly get my citizenship revoked, not that that matters now anyway. These are the words that have built up over the years, pressed down by fear, and a lack of understanding, but now I can say them; now I will be heard.

"To the watchers and Leaders in Primus, my name is Alpha Robins. My whole life I've been afraid of you—I've held onto credits that don't mean anything. I've learned all the lies that you wanted me to, and watched as my schoolmates and fellow citizens were murdered in front of my eyes, and I said nothing. But now I can... and I only have one thing to say to you, Revolution." My voice builds. "Revolution." And with a smile growing upon my face because I know they can hear me, and because I know how much they hate this word, and fear what it could do to them, in a soft voice, looking past Delta's eyes, I say a third time, "Revolution."

And Andrew dips down to the roof level without fully landing, and Tau and I wrap up quickly in the harness straps, dangling from the wings, and we're gone.

39

"I can't believe you would do that," Andrew says to me with his mouth still hanging open, like he doesn't know what else to say.

We've landed in the desert, in the cold hours of night: after flying for a few miles, then landing to readjust our harness straps, then returning to the field by the river to retrieve Sarah's extra bottle of water that she left when she was captured, then back to the sky, and flying until the battery charge on our solar-fueled drone finally ran out.

We are stranded in the desert until the sun can give us enough fuel to make it back, and Andrew is at last confronting me for what I did.

"It's like you stuck your thumb in an anthill, and you expect not to be bit," he adds.

"Why does it matter?" I say. "They wanted to kill us before. I didn't do anything."

Andrew scoffs. "No, they were annoyed with you before... But now you've got their attention. *Now* they want to kill you."

If he's right, if this has only been a slightly annoyed Common until this point, then I would hate to see what they'll try to do when they're mad.

Theta, from her small amount of medical rank training, is wrapping strips of cloth around Sarah's shoulder, trying to keep the pressure on it, to prevent the wound from reopening, and Tau is helping with what he can.

"He's right," Tau comments, turning toward me. "That was dumb."

I didn't know that the Common didn't care about us, but maybe it makes sense. If they had really cared to see us dead, then it's likely they would have found us already. And with that understanding, we'll have to be extra cautious heading back to Logos.

And in that same line of thought, Andrew tells Theta to hurry with her "nurse work" and that we'll have to take out her location sensor before we leave.

"Right here?" I ask. "We don't have any pain medicine. She'll—"

He cuts off my words. "I don't care," Andrew says. "I won't fly any closer to the city"—he points at Theta —"with this walking *homing beacon* here with us."

Maybe there's a different way to disrupt the signal without having to cut open the back of her neck.

Tau speaks up, as he's holding Sarah's bandage tight, while Theta ties a knot. "I think she can handle it," he says. "I cut mine out myself." Tau's voice is flat as he says it, not bragging, like digging a knife into the back of one's neck were as normal and average as taking a sip of water.

"I'm fine, Alpha," Theta says, securing the last knot on Sarah's bandages, to which Sarah gives a withheld yelp. Then Theta adds, "If this is what I have to do, then I'll do it," she says.

And the focus of her eyes settles onto mine—I wanted as soon as we rescued her for that to be the end of her pain, but I can't assure her of that, and she understands. Those are the sorts of things we can see in each other's eyes. After such a long time of not being able to speak in true complete sentences to each other, we've developed a skill to tell each other things without speaking.

"Who gets to be the one to do it, then?" I ask.

Tau says it should be he who does it, and I ask why. Though I must sound defensive, which I can tell by the vocalness of Tau's response. "Because I'm the only one of us who's cut one out before... and anyway, could you do it? Could you realistically stick a knife in her and know how much pressure to give it?"

All the defensive tension, I didn't even know I had, melts away. "No," I answer.

We find a spot on the open sand to do it, and wrap a blindfold around her eyes, because maybe that will help, and we place a folded piece of cloth in her mouth for her to bite onto. Tau asks us to help him restrain her, and I try to hold her arms, while Andrew grabs her legs. And Sarah, who can't do anything else because of her injuries, gives her best attempt at encouragement.

"You're doing great, Theta," she says. "You're gonna be strong. I know it," she adds.

Tau moves aside the red curls of her hair and begins the process. Immediately, the pain seizes on her face, contorting and twitching it.

"That's it," Sarah adds. "You're almost done."

Which is a decent thing to say, but I would rather keep her mind off the pain, perhaps if I can get her to think about something she likes, it will help.

The idea comes into my brain.

"You remember the..."—she yelps—"the sunsets we used to watch on the lawn?" I say. And she starts to try to reply, but Tau is warning her not to talk. "Just listen," he says. And I continue, "You remember how flawless they were?" I say. And her face is changing as her mind shifts to the sunsets. "Well, I found out that they weren't real. They're only a..."—she whimpers—"a generated image on our visual sensors."

Theta is moaning in pain as Tau moves his finger under the skin to get the sensor out.

And Sarah interjects, "Really, Alpha, I don't think that's helping," she says.

But I don't respond to her, and continue talking to Theta, saying, "When we get to the city, I'll show you a real sunset. They're so much wilder than anything the Common could come up with, with colors you've never imagined."

Her face relaxes from the extreme pain.

"That's it," Tau says, and he has the sensor in his hand, which he shows to us, and he lets Theta feel it since she still has her blindfold on. It's a miniscule squared piece of material with thin gold lines running through it, and stretching out from the center are eight metallic wires, which makes the whole thing look, in fact, very much like a spider.

And Andrew and Tau dig a hole to bury it in, while Theta tells me how to wrap strips of cloth around her own head, and how to hold pressure on her neck to stop the bleeding.

"Are the sunsets really that great?" she asks, through gritted heavy breaths, that obviously still feel pain.

"You've never seen anything like it," I say.

And when Tau and Andrew return, Tau asks the girls a question, which none of us really want the answer to, but one that should be talked about.

"What were the graves like?" he asks.

And Sarah tells us the answer, and we all hate the answer, and the graves, and the Common for making us ask the question. And there is crying. And sometime in the hours before dawn, Theta falls asleep beside me, and I don't ask her about the graves, and she doesn't say anything... she's too hurt for that right now, perhaps eventually, if we can make it back to Logos, alive.

40

"Is the real sun always this hot?" Theta palm-writes into my hand. She still has her blindfold over her eyes, so she wasn't able to see the sunrise, but now we all can feel the rising desert heat.

"It might be hotter here, than other places," I reply in writing.

We aren't talking. It's been too many hours since we left Primus, and the Leaders have probably since then dispatched all their available drones to come look for us. And besides this, Theta and I still have active audio sensors, and Theta still has her visual sensors. So, she's kept on her blindfold, and none of us have said anything vocally since the sun came up this morning.

But now we're sitting in the heat of a lifeless desert, waiting for the solar fuel to fill into the drone batteries again. And in the in-between time while we wait, hiding beneath the drone wings for shelter, I try to tell Theta about Logos, about Chi's plan to rescue me, and about my escape from the School, and also whom each one in our group is: Tau she knows, and Andrew can be easily explained, as a one-time militant who's now a reliable helper, but Sarah takes more time—mainly because I have to explain the concept of sister, and with that what father and mother mean, and what it is to have a family.

After a few minutes of writing she says she understands, and I'm sure she does. But it's one thing to know the meaning of words; it's another thing to live with them in a way that they become real. So that for her, sister is simply an idea, but for me sister means Sarah, and that's probably a difference she doesn't yet understand.

From the corner of my eye, Andrew is making a motion with his hands—we're leaving. The hours in the sun have filled the drone batteries, or filled them enough. We help Sarah and Theta into their spot, because of their injuries, and Tau and I tie ourselves into the straps hanging from the wings. The engine engages, and the desert falls away below us. I'll be satisfied if we never return to it. And though the sand and the dunes have their own agreeable qualities from this high distance, I know better now. I know how much they drain your life away, and it's nothing I would like to see again.

After several hours, and passing over mountains, there is the Ocean far away, and coming closer. In the distance are the broken Pre-Common buildings of the Ruined City. From this height, it is easy to see that it is nowhere near the sprawling size of Primus, but the mind can better fill in the destructed pieces from this vantage point. In this city, there were large quarters and smaller quarters, but nothing so drastic, or delineated and segmented as Primus. If the Pre-Commons had their own version of Leaders, then the lines between them and their citizens were much more passable. Or at least it seems that way, when seen from the ruins of a deserted city: many, many generation cycles ago destroyed.

We lower and land in a place that will keep our drone hidden, as Andrew palm-writes upon our arrival. And we see no other drones circling for us, or seeking us out, and so it is safe to go below ground, back through the ancient Pre-Common waste tunnels, to the entrance for the underwater tunnel route to Logos.

And when we find it again, for several minutes Andrew is speaking through a disguised communication box, begging for the elected officials to deactivate the explosive lined corridor and let us back into the city.

"Have you been followed?" they ask.

"No," he answers.

"Convince us," they argue, and he does. And this goes on for many more minutes, until they finally agree to let us return.

Which is not a welcomed return, since immediately they force us to be brought to the six elected officials, all of us except for Theta, who is quarantined in a signal sealed medical quarters.

We are in the elected officials' meeting place, with their long table, still with seven chairs, but the seat in the center is no longer empty—it has been filled by the familiar balding male official who angrily does not give us much time to explain ourselves. And their militant guards are surrounding us on all sides with drawn and ready guns.

"Why did you go after her?" this leading elected official says.

And maybe this is a trap, but I answer anyway. "Because we had to help her," I say.

"Had to?... Had to?" he repeats. Then yelling out his thoughts, he says, "With you two"—pointing to Tau and me— "I can believe that, but Sarah... Andrew, you've put the whole city in real danger. For what, for some citizen girl?"

And no one else is saying anything, but I can't let this go unchallenged. "Her name is Theta," I announce, getting each of the officials' full attention, and still I speak, "...and if we're not going to risk ourselves for people like Theta, then for whom? Who is good enough to fight for?"

The lead official's fist pounds atop their long table. "You *half-breed*," he shouts at me. "You have no idea what you're saying."

Then the female official with pulled back hair, who was pleasant with me before we left the first time, she quiets the man and says at a softer volume, "You don't know how dangerous it is to fight them. They're too strong."

Through the doors behind us, the hub of technology ranks have entirely stopped typing on their mismatched outdated display monitors. The yelling must have distracted all their attentions, and so both rooms are completely quiet as I speak.

"Then they will always be too strong," I say.

There is nothing but silence. Although in the corner of the elected officials' meeting room is a half-filled bucket catching drips of water from the roof, and each droplet is crashing with an echoing reverberation because of the silence.

After several long seconds, the leading male official speaks pushing through the silence with his voice. "You cannot stay here," he says. "You all will be *exiled*."

Sarah gasps, because she likely knows what that means. "Please, Johnathan," she says, with a sad strain. "You can't make us leave—that will kill us."

"It's already been decided," he answers, then holds his bottom lip up tightly.

But Sarah won't take it, even with all her many recent injuries, and while seated in a medical wheeled-chair beside me, because of the wound on her leg. "Then I call for a citywide vote," she orders.

"It's already been taken, while you were gone," the softer spoken woman replies.

Sarah clenches her eyelids, as if the woman's statement was painful to her.

And Andrew finally joins in. "And was the ballot close? Would it matter if Sarah and I elected to stay?"

"No," the softer woman speaks. Then several seconds later, she adds, "I'm sorry—your votes wouldn't make a difference. But we will allow for surgeries first. Theta is already having hers as we speak."

How could they already be cutting into her, without us knowing? With all this voting, it seems like that would be something we'd get a vote on.

"Did you tell her about the risks?" I ask.

298

And she assures me that they did, and that Theta agreed, if that was the only way to be sure that the Common could no longer find her.

And that's it—the officials have finished speaking with us, and they won't hear Sarah's pleading, or Andrew's logical arguments, yet Tau never says a word. And the militant guards lead us away from the officials' meeting quarters: Tau, and Sarah, and Andrew to separate confinements areas, and me to my own medical quarters for surgery.

My surgeon, Doctor Smith, who is the same grey-haired doctor I had before, she says that since the supersonic pulse failed to break my audio senors the first time, then they can assume it would fail again, and so a brand new and experimentally untested surgical procedure must be implemented to sever my audial sensors from my inner ears.

"Brand new?" I say. "As in, I'm the first?"

"Well, there always has to be a first, Alpha," she says. And when I ask why the non-surgical method would have worked with Tau, and is planned for Theta, though not for me, she explains that because of my father's history with the Common, that they likely used a newer, more reinforced model of audio sensor in my ears, and that Theta and Tau had probably a more standard version of audio sensor. This seems to make sense, but after this the reality of having my eardrums sliced open begins to settle in.

"Will the surgery affect my hearing?" I ask. "Or, at least, is there a chance it will?"

This makes the doctor pause. She puts a finger to her lips as if to think of a best response. "Let me say it this way,

Alpha," she begins, "...if you leave the city without having the surgery, there's a one hundred percent chance of you being discovered by the Common. And I would take a little bit of hearing loss over that any day."

Though "a little bit of hearing loss" might be a more sympathetic way to say complete deafness. And it's easy for Doctor Smith to say that that's what she would prefer, when she doesn't have to be the one to live with it.

Yet, even still, there are a decent amount of things that I would never care to hear again: the screeching sound that blares in my ears when the Common confiscates my hearing, the monotonous dull of unending pointless lectures, the noise of howling animals as they chase through the Ruined City. But there is only one sound that I have to hear again, a voice that I would risk the Common finding me for, if it meant I could hear it.

The double signal-sealed doors of my medical quarters open and shut, bringing in assistant medical ranks for my surgery.

"Can I talk to her before we begin?" I ask the Doctor, forgetting to qualify that "her" means Theta, but I think she understands.

"No," she says, and stares at me with sad eyes, likely mimicking my own. "And besides she's under such heavy medication that she'd never be awake enough to hear you speak, or if you could wake her, she'd be in such pain that you wouldn't want her to be awake to hear you."

I wish there could be another option, in which she could be awake and not in pain, but that doesn't seem possible.

"Then, can I just speak to her as she sleeps? Even if she can't hear me, or remember that I spoke, I would know. Please..."

This request finally breaks through her strict medical training, that would inform her that my request is a ridiculous one. But what is one more ridiculous endeavor, among so many others?

I am led quickly into the nearest medical quarters. Theta is on an operating bed, tubes flowing in and out of her body, and the reddest most violent bruising around her swelling eyes. The other doctors in the room are removing gloves, and rinsing doses of blood from their hands.

Doctor Smith goes to one of the other doctors as he's washing in between his fingers and around the nails. "How was it?" she asks, and they discuss the flawlessness of the procedure, and their expectations for her recovery. But I am only looking at her.

She has tubes drawn into her nose, and display monitors of every sort positioned around her, some dripping liquids into her veins, but her nearest hand, if looking at her hand and at nothing else, it looks about the same as it always has. I take it and write a message in her palm, something only we would know and understand, "No more bad dreams, ever again."

And my hand stays wrapped around hers—if she can't hear me or see me, then maybe she can feel my hand around hers. And then I speak aloud, "I'm here... You're alright. The doctors say, your eyes will heal—just don't scratch them, no matter how irritated they feel. Don't scratch." There is a pressure on my hand, a slow squeeze and then she releases. She can hear me; she wants me to know she can hear me.

My face glows with a smile. "She can hear me," I say to the Doctor, who is smiling at me now as well.

"Well, go on," she says, and glances her eyes to Theta.

And I continue, "They have to do a surgery on my audial sensors... and it's a new surgery, so they don't yet know all the risks." Her fingers squeeze my hand, and the beep that represents her heart shows a gradual increase. Her breaths are coming in more agonizing strains. My waking her must be making her feel the pain.

"Hurry, Alpha, you have to let her rest," Doctor Smith says.

And it all has to come out now: these might be the last words we ever say to each other.

"I know, if I can't hear, that we'll still find a way to speak—we have a code for everything else; codes for words shouldn't be that hard—and so, I'm not afraid of that. I just wanted you to be the last person I spoke to. I felt like it was something important that I could give to you, something that you deserved to have, and no one else."

The doctor tugs at my arm. Theta's heart is speeding and body rigid. Her hand squeezes continually now.

And my words stop... that's also something I can give to her, and there're only so many words that can fit into the time we've had, and that time is ending. I can feel the limit of it, like the limit of air in a single breath, that once it is expelled is gone forever. But all the while it was in my lungs, it helped me to live.

Doctor Smith says I have to leave, and I nod in agreement. And the last part of Theta I hear is the steady beep of her heart rate monitor: A single solitary sound that I play over and over in my head, until the sharp surgical knife pricks into my tender eardrum.

41

A rumble, a vibrating shock pulses through my bed. My eyes open with the shake still felt through my body. Display monitors tip and crash to the ground. The lights transition from dim eeriness to complete blackness, in odd, immeasurable increments.

And there is no sound, absolutely nothing. Not even the sound that silence makes in your ears. There is definitely zero noise, as if I'd never had ears at all. The whole flashing room with falling and shattering glass, which I know has sound, has nothing. My mind fills in the sounds that would be here within the rattling underwater city: with falling objects breaking, and the ominous rumbling boom, and the screeching of shifting metal roof panels. But these sounds can only fill my imagination, for in my ears there is no sound that can reside, nothing. Complete nothingness, and a level of deafness, unimaginable until now.

Another rattling, an explosive shake happens again, except this time more brutal. The city is unsafe. It is impossible that the dilapidated structure can handle this much violent force. Even under regular conditions, there were leaks and unsettling creaking noises, but with these rumblings the city must be coming to its end.

My feet leave the bed and sink into puddles of water to the ankles. The lights of my room continue in unreliable sequence, and I have just enough time to see my feet sink into the cold dark water, before the lights shutter into solid blackness.

Tubes and imbedded needles are pulled from my veins without a care for the pain that emanates through my body.

The chilled water that was only to the ankles when my feet first dipped below it, is now inches above that and rising. The city is sinking. Theta! My feet slosh in the frigid water. My hands pull open the double sealed doors and as I wade into the hallway. To the right, to the nearest door, my fingers feel along the wall, Theta's door, and I enter.

My toe kicks a fallen object, jamming the joint. Uncontrollable, silent screams burst from my mouth, though only silent to myself, to everyone else they must be audible bellows of pain.

Moving forward, the bed, her hand.

"I'm here," I write.

She squeezes with a trembling grip and writes in painfully slow, almost indecipherable letters.

"A-L-P-H-A?" she writes.

"Yes," I answer at a written pace that she might be able to comprehend. "Leaving. Danger," I add, and I pull the needles from her arms, much more slowly than I pulled them from my own arms.

She doesn't try to stop me. She must trust the reality of our danger, and she helps as I pull the tubes from her nose. As uncomfortable as that is, she doesn't struggle. In the all-encompassing darkness around us, she must be able to hear the collapse of Logos: maybe she hears the rush of flooding waters, which now go up to my knees, maybe she hears the crumpling of the city's structure. Whatever she hears, it is enough to welcome the removal of her pain medication supplies, so it must be abhorrently terrifying.

I help her from the bed, but her limbs cannot make their regular movements, and she drops into the water that to her must be waist deep.

I lift her out of the deathly water, and her fingers grip my hands with such agony that she could almost break the bones. She cannot walk. I drag her out of the water and into my arms. We are so weak, and our bodies racked with such trauma, but somewhere inside myself is a strength reserved for this moment and for her.

The vicious cold water struggles against my legs as I push them ahead. We are out of her medical quarters and the water now flows with an obvious current around the mid-portion of my belly.

The city is black and drowning. Another rumble shakes through the water that is rapidly burying me. We are lost; and the rising flood will soon overtake us. Even if the lights were on, I would have no idea where to go.

My mouth drops open, and shouts I cannot hear pour out, as I try to keep Theta above the water line.

"Help! Sarah! Tau! Andrew!" I know the words I'm yelling, but I cannot tell how loud they are. And so I scream until the words feel raw in my throat.

"Help! Help!" I shout. And on the third "Help!" I feel the grip of a hand reaching for me. These hands are rough, and too large to be Sarah's, and more calloused and worn than Andrew's, and too strong to be Tau's hands. They lift me up and Theta with me, holding up the both of us as we press through falling water that pours through the roof.

I know these hands. I learned them through hours of palm-writing, in our escape from the School and in our blindfolded journey through the forest. These are Chi's hands, made hearty from years of laboring in the lowest, most humiliating ranking.

And we are carried through the water, but still the level rises. It is now up to my ears, soaking the bandages and seeping into my opened ear ways. The instant shock of pain, almost shuts down my whole body, sending shivers down my neck and through every nerve.

But the complete darkness is now no longer as complete. We come around a corner and a single beam of light reflects on top of the water, through an opening at the far end of the hall ahead of us. Along this whole hallway there are sealed doorways, spaced close beside one another, and the only doorway still open is this last one. And there, inside what appears to be a tiny lit room, are Sarah, and Tau, and Andrew, waving for us to hurry ahead.

The chilled water splashes in through my nose, and burns as it chokes in my lungs, but this only happens once. And then we are carried safely into the tiny lit room, with measurement displays and handled levers all around us.

Tau and Andrew pull us in, with Andrew holding Theta's head and pain-ridden face above water, and Tau holding me up. And Sarah is standing on her one good leg, using a railing to hold herself above the still rising water level.

We are safe. We should shut the door before the waters can rise any further, but Chi doesn't come inside. He rushes out into the darkness once more.

Why is he leaving? A long way from us, at the very start of the door lined hall, our single beam of light rests on the miniature face of an infant girl. She is struggling to swim in the rushing flow, to keep her head above the surface. She is potentially four or five years of age. Her hair drenched, and little eyes wide open with fear. But her head sinks below the water before Chi is halfway through the hall. Seconds pass, and nearly a minute, finally he reaches the place where her tiny head had gone under, and he lifts up an unresponsive body, and carries her back to our quickly drowning room. We are breathing in the air at the ceiling, when he swims through the entry door, still holding on to the lifeless infant.

Then Sarah twists a wheel, and the outside hallway door is shut. The water stops rising. And she twists another wheel and a secondary, inner door is shut and sealed.

Sarah's mouth is moving, and Andrew responds, possibly to a question. Her hand pulls on a nearby lever, and the water level in our room starts to decrease.

My attention focuses again on the little infant. Her face is turning a shade of blue, or purple. She is held up in Chi's arms, and Theta says some frail words, and Chi responds, and she speaks again. It is almost impossible to know what they are saying, but it has to be about the infant. Theta's lips move and they form the shape of a word that might be "breathe."

And it must be that word, because Chi wraps his mouth around the infant girl's mouth and nose, and breathes in a full breath. Then, once more. And a choking gulp of water bursts from the girl's lungs and mouth. The color of her face is returning to normal with each vital breath. She is alive, and there has never been a happier pair of faces, both the little girl's and Chi's. She squeezes her weary arms around Chi's neck as the level of water drops below my waist.

Andrew engages another lever, and our miniature inclosed room shifts, detaching from the rest of the city. We are leaving. Our rapidly draining room is floating, or is being propelled, away from Logos.

The city that was supposed to bring us safety is dead and drowning below the deep water. But we are not. We are alive, all of us.

42

The little girl's name is Bridget. During the destruction of Logos, in the darkness and the crashing of water, in the commotion of fleeing crowds of people, she was separated from a woman she calls "Mommy" and a man she calls "Daddy"—which Sarah says means mother and father, respectively.

We float on below the Ocean for hours, and Sarah acts as my voice in the conversation, as we palm-write messages between each other.

After a while, she writes that Tau says, "Bombs." And Andrew, and everyone else but Theta, who is wearily asleep, agrees with him. The rumbling I felt, and that they heard, must have been bombs. The Common had discovered us, somehow; they had followed us through the massive desert and through the Ruined City back to Logos.

"They let us live in Primus, so that they could track us," I write, with Sarah speaking for me.

And Tau agrees, saying, "All those gunshots, and they never sent a drone. They wanted to kill us, but they were taking their time."

And Sarah speaks, then palm-writes so I can understand her words, "Yeah, in their eyes, better to kill a thousand innocent people than only five."

In all this devastation, and nervous exhaustion, it is hard to remember that it was the middle of the night in Logos time, but Bridget still remembers, as she curls up beside the sleeping Theta, laying her head in Theta's lap.

Andrew is mumbling to himself, and Sarah writes his words. "How did they find us?" His forehead rests in one of his hands, as he continues to mouth words, "They weren't following us..."

"Thermal scanners?" Chi asks.

"No... not at that distance," Andrew responds, still perplexed.

"Not Theta's visual sensors," Tau adds, counting through the possibilities on his fingers. "Those were blind-folded, and inactive.

"And not our audio sensors," I write. "They never tried to ping my sensors like they did before."

Andrew stiffens and looks up, with his eyes fixed onto Sarah, and he might be mad at himself for not thinking of it sooner.

"That only leaves one other option... another location sensor," he says.

And there is an interchange between Sarah and Andrew, that she forgets to write into my hand at first, but when she does, the summary of their conversation goes something like this:

"S- Why are you looking at me?"

"A- After you were shot, did you ever feel anything, like a bug trying to worm its way into your skin? Maybe on your way to the graves? Or while you were there?"

And this is when Sarah remembers to begin writing in my hand again. "Well that seems like an impossible question," she says. "There were swarms of bugs all over the graves—" Then she pauses, remembering a particular instance. "Actually, there was one time I thought I felt something bite my leg, but when I looked down, there was nothing there."

Andrew's face changes with terror. "Get it out, now," he says to Tau, frantically pointing toward Sarah's leg.

At this, Sarah stops palm-writing, but it's obvious what's happening, as Tau kneels down beside her and gently unwraps the bandages from her leg, where Delta shot her. Her recent wound was mended and stitched closed by the medical ranks in Logos.

Tau says something while holding the sides of her head with his hands, and Sarah nods like she understands the pain that she's agreeing to.

Then Tau takes out his tactical knife, and precisely cuts a portion of the stitching, just enough to fit his two fingers through the wound. Sarah sucks in, or bites her lip, trying to keep in a scream. But she can't keep it in entirely, which startles Theta, and the restful Bridget, waking them from their sleep.

The new blood dripping from Sarah's wounded leg and the sight of Tau with his fingers below the skin must be unbearable for an infant like Bridget, who has not seen the same amount of meaningless death and bloodshed like we have. Tears explode from her tiny eyes, and she reaches out her hands to try to help Sarah, or to try to stop Tau, but she can't do either, as Chi wraps her up in his arms and holds her weeping face to his chest.

Her tiny face that once was so happy is breaking. And a thought drops into my mind: it is not that she has not seen the same amount of death and violence as we have, or that we had seen at her age... perhaps the truth is that she's never seen any of those things at all. The whole of her young life has been lived in safety, away from the Common, but now that safety has been destroyed, she is flung out into the vicious world that the Common controls; and all this is because I made a plan to save Theta, not caring about the danger it would create for myself, and not thinking of the devastation it might create for others.

Tau turns his fingers below the skin, as Sarah's face cringes. And his grip fastens onto something, and his fingertips reemerge holding a miniature technology square with eight wiry legs like a spider.

Its legs tick and twinge, as if it is actually alive. Tau sets it on the ground, with its legs in the air. But as soon as he does, its multi-jointed legs bend downward and it scurries across the floor leaving a line of blood behind it. It runs around our shoes trying to hide, or trying to find a new place to implant itself.

Its metallic limbs lock onto the lace of my boot and it sprints up my uniform pant leg. My hand tries to swipe it away, but it holds fast to the cloth.

It wants me. It wants to go into my ears, and Tau won't be able to cut it out of my head once it burrows itself in. If it gets in, I'll be dead. I swipe again, but it leaps to the other leg and continues upward.

Chi's hand snatches it off of my mid-thigh, ripping fabric away. The spider sensor is flailing. It jabs its limbs into Chi's hand. And in one movement, he flings it to the ground and stomps it with the heel of his boot. One booming stomp that shakes through the entirety of our floating room.

The sensor is dead. And what the Common had planned for us is beaten. And Bridget gradually stops crying and falls asleep again with tear lines on her face.

"That was a new sensor," Andrew eventually explains. "New sensors burrow into pre-programmed places, or into openings in the skin, until they find a secure host, and then they 'die' under the skin. And most people all along are unaware this had happened."

But now that it's dead, we can float undetected below the Ocean. And one-by-one, after Sarah's leg has been rebandaged, we all fall asleep, except for Andrew, who steers us onward, searching for a new place where we can be hidden from the Common, and safe for now.

43

It is a week until Theta can remove her bandages. No one says it will work. They say the trauma during the bombing of Logos, and the water stinging in her eye sockets during the flood will all but guarantee her blindness, but I have a resilient piece of me that wants to think differently, even though all that I'm told and what I know says that Theta is blind: that she is blind in the same way that I am now permanently deaf, in an absolute and irremovable way.

But still I don't believe, not fully.

And when the day comes to remove her bandages, I take her from our new hiding place in tunnels below the ground, from our hiding place that Sarah calls Sea Caves, and I lead her out into the fading sunlight, onto a high cliff overlooking the ocean waters and the brilliant colors of a sunset.

And I slowly peel away her bandages.

"Are my eyes fully opened yet?" she writes into my palm.

"Yes," I answer.

"I thought so..."

A shudder overcomes her face, and I can tell that she's sad, tremblingly sad. Maybe there was a resilient part of her that believed as well.

And we sit for a long time not speaking, until she writes, "Tell me about a real sunset."

And I try to describe it with words but it is not enough, and so I lift up her hand, pointing her finger toward the location of the sun, and drawing her fingertip across the expanse of the sky, and writing in her palm the corresponding colors: red, purple, and burning golden red like the color of her hair, and blue at the top, and white where the sun hits its reflection on the water.

Her face is focused, trying to hold in all the colors I have mentioned, and then she smiles.

"I can see it," she says. "It's beautiful."

Yes, it is.

END OF BOOK ONE

Made in the USA
Middletown, DE
19 October 2015